Not Quite Mine

Also by Catherine Bybee

Contemporary Romance

Weekday Bride Series

Wife by Wednesday

Married by Monday

Not Quite Series

Not Quite Dating

Paranormal Romance

MacCoinnich Time Travels

Binding Vows

Silent Vows

Redeeming Vows

Highland Shifter

The Ritter Werewolves Series

Before the Moon Rises

Embracing the Wolf

Novellas

Soul Mate

Possessive

Erotica

Kilt Worthy

Kilt-A-Licious

CATHERINE BYBEE

The characters and events portrayed in this book are fictitious. Any similarity to real persons, living or dead, is coincidental and not intended by the author.

Printed in the United States of America.

Published by Montlake Romance

P.O. Box 400818

Las Vegas, NV 89140

ISBN-13: 9781611099515

ISBN-10: 161109951X

This one is for Kayce

My moral barometer and holiday sidekick.

Chapter One

Katelyn Morrison stood at the altar with tears welling behind her eyes. She forced her attention to the bride and groom and the vows they lovingly exchanged. Her brother, Jack, reached out to his newly adopted son Danny, and took the ring the six-year-old held in his hand. Danny beamed with pride, his smile and sigh caught the attention of everyone in the church. Katie felt the hair on her arms stand on end when Jack winked at the boy. Her brother deserved the happiness he'd found with his bride and her son. Katie couldn't be more ecstatic about the woman he'd chosen to make a Morrison.

The emotion that choked her up even more, however, Katie didn't want to name. She had no right to be jealous of her brother. Besides, green wasn't a color she chose to wear.

Squaring her shoulders, Katie witnessed Jessie place a ring on Jack's finger and repeat her vows. When the minister instructed Jack to kiss his bride, his dimples appeared as a wide smile spread over his face and he gathered her in his arms. True Texas catcalls and whistles lifted to the eves of the church when Jack dipped Jessie low and let everyone know she was his. When Danny lifted his hand to shield his eyes from their kiss, the cameras in the church went wild.

Katie let out a laugh and ignored the tears falling from her eyes.

Then she felt *him* watching, knew the weight of his stare as she slowly lifted her gaze to the best man.

Dean's gaze soaked her in. *Looked through her* would be a better way of describing the expression on his face. An unspoken understanding washed over his face and threatened a tidal wave of pain in Katie's chest. In that moment, Katie held more regret than she'd ever had in her entire life.

Jack and Jessie turned toward the guests at the ceremony while Monica, Jessie's sister and maid of honor, handed Jessie her bouquet. Katie pulled in her thoughts and memories and moved behind Jessie to fan the train of her dress so she could march down the aisle and not trip on the layers of fabric.

Thank God Jack picked Dean to be his best man and not a groomsman, otherwise bridesmaid Katie would be paired with him for the remainder of the evening. Being this close to him was hard enough. Standing side by side all evening would be torture.

Hell, it was still torture.

The photographer ushered the bridal party outside the church while the guests were funneled in another direction. The bride and groom posed in front of the marble columns and ornate doors. Monica stepped beside Katie with Nicole, the other bridesmaid. A buzz overhead brought everyone's attention to the sky.

A helicopter hovered over the church.

"Would have been asking too much for them to wait for a press release," Katie chided.

"I know you said to expect them, but a helicopter?" Monica tilted her head back and shielded her eyes from the sun with her hand.

"With a high powered lens snapping more pictures than the paid photographer." Having spent the greater part of her life attracting the attention of the media, both here in her hometown of Houston and wherever else she went, Katie was well rehearsed at ignoring their presence. Every mistake she'd ever made, nearly every kiss or affair she'd partaken in, ended up on the cover of a magazine.

"Take the damn picture and go already." Dean's voice, even when it was angry, shot up her spine with awareness.

Nearly every affair.

Dean, Tom, and Mike moved closer to the women and shot insults at the hovering chopper.

"Nothing's sacred," Mike said.

"At least Gaylord kept the paparazzi on foot far away."

"Daddy promised them a glimpse from the limo on the way to the reception," Katie informed the wedding party. "Or a trip to jail for trespassing if they stepped one foot on church property."

"A night in jail isn't usually a deterrent."

The three groomsmen had known Jack and Katie for years. Each one came from a family with money and power and knew the media better than their neighbors.

The noise from the chopper elevated, as did the wind it kicked up.

Danny ran up between Monica and Katie with a worried frown on his face. "Auntie Katie, is that helicopter gonna fall on us?"

She knelt down and took Danny's hand in hers. The role of auntie might have been new, but the fierce need to protect her nephew and ease his fears was as automatic as breathing. "They wouldn't dare risk it. Grandpa would tie them up and leave them in the sun to bake if they crashed this party."

Danny's eyes grew big. "Really?"

"Ask Grandpa to tell you about the paparazzi and my sixteenth birthday."

Dean and Tom cleared their throats behind her. She glanced over her shoulder and noticed both of them shaking their heads. A few misguided indiscretions of that day drifted to the surface of her memory. "On second thought, never mind."

Monica leaned in and offered her own advice. "How about we make faces at them, Danny?"

He shot her a big smile before he lifted his head to the chopper and stuck out his tongue. Laughter filled the small group as each one of them wiggled fingers and contorted their faces toward the sky. Danny's giggles kept them all animated. Chances were, the photographer in the chopper wasn't focused on them, but Danny no longer seemed concerned that the hunk of metal was going to land on them.

Even if their faces did end up on the cover of the *Inquisitor*, Katie knew she looked fabulous. The floor length maroon silk dress hugged her curves like a lover's caress. Lorenzo, the designer, had taken all three of the women in the bridal party into his studio and crafted identical dresses to work perfectly for each of their shapes. How he did it was a mystery. Not that he had to work around anything impossible. Both Monica and Nicole were over five seven and slender. And after a little work, Katie had shown them both the pleasure of designer heels. There was nothing sexier than a shoe that brought a guy's attention to a shapely calf before sending that attention zinging up a thigh and straight to one's ass. The second Katie had slid the two-hundred-dollar pumps onto Monica's feet, she knew she had a partner in crime.

Katie made sure the length of her leg peeked through her dress as she wiggled her fingers by her ears for the paparazzi.

As their laughter ebbed, the photographer waved them all inside the church for more pictures.

Danny took Monica's hand and pulled her with him as the rest of the party followed.

Katie adjusted her dress to make certain the low cut angle didn't reveal too much.

"You look amazing." Dean's voice was low and heated as he slid up beside her.

She hadn't realized he'd hung back, and she felt a little trapped in his presence. "You clean up well yourself, Prescott." Boy, did he clean up. He brushed his dusty blond hair that always seemed a little long, but at the same time, perfectly right, out of his eyes. His Texas drawl reminded her of home. She'd worked hard to rid herself of her accent when she was younger, thinking it made her sound stupid. Blonde and rich labeled her as dumb, which she fought for some time. It wouldn't have mattered if she'd become a doctor or a rocket scientist. The world looked at her as an heiress and treated her differently. Around her sixteenth birthday she'd snapped. Her hormones started to rage and her desire to be noticed ruled her brain. Her skirts rode high, her pants skintight. Those designer heels she loved so much pushed her height past most of the boys in school.

But the ones she wanted to look, didn't.

Katie glanced into Dean's eyes and quickly looked away. Her body tingled knowing he stood so close. The spicy scent of his skin made her want to lean in and take a deep breath. She fought her desire and found the silence between them painful.

She said the only thing she could think of, and then regretted her words instantly. "I'm sorry about Maggie."

Dean's jaw tightened. "It wasn't meant to be." Maggie had broken off her engagement to Dean a week before their wedding. According to Jack, there wasn't an explanation as to why. Then she'd disappeared and asked that Dean not contact her.

"It must have been hard for you…watching Jack and Jessie."

Lord knew if she'd been snubbed that close to matrimony, she'd never go to another wedding again.

The smile that always played on Dean's lips fell. "It wasn't hard at all."

Katie wanted to tell him he was full of shit. If anyone knew his dreams, it was her. A wife and family had always been in his plans.

"Are you two coming or what?" Tom called from the door to the church.

Dean tilted his head, acknowledging Tom, then spread his fingers low on Katie's back to usher her inside.

Heat spread up her body and licked every nerve ending in her skin. The memory of his hands slipping low on her hips, as he explored her lips with his own, washed over her. His hand jerked, as if he, too, shared the memory. He flexed his fingers and guided her forward.

Their time together was in the past, and best forgotten.

"So, what's with you and Katelyn?"

The question hit Dean in the center of his chest and caused his feet to move in a direction he hadn't planned. Luckily, Monica was ready for his dance floor flop and sidestepped his foot to avoid a broken toe.

"What do you mean?" Dammit, he thought he'd buried his memories deep in his head where no one could see them.

He was wrong.

"For starters, considering you've known her since grade school, neither of you talk to each other unless you have to."

Dean glanced across the dance floor and watched Tom swing Katie around. The two of them were laughing and having a grand time being the center of attention. The only people currently on the dance floor were the wedding party. The traditional display of royalty every wedding reception took part in would probably be Dean's only time spent in a woman's arms that night. Despite his brevity with Katie earlier, watching his best friend get married had stirred memories best forgotten.

"And then there's *that*," Monica said.

"There's what?" What were they talking about?

"I think a novel would call it a 'stolen look.' No, they'd call it a 'stolen gaze.' When Katie isn't watching you, you're watching her."

Katie was impossible to ignore. Her long, shapely legs brought her height over five nine. Her curves had haunted him in high school, and threatened to destroy him as an adult. The blonde hair atop her head was as natural as her grace. She honed the ability to attract attention early in life and hadn't seemed to tire of the spotlight yet. Her claim to fame came from several appearances on a reality TV show featuring other silver-spooned teenage girls. The tabloids often pegged her as an unintelligent heiress, but Dean knew better. She'd gone to college like all of their mutual friends, graduating with a degree in design and business.

Dean skirted his thoughts and focused on Monica. "You know, Monica, even *I* know it's bad form to be dancing with one beautiful woman while talking about another."

Her shoulders folded in with her laugh. "You're dancing with me because you have to. Luck of the draw being paired with the maid of honor."

"And here I thought you liked me."

Monica was charming, witty, and beautiful. In another life, he'd have jumped at the chance to get to know her better. His record with Jack's family and friends wasn't exactly stellar...well, with Katie anyway. He knew better than to get involved with someone he'd have to see on a regular basis after the breakup.

His eyes drifted to Katie again.

Monica cleared her throat, snapping Dean's attention back to her.

"My question is, are you thinking about what was? Or what might be?"

Dean danced around the query by reaching for Monica's hand, spinning her. He knew for a fact Katie didn't speak of her time with him any more than he did.

Monica slid back into his embrace with a smile. "I'm staying the whole week with her. If you won't talk, she will."

The confidences women laid out to each other were up to them. Being the home of a Y chromosome gave him the right to keep his feelings to himself.

Dean perfected the tight lip in high school. Too bad he hadn't kept it that way over the last year. Now he lived with his mistake and went back to life's early lessons. *Mouth shut, ears open.*

"Oh, fine," Monica grumbled, giving up her quest for more information. "Give me some dirt on Tom."

Dean hadn't seen that twist coming. "So you like Tom?"

Monica managed one of those stolen glances over her shoulder, not realizing that Dean watched. "I didn't say that. I'm just making conversation."

Dean allowed a true smile of amusement to crest his lips. "Oh, darlin', you're a terrible liar."

The dance ended and before long Jack had rounded up Dean along with Tom and Mike. He handed each one of them a shot of whiskey and stood back with a silly grin on his face.

"What are we toasting?" Mike asked before Dean had a chance to voice the question himself.

Jack lifted his glass. "To good friends. You guys made this day even better by being here."

"Oh, Lord, he's getting all sentimental on us," Mike joked.

"You laugh now, Mikey. Just wait and see how bright your future looks when there's a beautiful woman by your side to share it with."

Dean leaned over to Tom. "Is he gonna start crying?"

"He might if he drinks too many of these."

"He won't get drunk if he's looking forward to his wedding night." Something told Dean that Jack was more than happy to fulfill his husbandly obligations.

"Knock it off," Jack told them. "To friends."

"To friends!" They all lifted their glasses and drank the amber liquid with one swallow. Dean let it slide down his throat with a nice, comfortable burn. Outside of the champagne for the toast, he hadn't had a lick to drink all night. He took his role of best man seriously. Maybe after the bride and groom left for their monthlong honeymoon, he could kick back a few more.

"Speaking of friends," Jack started. "I have a favor to ask you guys."

Dean noticed the switch from carefree to serious cross Jack's face.

"What's that?" Mike asked.

"It's Katie."

The liquor in Dean's stomach hit bottom and started to hurt. "What about her?"

"Something isn't right with her. She hasn't been herself."

All four of them turned to search out the woman in question. Dean's radar found her quickly. She stood next to her father and Danny with a silly grin on her face.

"She looks fine to me," Tom said.

"She's not. Her smile isn't as big, her usual eccentric self isn't as large. I'm worried about her."

"Maybe she's growing up, Jack," Tom said. Which translated in Dean's brain to mean, *growing out of her reckless ways.*

Tom reached around to the bar and took another shot from the bartender. "I haven't seen her in any headlines in quite some time. Maybe she's bored with the spotlight. It does get old after a while."

Dean kept his mouth shut. He'd noticed the shift in her personality as well.

"She asked me if she could design the interior of the new hotels." Jack had started a new chain of family friendly hotels to add to the Morrison Empire. His first baby was nearly finished with the initial phase of construction. Dean knew the project well. Prescott Construction ran the job site in Ontario, California.

"Katie wants a job?" Tom asked.

All four of them twisted toward Katie again. Just thinking of her sexy ass in high heel shoes parading around the workers at the hotel made Dean cringe. Work would grind to a painstaking halt faster than lightning could strike the Empire State Building.

"Has a job," Jack corrected. "Design and fashion are her gig. It isn't like I could say no."

Damn. "That means she'll be staying in Ontario for a while." Southern California was where Dean had moved his life after he and Katie went their separate ways.

"I was hoping you and Mikey could keep an eye on her while she's there."

"I'm not sure what you want us to do, Jack. Katie's never lonely for company and chances are she'd see right through us if we knocked on her door and asked her if she wanted to hang out," Mikey said.

"Just keep an eye on her, will ya?"

"We will," Mike told him.

Dean nodded.

"Looks like I'm off the hook with this one." Tom reached for a third shot of whiskey. Tom lived in Houston.

Dean glanced up as Jessie walked toward them. Jack stepped forward and brought his wife into his arms.

"They want us to cut the cake now."

Jack wiggled his eyebrows. "I've been waiting to squish cake on your nose all night," he teased.

Jessie narrowed her eyes at her husband. "Careful, cowboy. You have to live with me for the rest of your life."

The couple laughed as they walked away.

Katie toed off her heels and fell onto her couch.

"You Texans sure know how to throw a party." Monica melted into the soft leather beside Katie.

"Big, loud, and never ending. But damn it was great."

"I don't think Jessie could be happier."

"Jack either."

"I think the two of them are going to be the rare ones that keep it going forever."

Katie agreed. She and Monica both knew what it was like to come from a broken family. Katie's mom had walked away from her husband and kids and never really looked back. She couldn't even be bothered with showing up at her own son's wedding. Same could be said for Monica and Jessie's dad. They didn't even know how to get hold of him.

"I'll bet Jessie's pregnant within the year."

"Less if Danny has his way. He and my dad were already hinting about Danny needing a baby sister or brother."

Monica tucked her feet under her bum. "You'd think he'd have waited for the wedding cake to digest before talking about babies."

"My dad drove himself hard for a lot of years. I think he wants to make up for lost time now that he's older. He loves Danny and can't wait for more grandkids." *Grandkids he'd have to get from Jessie and Jack.* The thought sobered her and brought a thick ball of emotion to the back of her throat. The whole night had been an emotional roller coaster. "I'm beat," she said, pushing off the sofa.

"Me, too."

As both women started down the hall of the high-rise hotel penthouse Katie lived in, the buzzer on the front door rang. Both of them jumped at the noise. It was one thirty in the morning.

"What the…?"

Monica followed her to the door. The complex had the tightest security money could buy, so concern for her safety didn't enter her mind as she opened the door.

The landing between her door and the elevator was empty.

A tiny noise drew Katie's attention to her feet.

Behind her, Monica gasped.

Cradled in a bundle of brown and pink blankets and nestled in a car seat was the most delicate tiny baby Katie had ever seen.

She dropped to her knees and lifted the blanket away from the infant's face. Slow, even breaths blew through pink lips. Tucked beside the child was an envelope. Katie lifted the paper away from the sleeping baby, careful to not wake her.

Katelyn Morrison was written in a flowing script.

"Oh, my God." Monica voiced Katie's exact thoughts.

Chapter Two

Monica lifted the car seat and brought the baby into the penthouse.

Katie's hands trembled as she flipped over the envelope.

"Get that," Monica told her while pointing outside the door.

Sitting on the hallway floor was a large plush diaper bag with sheep printed all over the exterior.

Grabbing it, Katie shut the door behind her and stood next to Monica. Both of them stared down at the baby as if neither of them knew what it was.

"Who would leave their child on your doorstep?"

She had no idea. "I'll call down to the doorman and ask if anyone has entered or left the building with a kid."

"Good idea." Monica sat beside the baby, careful not to wake her while Katelyn crossed to the phone and called downstairs.

"Good evening, Miss Morrison." The cheerful voice of the graveyard shift doorman didn't sound alarmed. In contrast, her heart was pounding in her chest and her voice was anything but calm.

"Hey, Alex. By chance has anyone come up in the last ten minutes or so?"

"Only you and Miss Mann. Why? Is everything OK?"

No, everything was definitely not OK. "Are you sure there hasn't been anyone you didn't recognize come in tonight? Anyone with kids?"

Alex's tone turned tight. "No one that wasn't expected. You sound a little worried, Miss Morrison. Would you like me to send up security?"

"No. No, we're fine. I thought maybe…" Oh, boy, what could she say? "Good night, Alex."

"G'night, ma'am."

"He didn't see anything?" Monica had listened to the conversation.

"Nothing."

"How can that be? They practically asked for my firstborn when I came…" Monica glanced at the infant. "Oh, bad joke. They seem so on top of things here."

"It's not the first time someone has gotten past security."

Katie pushed aside the magazines sitting on her coffee table so she could sit and stare at the child. The porcelain, perfect skin and fluff of pale hair on the top of her head were so beautiful. Unable to stop herself, Katie reached out and ran her finger along a tiny cheek. The smooth texture sent a zing up her arm and added to the rapid beat of her heart.

"We need to call the police."

Alarm spiked inside Katie's head. "Why?"

"Katie, someone abandoned their infant on your doorstep. We need to notify the authorities."

When mothers abandoned their infants, they did it on church steps or hospitals…or worse, garbage cans or public bathrooms. Katie's eyes inched away from Monica and glanced at the envelope clutched in her hand. She'd almost forgotten about it.

She ripped it open and removed two pieces of paper. One looked official, while the other was a handwritten note.

Dearest Katelyn,

Please read this letter before giving my child to complete strangers to raise within a broken system. I'm not a star-crazed kid pushing her unwanted baggage on someone with money, or a nut who will come back into your life screaming foul play. I am a mother whose heart is breaking as she writes you this letter in a desperate attempt to make you understand.

I am unable to raise my daughter, to love her, to guide her in life. No one is more sorry about that than I am. You can do what I can't, Katelyn. I've seen to it that no one will question who her mother is. All you have to do is take her.

Savannah was conceived with love, albeit one sided, and deserves a mother who can give her everything. I know things about you that I probably shouldn't. I know how much you want a child of your own, how impossible it is for you to do so. If you open your heart to my tiny miracle, she'll win you over before dawn. Her father isn't ready for her, but if my instincts are right, he will be one day. And when he is, the two of you will give Savannah the loving home she needs.

I've arranged everything. No one will question the parentage of Savannah, and even if they did, I believe you'll find a way to keep her.

Please…I beg you.

Love her, Katelyn. If the day ever comes, tell her I loved her, too.

There wasn't a signature. No name to give to the woman who had written the letter.

Katie glanced at the second paper, which was a birth certificate. Her back teeth ground tight and her head started to pound.

The words "Closed Adoption" stood out in bold print. Under "Child's Name" was "Savannah Morrison, no middle name." Under "Mother" was "Katelyn Marie Morrison." Katie shifted her eyes to the space for the father's name and found it blank.

She blew out a long, shaky breath.

"What does it say?" Monica sat anxiously waiting.

There would be no need to hide anything from her new sister-in-law so she handed over the papers. As Monica took in all that the letter said, Katie stared down at Savannah and allowed her heart to open a tiny crack. Who was Savannah's mother, and how did she know Katie's deepest secret?

"Holy shit."

Understatement of the year.

"Do you have any idea who the mom is?"

"None."

"What about the dad? Sounds like the mom thinks you know him."

Katie rubbed the back of her neck and tried to stop the nagging feeling of dread. "I know a lot of guys who aren't ready to be a father." No reason to tell Monica everything. Until Katie knew more about the mother and the reason for Savannah ending up on her doorstep, she'd keep quiet.

"How can someone do this?" Monica repeated the question a few more times as she stood and paced the room. "And what did she mean when she said that it's impossible for you to have your own kids?"

Savannah puffed out her tiny lips in her sleep as if she were sucking on something. Monica's question registered. "I can't have children." Saying the words aloud always hurt, which was why Katie never did.

"Are you sure?"

Karma had a way of slapping her in the face. "I'm sure." Since her own mother couldn't be a good mom, life decided to take the option away from her, too.

Monica sat beside her on the coffee table and grasped her hand. "I'm so sorry."

"Me, too." And she was. More than Monica could ever imagine.

Both of them turned to face Savannah and stared. The thought of putting her into the arms of a police officer, who would then place her into a home where people took in unwanted children for a price, raced through Katie's mind.

What if she didn't do that? Right in front of her was a miracle Katie could never have on her own. She knew that one day she'd look into adopting, maybe even a surrogate birth. Hell, she'd be a mother already if life hadn't killed that dream.

Bundled up in a neat little package was a dream realized. A dream that money really couldn't buy.

Savannah wiggled in her sleep, the movement had both Monica and Katie leaning closer. Within seconds, the infant started to blink and open her beautiful blue eyes.

Katie felt her breath coming in short pants. She was so amazing. So perfect. Savannah stretched her arms wide and opened her mouth in a yawn bigger than she was. Then a high-pitched squeak erupted from her mouth.

Katie reached for the buckle and unsnapped it. Savannah watched Katie as she pushed the blanket away and wrapped her arms around the baby for the first time.

"Watch her head," Monica instructed.

"Right."

Careful to support Savannah's neck, Katie lifted her onto her lap. Her tiny arms swam in the pajamas she wore. Little legs kicked Katie's stomach with a tiny pat. She leaned down and kissed Savannah's forehead and drew in the fresh, clean scent of her skin. Everything about her was so new. "When was she born?"

Monica picked up the birth certificate and said, "Two weeks ago today."

Savannah's hand curled around Katie's finger and gave a squeeze as if to say, *Don't let go.*

"You're going to keep her, aren't you?" Monica's question didn't have an ounce of judgment in it.

Katie shook her head no, then yes. "Her mother must have been desperate to leave her at my door. I think I should try to find her, find out what her letter meant."

"And keep Savannah while you're looking?"

"The police would put her in foster care. I can take better care of her than someone desperate for the money the state gives them."

"What if you don't find the mom?"

"Someone left a baby on my doorstep at one in the morning. There are cameras all over this complex."

"In your foyer?" Monica glanced toward the front door.

"At least one, plenty more in the lobby, the main hallways… elevators." There had to be someone with a baby caught on film.

Savannah squirmed and sputtered out a cry. Katie's attention went back to the child in her arms. "Are you hungry?" she asked in a voice a full octave higher than her normal tone. What was it about babies that had people talking in voices that weren't their own? "I'll bet your mommy has something in this bag for you to eat."

Monica's hand dipped into the bag and removed a bottle and a container full of formula. "I'll get this ready. Why don't you see if she needs her diaper changed?"

As Monica stood to work her way to the kitchen, Katie stopped her. "I'm doing the right thing, aren't I?" The question was foreign coming from her lips. Katelyn Morrison, millionaire and heiress to half of her daddy's estate, had always run through life completely confident in everything she did. Yet with the package weighing less than ten pounds sitting in her lap and starting to fuss, she felt clueless about her next move.

"I have no idea."

"What would you do?"

"I'd call my sister and ask her advice." Monica and Jessie were very close. Up until Monica finished nursing school, she lived with Jessie and helped take care of Danny. They had struggled for money every day of their lives, but they loved each other, depended on each other.

"I don't have a sister," Katie stated the obvious.

Monica shook her head. "You do now. I say we sleep on it. If Savannah is going to let us sleep, that is. We'll figure this out together."

"OK." They could do this. Katie reminded herself to kiss her brother when he returned from his honeymoon. Marrying Jessie was the smartest thing Jack had ever done. Monica was quickly turning into a true friend.

Dean reduced himself to stalker status. Outside of Katie's penthouse suite, he waited for Monica to exit the building for her morning run. He'd extracted the information about her exercise routine during the previous evening so he could corner Katie alone.

Jack's concern for his sister squeezed a nagging trigger inside Dean's head. A trigger he wished weren't there. He had to know for himself that his ex wasn't in any real trouble. Dean told himself it was for friendship's sake. Hell, it was his friendship with Jack that had kept Katie and Dean apart for a small lifetime. And when their affair fell apart, Dean couldn't even drink through the pain of the breakup with his best friend, because his best friend had no idea about the relationship.

Still, in the year and a half that he and Katie hadn't spoken outside of obligatory time together getting ready for Jessie and Jack's wedding, Dean had watched and kept up with Katelyn Morrison's life. What he could see from afar, that is.

The papers grasped onto every torrid and newsworthy turn in the heiress's life. Dean knew that when she'd broken off with him, she'd rushed back into the arms of an old lover, proving that she'd never felt the same for Dean as he had for her. Looking back, he knew he'd rushed into a relationship with Maggie, and their breakup was probably for the best. What was wrong with him that women didn't want to stick around? He'd pondered that thought for months until he simply turned his back on *happily ever after*. Sure, Jack made it look like fantasy material with Jessie. But Dean was done with long term anything when it came to the female gender in general. No-strings mutual affairs he could handle.

Commitment and promises of tomorrow, no way.

So what the hell was he doing suffering the early morning heat of a Houston summer waiting for Monica to jog her skinny butt around a few city blocks? The question swimming inside his head had him pushing off the building and turning to walk back to his rented car. Then Monica swung out of the building, waving at the doorman as she rested her sunglasses on her nose.

As Monica took off in the opposite direction, Dean removed his sunglasses and made his way inside the elite high-rise.

Dean walked up to the reception desk, praying the staff hadn't changed over the last year.

"Mr. Prescott, how nice to see you again." *One hurdle down.*

"Hello, Miss May. I see you're just as lovely as ever." Miss May was on the far side of sixty…and even further from "Miss" status.

"You always were a tease." She winked at him. "Shall I let Miss Morrison know you're on your way up?"

Dean waved her off. "No need, she knows I'm coming," he lied.

"Have a nice day, Mr. Prescott."

Dean tipped his Stetson in her direction before moving to the bank of elevators. When he stepped inside, a green light went on indicating that Miss May had offered him access to Katie's penthouse as she'd done many times in the past. At least when he wanted the staff to know he was visiting Katie. There were plenty of other times he'd made his way into the hotel penthouse without anyone knowing he was there. He and Katie had liked the game of being secret…at least in the beginning. Within seconds, he stood outside Katie's door, his hand hesitating midway to the oak entrance to her home.

Suck it up, he told himself as he let his knuckles scrape against the wood.

A few seconds passed without Katie showing up. He knocked again, this time with more urgency. Just as he reached for the doorbell, the door flew open. "What?"

Dean stood back; his eyes ran down the length of Katie and took in her disheveled appearance. She was in a bathrobe, which wasn't a surprise considering her playgirl lifestyle, but the way her hair was messed on top of her head, and the dark circles under her eyes, made him consider Jack's words even more.

"Katelyn."

Instead of opening the door wide, Katie shrank behind it and used it as a barrier between them. "What are you doing here?"

What *was* he doing there? "Jack wanted me to check in on you."

Her gaze narrowed, suspicion laced her brow. "You saw me last night."

"Right. But we couldn't exactly talk there, could we?"

Katie hid a yawn behind her hand and shook her head. "I'm not sure what we have to talk about, Dean. I'm fine. Jack should mind his own business." She glanced behind her shoulder and held the door tight as if to keep him from barging in.

"He's worried about you and so am I. Are you going to let me in or are we going to have this conversation in the hall?" He was starting to wonder what she was hiding.

"Now's a bad time." She nearly whispered her words.

Realization dawned on him like a splash of ice-cold water.

"You're not alone," he said, feeling something inside him ache. Dammit, he had no business aching.

"No, it's not…yes, that's it. So, if you'll excuse me."

As Katie started to close the door, Dean stuck his foot out to stop it.

She was lying. Her left eye did this little twitchy thing when she was being untruthful. It was something that he'd noticed early on when they'd flirted with each other. "What are you hiding, Katie?" His voice rose in agitation.

"Shh!" She glanced over her shoulder again then zipped her gaze back to him. "It's a bad time, Dean. Why don't we meet up for coffee...later."

"I could use a cup now." Without invitation, Dean pushed back against the door, determined to see what she was guarding.

The living room of her penthouse was as he remembered. Nothing seemed out of place. He glanced around and noticed that Katie still stood by the door holding it open.

"What's going on?"

Katie placed her hands on her hips and pinched her lips together. It was her ticked off look. One he knew too well. "Nothing. Now will you please leave? I haven't even showered yet and I'm not ready to entertain *you*."

She shouldn't look sexy in the pink, fluffy robe with her hair scattered every way but down, yet she did. Dean despised that his body heated with the memory of him messing up her hair. A memory a year and a half old.

"I'll wait here while you get ready."

Dean sat on her sofa and lifted one ankle to rest on his opposite knee.

Katie pounded her foot. "I never realized how dense you were, Dean Prescott. I don't want you here and if you won't leave on your own, I'll have security escort you out."

Her threat was empty and they both knew it. Dean winked and removed his hat from his head.

"Dammit, Dean!" Her voice rose well above the whisper she'd been using.

As he started to laugh at her agitation, a foreign noise sounded from the direction of her room.

Katie eyes shot to her bedroom door and she went perfectly still, her face lost all color.

When the noise sounded again, her attention shifted back to him. Then she did something Katie never did.

She fidgeted.

Dean saw the moment panic set in and leapt to his feet, over the sofa, and beat her to the door to her room.

Her chest heaved against her robe as she fought for her breath.

Dean's hand grasped the doorknob and her hand shot out to stop him. The contact sizzled unwanted and unexpected awareness throughout his body.

He stared deep into her eyes and saw the same heat he felt staring back at him.

When an infant's cry shocked him out of his trance, he loosened his hold on the door and let Katie push him out of the way.

What the hell?

Chapter Three

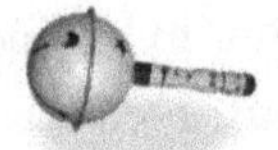

Left without a choice, Katie pushed around Dean and shot straight to Savannah to pick her up. She'd slept for three hours this time, the longest stint since she'd shown up in the early morning hours. Too bad she couldn't wait ten more minutes so Dean could have left clueless.

Now Katie was forced to come up with a viable reason why an infant was sprawled out in the middle of her massive king-size bed.

Katie leaned over and lifted the tiny bundle into her arms. The fatigue of moments ago evaporated like steam when Savannah's cries muffled to only whimpers once she was drawn close to Katie's chest. "Are you hungry, baby girl?" Katie lifted her little finger to Savannah's mouth, just like Monica had shown her, watched Savannah bite the tip and give it a hefty suck. "C'mon, let's get you something to eat."

Katie fidgeted until she successfully tucked Savannah into the crook of her arm and turned to leave her room. Her eyes collided with Dean, who Katie nearly forgot was there.

"So this was who you were hiding?"

"Not hiding," Katie said a bit too quickly. "I just didn't want you to wake her up." Let him think what he would, she'd keep the information to a minimum to avoid a waterfall of lies that would surely catch up with her.

She made her way to her kitchen, all the while holding Savannah. It was crazy how after only a handful of hours Katie had the ability to hold Savannah with one hand and work with the other. The task wasn't effortless, and she was slow with the multitasking, but it was getting easier.

Behind her, Dean followed. What he was thinking was a mystery. Which was just as well.

"Who is she?"

"Her name's Savannah." Katie kept her back to Dean knowing he always caught her when she lied. "I'm watching her for a friend."

"Who?"

"No one you know. Can you hand me a bottle from the fridge?" She hoped putting him to work would stop his questions.

Dean handed her a premade bottle, which Katie put in a pot of water on the stove to warm.

Savannah started to fuss and Katie found herself rocking back and forth to keep her quiet. "It will just be a minute," she cooed. "Oh, I'll bet you need to be changed." *They eat, sleep, and need to be changed. Welcome to motherhood.* Monica's words ran like a tape inside Katie's brain.

"Watch this, will you?" Katie gestured toward the bottle before walking around him to tend to Savannah's needs.

Back in her bedroom, she went to work on the diaper with a surprising smile on her face. Dean seemed to take the "babysitting" excuse. Why wouldn't he? He certainly wouldn't believe the truth.

Focused on changing Savannah into one of the few outfits in the diaper bag, feeding her, and then ushering Dean out the door, Katie outlined the next half hour in her head.

The tiny pajamas were kicked free of Savannah's skinny legs. Katie leaned down to kiss her baby toes. What a precious gift. How could anyone give her up willingly? The thought never left Katie's mind. Even in the stolen moments of sleep, Katie dreamed about a desperate mother walking away from her door in the middle of the night.

Then again, not all mothers were the same. Katie's own walked away years ago, never looking back. Even before she left, Katie remembered the cold disapproval that hovered around her mother like an aura. Hell, Katie felt more love from her daddy's housekeeper, Beth, and her Aunt Bea than she'd ever experienced from her mother.

What if the letter left by Savannah's mother wasn't really heartfelt? What if Savannah's mommy wasn't ready to be a mom and she left her baby and never even glanced over her shoulder again?

Katie dismissed the thought instantly. Too many fingers pointed to this mother's desperate need to find a safe home for her daughter. The letter had said that Savannah would win Katie's heart by morning, and by God, that's exactly what had happened.

While Katie tucked Savannah into a lavender cotton shirt that snapped between her legs and fashioned a tiny skirt around the baby's waist, she thought of all the supplies needed to care for a baby.

She needed more diapers, wipes, and formula. Certainly a few more outfits were in order and a bassinet. Sleeping in the middle of a king-size bed wasn't safe. She could roll off and get hurt. Maybe a baby book with a list of expected milestones would be a good thing to have on hand. Monica seemed to know all about babies, but Katie wanted to understand Savannah's needs so she could meet them.

Back in the kitchen, Dean had removed the bottle from the pan and stood holding it with a faraway look on his face.

"Is that ready?"

"Couldn't tell you. But I'm pretty sure it isn't supposed to boil." He waited for her to sit down at her kitchen counter before handing her the bottle.

Katie tested the formula like Monica had taught her during the night. The milk was still a little cool, but Savannah's fussing was turning into a full-blown *Give me something to eat* cry.

Once the nipple was in Savannah's mouth, she quieted and sucked down the formula in greedy fashion.

"You know, for a tiny bitty thing, you sure do eat a lot."

Savannah blinked her eyes, barely focused on the bottle in front of her.

"How long are you babysitting her?"

Katie swallowed and didn't meet Dean's eyes. "For today."

"How long have you been watching her?" Dean leaned against the counter and crossed his arms over his chest.

"Since last night."

"You were at the wedding last night."

Right. A post-midnight drop off wouldn't sound good. "I mean the night before last. She doesn't sleep for long, the hours kind of speed by."

Dean nodded, his expression unreadable.

Katie shifted in her seat, uncomfortable under Dean's stare. "Why are you here again?"

"In a hurry to get rid of me?"

"Yes, actually. I told you I wasn't ready for visitors and now you know why. So be a doll and show yourself out." The sappy sweetness of her voice with a little extra Texas twang usually produced exactly what she wanted.

Unfortunately, Dean wasn't one to bend to her charms easily.

"You didn't say anything about babysitting last night. I wonder why that was?"

"Go home, Dean."

"And since when does a new mother leave an infant with a friend overnight? That baby can't be more than a month old."

"Two weeks." Katie regretted her words the second they popped out of her mouth. Dammit, she really needed to shut the hell up.

"Has her cord even come off yet?"

Right, that's why Savannah's belly button was pink. Katie glanced down at her lap.

Dean advanced on her with slow, easy steps.

As he did, the room started to lose its oxygen and the familiar feeling of being trapped hovered all around her. He leaned in and rested a hand on the table behind her. He used his six-foot-two frame of solid steel muscle to intimidate her. Had she not been holding a helpless baby, Katie would have been happy to push Dean away and lay into him with her razor sharp tongue. As it was, her lips had already said too much so she kept her mouth sealed.

When Dean was close enough for Katie to scent the flavor of his toothpaste, he whispered, "That is a heaping lump of bullshit spewing from your mouth, Katelyn, and I'm determined to find out what the truth is."

Savannah took that second to finish the formula and suck in a few swallows of air. Katie removed the nipple and lifted her to her shoulder. When she did, Dean backed away.

Determined to keep Dean from learning anything more, she rubbed Savannah's back to coax a burp. Instead of a little gas to match her size, Savannah let out a sound bigger than a bark. With it came half the formula she'd drunk, which soaked both Katie and the new outfit Savannah wore.

"Well, damn." Katie used her sleeve to wipe up some of the mess on Savannah's chin.

When Dean cracked a smile, Katie lost it. "Get out of my house."

"Not until you tell me what's going on."

"I'm a little busy, Dean. Dealing with your paranoia isn't on my list of things to do today." She marched out of the kitchen and walked to her front door. She shifted the baby in her arms and tossed open the door.

"Fine, I'll go. But when I come back, if your explanations don't measure up, I might have to do some of my own investigating to determine the truth."

"Really, and how do you plan on doing that?" He was really starting to piss her off.

"I'll start with Monica." When she smiled, knowing Monica would be much better at keeping her trap shut than Katie had been, Dean added, "Then I'll move on to your father. My guess is Gaylord would be very interested in his daughter playing house with a *Barely out of the womb* baby."

Her jaw tightened. The last thing she needed was her daddy poking around. He'd scrape the truth out of her in a matter of minutes.

Smiling smugly, Dean waltzed past her, stopping only to glance down at her arms, then winked before walking away.

Katie shut the door on his back…hard.

Back in stalker mode, Dean leaned against the outside edge of the hotel Katie called home in order to corner Monica. If there was one thing he'd learned from his friend Jack's relationship with Jessie, it was that sisters, even newly in-lawed sisters, talked.

He needed answers and the best way for him to obtain them was through manipulation. He knew it wasn't noble, but he didn't give a damn.

Seeing Katie holding Savannah, cooing over the infant with an expression Dean could only describe as bliss, evoked pain, anger, and even a bit of hope. Pain and anger he could deal with. Those emotions he understood. The pain at witnessing Katie hold on to something he'd always wanted for the both of them. His anger stemmed from how she'd reacted after her miscarriage, after their baby had slipped from her womb.

But hope? Hope for what?

He'd wanted a family, a life with Katie by his side. In the beginning, he thought she was right there with him.

Sex with Katie had always been spectacular and sinful. Just thinking about how Katie responded to his touch shot unwanted desire through Dean's body as he waited for Monica to finish her run.

For Dean, his relationship with Katie was founded on friendship, exploded in passion, and evolved into love.

For Katie it was only about the sex.

Where was the *hope* in that?

Monica's blonde head bobbed up and down as she rounded the corner, her presence forcing Dean's attention to his recent goal. He eased from the side of the building and placed himself between her and the entrance to the lobby.

Recognition shifted over Monica's face like a curtain falling on a stage. It slowly fell over her eyes first, causing her lips to turn into a grin. And when Dean purposely shifted his gaze up the side of the building, then back to her, she slowed her pace, and let her smile fall. Like a switch, her guard went up.

"Hi, Dean. W-what are you doing here?"

He hit her hard with quick questions, to see how fast he could catch a lie. Then he'd know for certain Katie's story about the child was bogus. "Checking on Katie for Jack. You didn't tell me you guys had a roommate."

"A roommate?"

"Savannah."

"Ah…" Monica looked over her shoulder and back. "Savannah?"

"Don't be coy, Monica, I've already seen Katie."

"Oh, well."

"I'm surprised you didn't tell me last night about your guest."

Monica shifted on her feet. "It was a last-minute thing."

"Right, Katie said Savannah has been here since…when was it?"

"Yesterday."

Dean nodded. "Right. When is the mom coming to pick her up? Katie is supposed to be designing the interior of Jack's hotel."

"Why didn't you ask Katie these things?" Monica was catching on to him, and drying up her information. She'd already confirmed that Katie was lying through her teeth. But why?

"She had her hands full." *Literally.*

Monica moved around him, so she was angled close to the door. "I'm sure Katie will tell you all about it when she's ready."

"So there is something to tell."

"I didn't say that."

"Yeah, you did, darlin'. But don't stress yourself out. I already knew Katie wasn't telling everything. She's a lot easier to read than she thinks she is." Dean figured that, once these two started to talk, he wouldn't get another chance at any information. He might even find himself barred from Katie's door.

"Why do you care?"

Good question. "Jack wanted me to check on her. He's worried about her."

Monica shook her head back and forth in confusion. "Jack? How could he know anything? Savannah arrived after the wedd…" Her voice trailed off, her eyes shot to his.

After the wedding would have been in the middle of the night. And no matter how you spun that bottle, it landed on trouble. "Listen, Monica, if Katie's in some kind of trouble, you've got to let me help. Jack would kill me if I let his kid sister—"

"Katelyn isn't a kid, Dean. She'd a grown woman with a mind of her own. If she wanted your help, she'd ask." It was then that Dean noted the flash of concern embedded deep in Monica's eyes. The same look that passed over her face and Katie's when they'd noticed Danny's concern over the helicopter landing on them at the reception.

Dammit. Katie was in trouble. The question returned. What kind of mother left her infant with someone less two weeks after they were born?

"At least tell me how long the baby is going to be here."

Monica started for the door.

Dean placed a hand on her arm to stop her.

"Talk to Katie."

Which meant Monica didn't know.

As she walked into the air-conditioned lobby, the knot inside Dean's chest started to rise in his throat like the Texas heat.

Chapter Four

Katie's mind ran in so many different directions she didn't know which way was north. Savannah lay in the center of the big bed again, this time wide awake and sucking on her fist. Katie didn't know where to start. She needed to leave, they all needed to leave as quickly as they could pack and make excuses. If Dean called her daddy and he blessed her with his presence, keeping Savannah wouldn't be an option.

Katie needed time to think. Time to plan. That wasn't going to happen in Houston where everyone knew her and expected a certain persona. That facade didn't include a diaper-changing mama.

In the back of her massive walk-in closet, she found her largest suitcase and moved it to the bench at the end of her bed. She indiscriminately scooped underwear from her top drawer and tossed the lot inside the case.

She would go to California early, before Dean had a chance to inform her dad about the baby. The excuse of working for Jack would explain her rapid departure if anyone cared to ask.

From the front door of her suite, Monica called out. "Katelyn?"

"In here." She hung a garment bag on a hook and unzipped it. Bypassing her skintight dresses meant for the club scene, she packed longer skirts and pantsuits.

"Guess who ambushed me at the door," Monica said as she walked into bedroom.

Katie stopped midstride and turned to face Monica. "Oh, no."

"Oh, yes! I take it you and Dean had a conversation."

Her heart squeezed in her chest. "You didn't tell him anything… did you?"

"He asked questions. I avoided answering. I'd be lying if I told you I steered him off, though. He didn't believe the babysitting thing for a minute." Monica's gaze moved to the bed, then the suitcase.

Katie squeezed her fist. She needed to leave. Now!

"Help me pack." Back in the closet, she opened another suitcase and started to fill it with shoes.

"What are you…where are you going?"

"California. With you."

"But…"

"Please." She dangled a pair of Jimmy Choos off her index finger. "I can't take the chance of Dean returning here with my father. In order for the babysitting excuse to work, and for him to forget about Savannah, I need to get her out of here."

"I don't know, Katelyn. Taking a baby that isn't yours out of the state has to be against the law."

"I have a birth certificate."

"That you know damn well is a lie. You didn't adopt Savannah. And you sure as hell didn't ask for her."

She chucked Jimmy into the suitcase and stood closer to Monica. "Someone went through great lengths to create this lie. I owe it to Savannah to find out the truth."

"You don't owe anything to Savannah."

Katie glanced over to the bed. Savannah was staring at her fist.

"Are you telling me, if you were in my position, you'd just give her up? Take her to the nearest police station and tell them to deal with it?"

Monica released a frustrated sigh.

"Exactly. Help me pack."

They worked in tandem and finished the job quickly.

"You can't take your dad's plane. The pilot would confirm that Savannah was with you."

She hadn't thought of that.

"And if you take her to the hotel, word will get out."

She hadn't thought about that either.

"I've always stayed at the hotels. If I don't, someone is going to get curious."

Monica sat on the edge of the bed and tickled Savannah's feet. "I have a second bedroom. You can hide out with me for a couple of days." Monica and Jessie had shared an apartment while Monica was in nursing school. Now that she was out and Jessie had married Jack, she had the place to herself.

Staying with Monica would solve the problem of hiding Savannah, at least in the short term.

"Are you sure?"

"No. I think this is crazy. But I can't walk away now. Besides, I doubt you know a whole lot about babies and at least I know what Jessie went through with Danny." Monica placed a thumb into Savannah's hand and kissed her tiny fingers. "She may look small, but she's a full-time job."

"So you'll help me take care of her?"

Monica leveled her eyes with Katie. "I'll help you get situated. If you plan to work on Jack's hotel and find out who Savannah's mommy really is…plus take care of her, you're going to need six hands and three heads. Actually," Monica moved off the bed. "This is a crazy idea. I work full-time and finally landed the day shift. Plus I pick up overtime whenever I can get it to pay off my college loans."

Katie felt her ally fading fast. "I'll hire a nanny." Just until she found a rhythm that worked. The last thing Katie wanted was for Savannah to be raised by strangers.

"In my neighborhood they're called babysitters."

"Babysitter then." That sounded better anyway. More temporary.

Monica clasped her hands together, doubt filled her gaze.

"Please."

Squeezing her eyes shut, Monica shook her head. "I'll shower and be ready to leave in thirty minutes. You need to turn on some of that Texan charm and wiggle your way into some last-minute flights or I have a feeling Dean will rat us out before dinner."

All the Texan charm and daddy's money didn't get them on a flight fast enough to suit Katie. First class was sold out but they managed a flight in economy with Monica seated several rows behind her and Savannah. It had been so long since she'd crammed into a commercial flight that she'd forgotten how cramped it was. Not to mention the baggage restrictions. She checked two bags under her name, and two under Savannah Morrison. The elderly lady in the window seat cooed over Savannah the moment the flight attendant finished helping Katie buckle the car seat in.

"Oh, isn't she precious."

She juggled the diaper bag under one seat and her oversized purse under another. "Thank you," Katie managed to say before taking her seat.

"How old is she? One month?"

"Two weeks." The answer was instant, and after the words escaped Katie's mouth, she cautioned herself to keep quiet.

"Isn't that a little young to fly?"

Katie's right eye twitched. "The, ah, doctor said it was fine."

"I have three grandbabies. Well, they're not babies any longer. Two in high school and one finishing up college now, but they will always be my grandbabies." The happily plump woman talked about her grandchildren, two boys and one girl, and made kissing noises to Savannah whenever she turned her head toward the woman's voice.

Katie clicked her seat belt and rested her hand on Savannah's tiny leg.

"They grow so fast," the woman went on.

"Yes, they do." Or so she'd heard.

The older woman paused and took in Katelyn's frame. Her eyes narrowed. "You don't look like you just had a baby."

Her heart leapt. The woman's observation wasn't something she'd seen coming. "I adopted." She said the first thing that popped in her head. Sticking close to the truth would probably be best anyway. Thinly veiled truth was better than a flat out lie. Many years of skirting the truth would come in handy to keep Savannah's identity hidden.

Katie glanced over her shoulder and found Monica peeking over her seat. After sending a reassuring smile, Katie swiveled forward and tilted her face away from the people surrounding her. She wore little makeup and dark sunglasses in hopes of avoiding anyone recognizing her on the plane. If someone did notice her, they'd probably second guess who she was based on the sole fact that Katie never flew anywhere but on her daddy's plane. Not to mention she was wearing sweatpants…workout clothes in public for God's sake. Even the T-shirt she was wearing belonged to Monica and sported some of Savannah's lunch.

Before boarding the plane, Monica and Katie had taken turns walking Savannah around, hoping that, when buckled in a car seat, she wouldn't grow restless and call more attention to herself than necessary. A baby, especially one as tiny as Savannah, drew attention and more than one neck craned to get a glimpse.

The last of the passengers took their seats.

Grandma kept talking about her grandchildren, the soothing voice seemed to be putting Savannah to sleep.

Maybe the flight won't be so bad.

The words no sooner fled her mind before the captain's voice swam over the PA to welcome them aboard. Sadly, the intercom squeaked at a high pitch and jarred Savannah to a full-on wakeful scream.

Passengers turned toward her as Katie attempted to coax a pacifier into Savannah's mouth. She wanted nothing to do with it. The plane taxied from the terminal and the noise of the engine helped cut some of the noise coming from such a small person.

The coy smiles and oohs and aahs over "such a tiny thing" swiftly turned to ugly looks and rolling eyes.

"Shh, it's OK..." Katie couldn't stop the pitiful wails any more than stopping the tide.

Grandma offered some encouragement. "Don't worry. Babies cry. Everyone knows that."

Still, every passenger within four rows honed their ugly stares on her.

So much for keeping a low profile.

As soon as they reached cruising altitude and the captain turned off the seat belt sign, Katie lifted Savannah from the car seat, laid her on her chest, and managed to calm her down. A little.

Half of the time in flight was soothing a fussy infant and dodging dirty looks. It took every ounce of decorum for Katie not to tell the people close by to mind their own business. Lashing out at them for their snide looks and not-so-quiet whispers about babies on airplanes would warrant more attention, not less.

With any luck, this flight would be the only commercial one Savannah would have to endure.

Even Grandma had hit her limit by the time they landed. Katie's nerves sizzled like onions at the county fair. As soon as the diaper bag, handbag, and Savannah in her car seat were shrugged over a shoulder or an arm, and Katie was laboring across the tarmac to baggage claim, Savannah then decided to go to sleep. It was dark, the peanuts on the plane not only didn't constitute an in-flight meal, they also gave Katie indigestion. She couldn't even enjoy a glass of wine. The thought of her drinking while a baby screamed in her lap felt irresponsible, even to her.

Monica caught up to her and asked how she was holding up. Katie nearly decked her for talking so loud. "She's finally asleep! Keep it down."

The noise of the airport and all the travelers wasn't bothering Savannah one bit, yet somehow Katie knew that Monica's inquiry would.

Monica's jaw drew down as she peered over the edge of the car seat. "We didn't hear her very much where I was."

"You're full of shit." The whole damn plane scowled at her as she walked off.

"Babies cry. No biggie."

"She's too young to be traveling." Katie repeated the words murmured between the lips of several women on the plane. Women who were obviously mothers. Mothers who obviously knew babies better than her.

"The biggest problem with babies traveling is illness. Lucky for you…" Monica grabbed one of five bags rolling on the conveyer belt in baggage claim. "…I'm a nurse and can clue you in if little Vanna here gets ill."

Little Vanna, as Monica called her, was now sound asleep. Her hands would twitch when a loud noise sounded inside the huge building, but she didn't wake. The strong urge to kiss her soft cheeks clutched Katie's heart but she didn't dare for fear she'd wake.

"We're going to have to grab a cab," Monica said after hoisting every bag to their side. "I wasn't expecting to come home for a few days and my ride was busy."

Katelyn sighed. Now this was something she could handle. And a smelly cab wasn't going to disturb the peace of a sleeping child. She handed the car seat over to Monica. "Wait here. I'll get us a ride."

Ten minutes later they were seated in the back of a stretch limousine with Savannah puffing little breaths through her pouty pink lips.

"Where to, Miss Morrison?" the driver, asked.

Monica rambled off her address before closing the clear window between them and the driver.

The limo was from the Ontario Morrison Hotel. Although Katie didn't know the driver by name, she would by the time she showed up to the hotel, and she'd buy his loyalty one way or the other.

"He thinks the baby is mine, doesn't he?" Monica asked.

Katie glanced at the back of the driver's bald head as he pulled away from the curb. "He sees two women with a baby. I'll say enough to throw him off. Don't worry." Laying the groundwork for an affair wasn't as complicated as it was for hiding a baby. Katelyn's thoughts traveled the tide to Dean. Now hiding the baby from him took a complicated weave of lies. Hiding Savannah from everyone else would take more time, more effort.

So why was she doing it? Why work so hard to keep a baby that wasn't hers?

The sun had set and the lights of the suburbs of Los Angeles sped past the windows of the limo. Her entire life had been spent in limos and surrounded by other luxuries her father afforded her. She'd seen the world, twice. She'd dined with the rich and famous, skied the Alps, and sailed in the Grecian Sea. She spoke enough French to buy expensive clothes in Paris and order a decent meal there as well, but she wasn't happy.

Seeing Dean at the wedding jump-started her emotions and reminded her of better times—times with him. As luck would have it, Savannah arrived and gave her something else to focus on other than her history with Dean. Something other than her failures.

Not a peep emitted from the car carrier. All that silly crying on the airplane wore the poor thing out.

The ride from the airport to Monica's apartment passed in blissful silence and didn't take long.

"Thank you, Gerald." Katelyn sank the driver's name into her memory by using it. "I'll be staying with Monica tonight. Can you arrange for the rest of my things to be placed in the family suite?"

The family suite was one of the penthouse apartments at The Morrison. Jack had previously occupied it while he supervised the beginning stages of construction of his hotel. Now that he and Jessie were married, they would be staying primarily in Texas. Jack had bought nearly five hundred acres just west of their father's ranch and, when he and Jessie returned from their honeymoon, they'd be deep into putting their own touches on the existing home situated on the land.

"Of course, Miss Morrison." Gerald carried her other bags as well as Monica's into the apartment.

Monica carried Savannah into a dark bedroom while Katelyn placed a hundred-dollar bill into Gerald's palm.

The man glanced at the denomination briefly before it disappeared into his pocket. "I'll be back on from three to eleven tomorrow, Miss Morrison. Let me know if I can be of assistance."

Just like that, Gerald was in her favor.

"I'll do that."

Katelyn closed the door behind Gerald and turned on her heel. The entirety of Monica's small two-bedroom apartment would fit inside the living room of the penthouse at the hotel. A kitchen counter separated the cooking space from the living space. A sofa bed filled the room with a reclining chair to its side. The only updated furniture was a midsize flat screen mounted on the wall. It was hard to believe that Monica had shared this apartment with Jessie and her son for several years. Her imagination wouldn't have to work hard for long. Until she figured out exactly what Savannah's future held, the two of them would live here most of the time.

Monica closed the door to the spare room. "She's sleeping so I left her in the car seat. First thing tomorrow you're going to have to buy a few essentials. Jessie didn't keep any of Danny's baby things he outgrew since there's not enough storage space."

"Shopping I can handle. What I really need is a sitter."

In the kitchen, Monica ran a kettle under the faucet before turning on the stove to boil water. "Mrs. Hoyt lives down the hall. She sat with Danny when my schedule collided with Jessie's. I'll call her in the morning."

"Seriously?"

"She loves babies and could use some extra money. Her husband passed away a few years ago and her fixed income barely does it, from what I can tell."

Katelyn leaned a hip against the counter. "It all feels so easy."

Monica laughed aloud. "Easy? Oh, sister, getting a sitter and a crib is the easy part. Juggling a job, the staff at the hotel who need to think you're living there when you're not, and dodging baby questions from the people who know you…that is gonna take some serious work. Not to mention that pint-size living, breathing, demanding infant. You can kiss off those stilettos and silk pantsuits for a while and embrace your T-shirts and jeans. Raising a kid is hard, grueling work. The hours are long and the pay is shitty."

Monica's words would have scared off a lesser person. Not Katelyn. She squared her shoulders and put her best Morrison foot forward. "My father didn't raise a quitter. Savannah is not quite mine…yet. One way or another, I'll find her mama and the meaning behind the message in her letter. When that happens, I'll either hand her over or give her the Morrison name permanently."

The steam from the kettle started to whistle and Monica quickly turned down the fire.

From down the hall came Savannah's pathetic cry.

"That's your call, Mommy. It's time to see what all that Texas determination can do."

Chapter Five

According to Miss May, Katelyn and Monica left the hotel with enough baggage to last a month. Dean ascertained that information after leaving two messages on Katelyn's home answering machine. Messages he wouldn't have bothered with if Katie had left her usual response on her machine. It wasn't unlike her to leave Texas for weeks on end for extended trips abroad. This time, however, she didn't leave the typical explanation…"I'm drinking wine in Italy. Call you when I fly home."

No. This time Katelyn left no such message on her personal line and Dean thought the worst. He knew something wasn't right. He didn't relax until Miss May revealed that, although Katie left rather abruptly, she at least disappeared with a friend.

Dean talked with some of Katie's friends, none had recently given birth, or even knew anyone who was expecting. So who did Savannah belong to? And why was Katelyn so determined to keep the baby's identity from him?

On a hunch, he called The Morrison in Ontario and asked if Katie had checked in. Sure enough, the staff had seen her and expected an extended stay.

"Can you leave a message for Miss Morrison, please?"

"Of course, Mr. Prescott."

"Inform her that she's not to step foot on the site until I arrive in town." If her only business in Ontario was to help Jack with his hotel, she would ignore his demand…if she were keeping something from him, she would avoid confrontation. At least he thought she'd react that way.

"Excuse me?" The receptionist had heard him. Chances were she didn't want to relay his words.

"Not one foot. I'll be there Monday afternoon. Have her call me."

"Does she have your number?"

He hadn't forgotten hers. "Yes."

The receptionist disconnected the call and Dean stared at the phone in his hand. What put the fire under Katie's butt and made her run?

He made a quick call to the airline and moved his flight up a full day. Even then, she had two full days in California before he arrived.

Jack always had a sixth sense about his sister's well-being and Dean was determined to keep an eye on her. From what he'd seen so far, he agreed with Jack. Something wasn't quite right about her.

"Is that so?" Katelyn tapped the edge of her sunglasses against the reception desk.

"Those were the very words Mr. Prescott left for us to deliver." The young woman behind the desk lifted her brown eyes and appeared to fade before Katelyn's.

"Not one foot?"

"Yes, ma'am."

If there were two things Katie couldn't stand, it was someone telling her what she couldn't do, and the other was to be called *ma'am*.

She glanced at the woman's name tag. "I'm going to need a favor, Naomi."

Naomi's eyes grew wide. "I'm told the hotel is at your disposal."

"Right." It was…but it also needed to be her ally. "I'll need a rental car while in town. My preferences are in my file. I'd like the lunch special delivered to my room in thirty minutes and I need you to deliver a message for Mr. Prescott if he calls again."

Naomi poised a pen over a hotel pad of paper and waited.

"Let Mr. Prescott know that I take orders from no one." She turned and strode to the bank of elevators. Her stiff disposition fled once the elevator doors shut.

She was exhausted. Leaving Savannah in the care of Mrs. Hoyt while Monica left for work had to be the hardest thing she had ever done. Staying with Monica wouldn't be within her character and red flags would be flying with the likes of Dean if she didn't pretend to be staying at the hotel.

Once inside the family suite, she stashed her suitcase deep in the closet, removed several outfits, and hung them up. She selected what she considered a typical Katelyn Morrison skirt that reached a full hand span above her knees and hugged her hips like a second skin. The cream color brought out the bronze of her skin, kissed by the Texan sun. After slipping into a silk shirt and applying a dab of lip gloss, she called housekeeping and asked them to press the outfits that hung in her closet while she was out.

She slipped on her high heels as room service arrived. She thanked the waiter she recognized from the last time she'd stayed with her brother in Ontario. "Thank you, Mario. You can return in an hour to retrieve the dishes."

"Shall I put in your order for dinner?"

Katelyn lifted her chin and offered a smile. "That won't be necessary. I have a…companion in town and probably won't be back in until late. But thank you."

Mario had been with the hotel staff long enough to understand the undertone of what Katie had told him.

Companion meant *lover…later* meant *in the morning if at all.*

Katie had told many a staff member these things in the past and had never been questioned. There was no reason to believe anyone would start to now.

Mario tilted his head to the side and let himself out. Twenty minutes later, she pulled out of the hotel valet in a red convertible and let the top down.

Don't step one foot on the property until he arrives, my ass.

Dean must have forgotten who he was talking to.

She might be tired for lack of sleep, but she wasn't catatonic… not yet anyway.

Dean knew the moment he spotted the red sporty convertible with a rental car sticker on it, that Katelyn had ignored his request. In a strange way, he was pleased. Maybe all his worries about her were for nothing. Jack's worries, he corrected himself. It was Jack who thought something wasn't right with his sister.

Dean swung out of his truck, reached into the backseat of his extended cab, and grabbed a hard hat before plopping it on his head.

Under his feet the dirt mixed with weeds as he made his way to the construction trailer on the site. He assumed Katelyn would be in the air-conditioned office since there wasn't much for her to do inside the hard shell of Jack's hotel. The rough framing had been done with exterior walls added for support. The plumbers and electricians were scheduled to start work within the week on the interior building. Already miles of pipes crisscrossed the grounds delivering electricity to the exterior lighting. Everything about the job site was a well-orchestrated symphony of work. *Organized chaos* he often called it. It calmed him, in a strange way. He enjoyed watching a project come together like an artist enjoys the last stroke of the brush to a canvas.

Working with Jack had been a dream so far. They both talked about the project and had a clear picture of how the hotel would work and run after it was completed.

Jack wanted a posh hotel for families. He wanted something most could afford or, at the very least, save to splurge on. The hotel would host many of the amenities of his father's fancier establishments. There would be hotel cars, with car seats, and minivans. Each room was a suite complete with a door between the rooms so parents could close off sleeping children, or children could close off noisy parents. Child safety was paramount but that didn't mean every corner and edge of the hotel had to be rounded. It simply needed to be constructed with safety and families in mind.

Dean was the oldest of four kids. His baby sister was already married and on her second pregnancy. He loved his nephew, Robert, and couldn't wait for the birth of his niece. Syrie, his sister, already knew the gender of the baby but still had a few months left before the birth. She and Dean had had a couple of conversations about three-year-old Robert and how fast he could escape her childproof home. Some of her suggestions for safety had been implemented in the plans for the hotel.

Dean kicked his steel-toed boots onto the straw mat at the door leading into the trailer and braced himself to see Katie.

Jo, his on-site receptionist, sat at her desk right inside the door. She glanced up when he walked in. "Morning, Mr. Prescott."

"Hey, Jo," he said, glancing around the room. The door to his office was closed, the one to the center of the small building was wide open. Plans were spread out all over the desk, which wasn't abnormal, but no one hovered above them as he expected.

Where was Katelyn?

As he removed his hat, Jo stood and gathered a bunch of papers in her hands. "I placed the messages that could wait on your desk. Mr. Simpson called this morning to schedule the next inspection. I told him you'd call him later today. Faltworth came in this morning to tell me that half of the roofing materials that arrived over the weekend were the wrong color. He has already called the manufacturer and scheduled a truck to take the materials back." Jo took a deep breath and smiled. "How was the wedding? I'll bet Jessie was just beautiful. Did everything go without a hitch?" Jo was the best damn secretary Dean had ever had. He swore she had caffeine in her bloodstream and a firecracker under her ass.

"Jessie was the blushing bride. Jack's a lucky man." And because he knew Jo would ask he added, "Everyone arrived on time, and nothing happened that wasn't expected. It's almost like you'd planned it."

Jo was five foot four on a good day. She wore blue jeans and boots much like the men on the job site, and kept her hair in a simple ponytail. Dean had hired her right out of college without any secretarial experience at all. She'd responded to the employment ad he'd placed when he landed a strip mall contract outside Moreno Valley. The economy had already turned and Dean had to bid the job at a lower rate than he'd wanted to. The secretary in his main office had left unexpectedly, met a guy and ran off or some such thing, and Dean had been left without help. Jo showed up and explained, in detail, just how efficient she was at running damn near everything. In years past, his secretaries would run their end of the business from a central office. Jo didn't understand running his office from anywhere but a job site. She had no problem traveling to wherever his latest and biggest project was being built. For a little thing, she wasn't intimidated by men twice her size. She reminded Dean of his other sister, Ella. Jo turned a head or two, but didn't seem to notice.

"Have you met Jack's sister, Miss Morrison?"

Jo's eyes grew wide as she nodded. "I told her that she needed sensible shoes and to wear a hard hat. She politely ignored me, took some plans, and headed toward the main lobby. I didn't think we'd see her until the drywall was up."

"I didn't either," he said while placing his hat on his head again and then turning toward the door. "How long has she been here?"

"About an hour." Jo removed a second hat from a hook and handed it to him.

Dean could only imagine what shoes Katie had on and how her waltzing through the construction zone was affecting the workers. He pictured her infamous tight skirts, the ones that screamed to every man with a pulse to stare and weep with want, clinging to her skin. The first time he'd seen her wearing one was at a barbeque at the Morrison ranch. He and Jack were deep into the summer before their senior year of high school. Katelyn was a couple of years behind them but that didn't stop her from sticking close to her brother and his small posse made up of Dean, Jack, Tom, and Mike.

She'd stepped from the massive oak doors of her father's ranch home wearing a thin layer of black leather over her ass that curved so tightly there was no possible way she wore panties. Her father, Gaylord, spotted her from across the expansive yard and fell on her like flies on raw steak. Although Gaylord wasn't a pushover, he didn't know how to diplomatically make Katie change her clothes. It didn't help that her friends wore virtually the same outfit, though a tad longer and not nearly as inviting, as Dean recalled.

Katie loved the spotlight, reveled in the attention of the media and all members of the opposite sex. There was no reason to believe she wasn't traipsing around *his* job site in a tight little number that would grind work to a halt.

The sound of pneumatic hammers slamming nails into wood grew as he breached the outside walls of the main lobby. A couple of construction workers with slack jaws and wide eyes stared toward the east side of the building.

Dean followed the pattern of awestruck men until he found her.

Bent over a railing on what would be one of the many ground floor suites, Katie's short, cream-colored skirt rode midthigh. The sight of her slammed his breath from his lungs. Her long legs appeared to ride for miles and the four-inch heels extended them even farther.

Her butt flexed as she straightened and looked up to the ceiling. She reached above her head as if measuring the height of the room.

The memory of her stretching in bed, naked, after they'd made love swam in his mind.

Get a grip, Dean, he chided himself. Drowning in those memories would only lead to heartache. And he'd had his share of that, enough to last a lifetime.

"You need to wear a hat," he all but yelled in her direction.

Katie jumped and swiveled in his direction. "Dammit, Dean, you scared me." She brought a hand to her chest as if calming her heart from the shock of him being there.

"If an inspector were here, he'd shut me down if he caught you without a hard hat."

He took two purposeful strides in her direction and thrust the hat in front of him. He avoided her personal space but couldn't keep her floral scent from reaching his nose.

She always smelled like spring.

Dean wiggled the hat in his hand.

She sneered at it as if it were a snake. "Who else has worn that thing?"

"I have no idea."

"I'm not touching it."

He rolled his eyes and let his arm fall. "You wear a hat, or get off my job site."

Her mouth dropped. "You can't fire me."

"I'm not firing you, I'm telling you the rules. And those shoes have to go, too."

She stuck out a hip and rested a hand on it. "Will an inspector shut you down for my shoes?"

He wanted to tell her yes, but he'd be lying. "The ground is uneven and there are nails everywhere. Twisting an ankle and contracting tetanus are the most likely by-product of stilettos on the site."

Katie lifted a leg and examined her own shoe. Her skirt slid farther up her thighs.

Dean groaned.

"I've run from half a dozen paparazzi on the cobblestoned streets of Italy in heels like these. I'll take my chances."

He thrust the hat in her direction a second time and dismissed the footwear argument. "They're your feet. The hat isn't optional."

After sniffing the air and finding it unsavory, Katie glanced at the top of his head. He read her thought before she managed to voice it.

"Has anyone else worn your hat?"

It had his name on it. No one would consider putting it atop his or her head. "No."

A slow Southern smile met her lips. Avoiding a forgotten two-by-four, she shortened the space between them and stared at his hat.

This was not a fight he was going to win. He could insist she wear the hat in his hand, but knew he'd end up tossing her over his shoulder and removing her from the site because she wouldn't wear it. It wasn't that she was a snob, just particular about what touched her skin.

No matter how the hat ordeal played out, the men on his crew would be talking by the end of the day. Carrying her off the site or letting her wear his hat for the day…those were his options.

He mumbled under his breath and removed his hat before plunking it down on her stubborn head.

She stood a little taller and wore a satisfied smile.

"How do I look?"

Good enough to eat, he thought but didn't say. The hard hat should have looked ridiculous on her. It didn't. A completely unwanted sense of pride sparked his ego when he glanced down at his name atop her head. The hat claimed her as his in a completely high school way.

He shook the thoughts from his confused mind and quickly said, "Fine."

She tilted her head to the side and considered him for a moment before turning back to whatever it was she was looking at when he had first walked in behind her.

"Is this the standard size of all the rooms?" she asked.

"All but the two and three bedroom bungalows that are outside of this building. Those have small kitchens."

She nodded and crossed the room to her purse and removed a pen. After writing something down, she tapped the pen against her bottom lip. "Is there a penthouse?"

"Not in the traditional sense. Jack wanted individual single dwellings, the bungalows, for patrons with deeper pockets and space needs. There is one suite on the top floor, but it's only half the size of the largest single standing suite structure. The rest of the top floor is dedicated to dining, a bar, and a teen club hangout."

"Teen club?"

Dean smiled and crossed his arms over his chest. "Family first. That's what Jack wants. This is a destination experience. Something for everyone in the family to enjoy." Unlike any other project Dean had been a part of building, this hotel felt more like building a fantasy. Fancy hotels catered to the rich and adult. There wasn't a place for the kids to go and be kids.

"How soon before I can get up there and get a feel for the space?"

"Once all the exterior walls are up."

"How long will that be?"

"A couple of weeks, give or take."

She jotted down a few more notes and narrowed her eyes. Katie sounded so professional and ready to take on the project, Dean had to remind himself who he was talking to.

"The hotel isn't anywhere near needing your hand. I'm surprised you flew out as quickly as you did."

"I'm anxious to get started," she said before turning her back on him.

"Why?" He'd asked himself why she wanted a job ever since Jack told her that she'd been hired. It wasn't like she needed money. In fact, she wasn't getting paid.

She ignored his question and asked one of her own. "How many square feet are the rooms?"

He told her and asked her again, "Why?"

She continued to scribble notes as she spoke. "I know you don't want me here."

"I didn't say that."

"So you do want me here?"

"I didn't say that. I asked why you want to do this. Why put out all the effort when you could be flying to France or dodging photographers in Italy?"

Blue eyes met his and held. "If I were a man, you wouldn't ask me why I was doing this. No one asks Jack why he wants to build his own hotels when he has Daddy's to fall back on."

"You'd be hard-pressed to pull the women libbers' card wearing that skirt, darlin'. I've never known a female more proud to be a woman in my life." It was one of the many things he admired about her. She wore womanhood like a thick fur and dared anyone to say a thing about it.

Her eyes softened. "Maybe I'm bored with France."

Ah, now they were getting somewhere. "People are going to depend upon you here. This isn't something you can get bored with and move on."

"Have I ever walked away from my obligations?"

You walked away from me. From us.

Hurt swelled in his chest and he needed to remove himself from her side before he revealed any of his undesired thoughts. "Return those plans to my desk before you leave."

Chapter Six

What felt lower than dirt? Mud…definitely mud. Worm-filled mud crawling with insects might be the closest thing Katelyn could compare herself to as she watched Dean walk away.

She could convince herself all day long that Dean had run full speed into her ego, knowing damn well she had one and would defend it to the death. But the look of longing that had passed over his beautiful gray eyes before he told her to return the plans to his desk would live inside her for some time to come.

The last thing she wanted was to involve Dean with her life. He needed to be free to find a life with another woman, one who could give him the large family he wanted.

That wasn't her.

It didn't escape her notice when his eyes followed the length of her legs and settled on her breasts a time or two during their brief conversation. Oh, he'd been tactful, but he hadn't been invisible. Maybe she should wear something a little less *her* while at work.

Dealing with Dean on the job site would be complicated, but she assumed he'd see her in passing. She did the finishing work and he did the major construction. Yet as she looked deeper into what it would take to pull off designing the hotel after construction, she knew she needed to have more involvement from the beginning.

A teen club would require more lighting, more soundproofing. Katelyn was certain that Jack and Dean had considered some of these things, but not the design aspect of them. Her being involved this early on would save money in the end and make her job easier once Dean completed the job.

Putting emotional distance between her and Dean was a must from the beginning. For more reasons than he would ever know. It didn't matter that their chemistry had always been combustible. Hell, she remembered phone conversations with him that left her breathless and wanting.

All of that was before. Before she learned just how inadequate she was to be with anyone, let alone a man as good as Dean.

After shifting the papers in her hands and gathering her purse, she left the shell of a room and took one more walk in what would be the main lobby.

A couple of construction workers craned their necks to watch her as she avoided multiple hazards in her high heels to visualize the space. With the right lighting, table lamps wouldn't be necessary. She wrote a note to herself to ask about the electrician's plans. She'd taken one course in architectural design and could fake her way around a set of blueprints. But she'd need a hell of a lot more knowledge if she was going to make hotel design her life's work in the next few months.

She tucked her notebook into her oversized purse and strode from the room. She had a couple of days' worth of homework she needed to do before involving Dean.

Maybe by then she'd forget the look in his eyes before he had left.

There was a slight hesitation in her step as she neared the stairs leading to the construction trailer. Dean was probably in there… doing whatever it was that he did. She'd see him again and need to meet his gaze without emotion. With anyone else, that was easy. Not with him. Never with him.

The cool, dry air of the trailer met her skin with welcome relief. She hadn't realized how warm it was outside. Texas heat was so much thicker. The dry Southern California air might be warm, but it didn't weigh on her.

"Hi, Jo," she addressed the surly secretary. "Dean wanted me to return these before I left."

Jo didn't look up from her computer. "Leave them on his desk."

Katie looked toward his office, the one where she'd found the plans earlier that morning. The door was nearly closed and she couldn't tell if he was in there.

"I wouldn't want to bother him. How about I leave them with you."

Jo released a gruff laugh. "He doesn't hide inside all day. Leave them on his desk. He'll find them when he gets in at lunch."

Oh, good, he's not here.

Instead of voicing her relief, she quickly returned the plans to his empty office and left the trailer.

It wasn't until she'd pulled out of the parking lot, and the hard hat on her head started to slip in the wind, that she realized she still wore his stupid hat.

She tossed it into the passenger seat and turned the car toward Monica's apartment.

Katelyn avoided the job site for two days. Which wasn't difficult considering the life-changing event known as Savannah.

In the corner of the small room, Katie placed a bassinet adorned with pink and brown baby blankets. A plush pad had been affixed to the top of a dresser for use as a changing station.

She'd taken a crash course in all things baby in the past week. She'd purchased a stroller, a reclining swing, and more clothes than the infant could possible wear while she stayed in the zero- to three-month age range.

A trip to the bookstore resulted in half a dozen parenting books along with developmental expectations in children. And a baby milestone book.

The baby book she pondered. What would happen if the mother returned for Savannah? Writing down milestones and taking pictures somehow cemented her in Katie's life.

It was silly to think a baby book was some kind of glue. Already Savannah had wiggled her tiny fingers around Katie's heart and squeezed hard.

Monica returned home after seven that night. Her twelve-hour shifts had to be hard, yet Katie never heard her new friend complain.

"Look who's still awake." Monica motioned toward Savannah who was lying on a blanket in the middle of the floor kicking her feet.

Katelyn glanced up from the reference book she was using to understand Dean's construction plans. Blueprints and furniture catalogs were worlds apart.

"And quite content just sucking her fist for about an hour now. I'm hoping to keep her up a little later to see if I can get her to sleep for three hours in a row."

Monica placed her purse on the kitchen counter and poured herself a glass of water. "You look like you could use the sleep."

"I can." Surprisingly, the tiny smiles that greeted her at two a.m. were worth waking up for. The irony was, if Katelyn could have told the world about the baby from the beginning, she probably would have hired a full-time caretaker to help at night. Those two a.m. smiles would be awarded to a nanny and not her.

"If she doesn't sleep tonight, you can look forward to tomorrow at the hotel."

Monica had agreed to watch Savannah all night between her days off in order for Katelyn to keep the appearance of living at the hotel. She had yet to actually sleep in the penthouse suite since arriving in California.

She kept up the appearance of living there. She left laundry, ate lunch, and even messed up the bed so it appeared she slept there. She would arrive before one personnel shift ended, change clothes, and then leave a short time later.

Gerald drove her from time to time back and forth to the apartment, but Katelyn never let him see her with the baby.

"Did you call the private detective today?" Monica asked.

"I did."

"And?"

Katelyn pushed the book aside and focused on Monica.

"He's flying here on Monday to discuss the case."

Patrick Nelson came highly recommended. He was exclusive, discreet, and expensive. Hiring him to dig into Savannah's parentage was as necessary as eating. If Katie took the birth certificate and didn't question it, she would forever look over her shoulder. There were already times she felt like a criminal. She tensed when a police officer drove by and hid her eyes behind sunglasses when she bought diapers. It was crazy, and not the way she wanted to live her life.

Monica covered Katie's hand with hers. "It will be all right. You're doing the right thing. I spoke with social services today at the hospital."

Panic rose in Katelyn's throat. "You told them?"

"God, no. I'm getting our facts straight. What the laws are about abandoning infants. We have a safe baby surrender program here in California. Babies are dropped off in ERs and fire departments all the time. No questions asked. A baby isn't considered abandoned unless it's left to its own defenses. When we find Savannah's birth mother, she can't be prosecuted because she left her with you, gave you custody. There's a whole bunch of legal shit involved that I don't understand, but there are several cases of babies being given to someone without an adoption agency."

"The laws in Texas probably aren't the same as here."

"Probably. You might want to look into them…or have that PI look into them for you. The more knowledge you have, the better you're going to feel about it."

Monica had a point. Katelyn's education needed to involve infant care, construction plans, and legalese about adoptions or baby abandonment clauses. *I hated school when I was in it.*

Monica removed a frozen dinner from the refrigerator and popped it into the microwave. "Have you heard from Dean?"

Just hearing his name made her squirm in her seat. "No. Not a word."

"Don't you find that odd? I mean, you still have his hard hat and you haven't returned there since the first day."

Katelyn shrugged. "I'll go in tomorrow to see how far along they are. Jack made it sound like it was taking forever for things to move forward. I doubt I'm needed every day."

"You're avoiding Dean."

"I am not."

"Are, too."

Katelyn opened her mouth to protest again and promptly shut it. "Lord, Jessie must have hated growing up with you."

Monica smiled and winked. "I call 'em as I see 'em. Jessie tried to hide her true emotions about all kinds of things growing up, but I could see the truth in her eyes. You have a thing for Dean and don't even try and deny it."

"Dean is my brother's best friend."

"Doesn't mean you don't have a thing for him. The man is gorgeous. I'm not sure why you of all people would deny your attraction to the man. He obviously feels the need to watch over you."

"Misguided loyalty to my brother."

Monica snorted. "Bull. Dean might feel the need to *watch out* for a weak sister," she air quoted *watch out* with her fingers. "You're not weak. You might have lost a little bit of snark with the lack of sleep, but you're far from fragile."

No, she wasn't made of glass. She didn't go out of her way to gossip and let anyone inside her head either. Yet talking with Monica, living with her for the better part of two weeks, boiled the need to talk and spill the entire story about her and Dean.

Maybe if Monica knew their history, she'd understand how desperate Katie was to keep Dean at a distance now.

"If I tell you something, will you promise to keep it only between the two of us?"

Monica lifted her lips into a cat-ate-the-canary smile. "I'm almost offended you need to ask. You're living in my place with a child that isn't yours. I *can* keep a secret."

Katie glanced over at Savannah who hadn't made much of a peep since Monica came home.

"Dean and I…" Katie ignored the chill down her spine. "We, ah…"

Monica placed her hand in the air. "Wait. This needs wine."

Boy, did it ever.

Monica uncorked a bottle of wine and poured two glasses before settling into the sofa with her legs curled under her. It was as if she were getting ready to watch a movie. Her sharp gaze focused on Katie before she uttered the words, "Let me have it."

After drawing in a fortifying breath, Katie started again. "Dean and I dated…secretly."

Why Katie thought the sky would fall as she voiced her past, she didn't know…but she did.

Monica sipped her wine and smiled. "I knew it."

"We hadn't set out to. It just kinda happened. And no one, not my brother, not my diary, knows about it."

Monica put a hand in the air. "Why the secrecy?"

Katie shrugged. "We run in some tight circles back home. We thought it would be better to keep our relationship to ourselves to avoid any of those awkward *Do we invite Dean or do we invite Katelyn?* situations."

"Sounds like you anticipated the breakup from the beginning."

The memory of their first kiss surfaced in her mind. The softness of his touch, the pine scent of his skin. The way he cupped her head so she couldn't pull away…

"Oh, to be a fly on the wall of your brain," Monica said. "I don't think I've ever seen you blush before."

Katie sighed and covered her face with her hands.

Maybe Monica would understand if she started from the beginning. "Dean and my brother have been best friends since high school. Being the younger and annoying sister, the two of them didn't pay a lot of attention to me. But you've met all the boys and none of them are hard on the eyes.

"When I hit thirteen, my hormones went crazy. My mom, if you can call her that, had already run off. She'd call once in a while, but I didn't have another woman to confide in. My dad tried by having our housekeeper keep tabs on me, but I wanted nothing to do with her. I started wearing clothes that made me feel grown up and loved the attention the guys gave me. I'd be lying if I said I hadn't always had a crush on Dean. But he didn't look. Not once."

"He looked eventually," Monica pointed out.

Yes, he did. There were times over the years Dean would stand beside her brother Jack as the two of them confronted her with another tabloid article about her dating life. She took Dean's sharp disapproval like she had her brother's or her father's. She ignored it. Eventually Jack backed off…hell, even her father didn't bother with anything more than a grunt or a shake of the head these days.

But not Dean. He'd suggested she find a different guy to date, or different club to hang out at.

It was one of those *Change what you're doing, Katie* conversations with Dean that resulted in that first kiss nearly two years ago.

"This guy is scum," Dean had spit out between his teeth as he slapped the tabloid on the table in front of her. They were celebrating Jack's birthday at the ranch and Dean had pulled her into an empty room to talk.

Katie tossed her chin up in defiance. "I'm not sure who died and left you as my fairy godmother. Not even my father tells me who I can sleep with and who I can't."

Dean's face had grown even harder. The cleft in his chin was so tight she could probably bounce a golf ball off it.

"You're sleeping with him?"

The *him* Dean referred to was an actor. And in reality, only a friend. But the tabloid had snapped a picture of the two of them leaving a club and suggested that Mason was cheating on his current girlfriend and that Katelyn was the "other woman." It was laughable, really. The tabloids seldom painted a clear picture. Dean knew this but still raged on as if the magazine were gospel. A few times the rags would get the story somewhat right but she hadn't slept with nearly as many people as the public thought she had.

As Dean obviously thought she had.

"That," Katie poked her finger into Dean's broad chest, "is none of your business."

"It damn well is my business, darlin'."

"Oh, really? How so?"

"You're Jack's sister. I've known you since before you wore a training bra."

Katelyn glanced down at her ample cleavage and purposely tugged her shirt a little lower to reveal more skin. "Are you telling me you're looking out for me like I'm *your* sister?"

Dean opened his mouth and then closed it.

That was the moment she knew that Dean didn't look at her as a sister. His gaze had heated and desire flashed over his face.

Katelyn's knees suddenly felt weak. As if sensing her inability to stand, Dean slid into her personal space and cupped the back of her head. She froze, hardly believing he was touching her. Then his lips met hers in a kiss that defined the art of kissing. He was soft and warm and made her tingle. Her eyes closed while she opened to him like a flower did to sunshine.

It ended too soon. Both of them were stunned by the kiss.

Neither of them acknowledged what had happened the rest of that day.

Not twenty-four hours later, Dean knocked on the door of her suite. When she asked what he was doing there, he told her he wanted to kiss her again. To make certain he hadn't imagined the experience.

Suddenly Katie was a young girl again, giddy with his attention. He left her suite the next day, and she knew her life would never again be the same.

"We didn't date in public. When we were with friends, it became a game to tease each other without anyone noticing," Katie explained to Monica.

"How long did this go on?"

"A few months."

"What happened to break it up?"

Katie's gaze slid to the floor where she had been lying next to Savannah for the last hour as she talked about her past. Savannah had fallen to sleep, her pouty lips moved with every breath.

"We fought…things ended." She wasn't about to tell all her secrets. About how she'd ended up pregnant with Dean's baby only to have a miscarriage. About how the awful monthly cycles she'd endured were actually a severe case of endometriosis that messed up not only her fallopian tubes, but made her uterus inhospitable to carry a pregnancy to term. The fact she ended up pregnant to begin with was a small miracle. "Six months after our breakup Dean was engaged. He obviously wasn't heartbroken."

"But you were."

She shook her head. "No…please. We had a fling. That's it."

Monica was sipping her second glass of wine. "A fling? You sleep with your teenage crush and you think it's a fling?"

"Yeah, I do."

"Hmm. Do the two of you ever talk about your affair?"

"No." Not out loud anyway.

"Is it awkward? Working with him?"

"As much as can be expected. I'm sure it would have been worse had we told the world about us."

Monica moved off the couch quietly and placed her wine glass in the sink. "I'm sure you think what you had is over, but Dean watches you whenever you're in the room. I noticed it at the wedding. He obviously still cares."

"He nearly married another woman. If he felt anything for me, it was lust and that's it."

"Time will work that out."

"Time will work what out?"

"Whether he only wants you for the crazy-hot sex or something more."

"I didn't say it was crazy-hot."

Monica rolled her eyes. "You didn't have to. The temperature in the room rose five degrees while you talked about it. Listen, all I'm saying is this. If you're going to be working beside him for the next few months, and he still has a thing for you, you're going to find out about it. My gut says he does."

Katie started to shake her head.

"And…my gut is also saying you have a thing for him."

"*Had* a thing."

Monica waved her hand in the air, dismissing everything Katie was saying. "Whatever! *De'Nial* is a river in Egypt yet you've parked your brain right next to it. Deny you care about him all you want. But when he starts sniffing around asking where you're spending your time, you'll know without a doubt that he's thinking about you."

Monica slipped past her and started down the hall. "I'm taking a shower and going to bed."

"G'night, Monica."

Left alone with her thoughts, Katie wondered if it was possible that Dean thought about her at all. She'd severed their relationship with a hacking knife instead of a quick clean blade.

Two weeks after the miscarriage and all the follow-up tests her doctor put her through determined that she would never carry a child, Katie found Dean in her suite looking at pictures on his cell phone. They were pictures of his nephew and Dean's large family visiting the baby in the maternity wing at the hospital.

For the first time in weeks, Katie had felt like getting dressed and joining the world. She'd surprised Dean by coming up behind him.

He snapped his phone away, but Katie had already seen the pictures.

"Hey," he said, pecking a kiss on her cheek. "You're dressed."

He'd been strong, a shoulder to cry on…a friend. "I'm feeling better," she said. "What were you looking at?"

"Nothing."

"Really? Nothing?"

Dean tucked his phone into his jeans as he stood. He placated her with a smile, but it didn't reach his eyes.

"Just pictures. So, what do you have planned today?" His changing of the subject wasn't unnoticed.

"How old is your nephew now?"

Dean shuffled his feet. "A year and a half."

"You still keep a baby picture of him on your phone?" The hurt of losing their child hung just above the surface of her skin, it burned.

"He's a cute kid." There was more to his walk down memory lane than glancing at a picture of his nephew. Dean was thinking about the magnitude of Katie's problem. At least that's what she thought. If she asked him, he'd probably tell her she was wrong. But she knew he wanted to be a dad. He'd been right there with her from the beginning of the pregnancy and never once said he wasn't ready. Quite the opposite.

They'd never kept secrets from each other and the moment Katie suspected she was pregnant, she told Dean. They drove together to a drugstore far outside of town, hoping like hell that there weren't any cameras pointing her way. They'd been together when the double lines on the stick told her that her period wasn't late, it simply wasn't coming. Instead of staring at the stick and cursing it, Dean gathered her in his arms and kissed the living daylights out of her. "Yeah, we didn't plan it," he'd said. "But I was born to be a dad and you're going to be the best mom." He'd made love to her that night and the next morning she woke up to a plush teddy bear on the pillow next to her.

Within a week, she'd miscarried.

All the joy, all the excitement, left Dean's eyes. Until she'd seen him staring at the picture of his nephew.

Her inability to have kids was her problem.

It wasn't too late for Dean.

For the next few days, Katie cloaked her emotions with her debutant persona, slid into her tight skirts, and avoided Dean. No one knew about them. No one knew about the miscarriage. Katie knew she had to cut her ties and the only way she'd be able to do that was with bloodshed.

The nightclub was packed the night Dean found her. She'd had a couple of drinks, but was far from drunk. She was contemplating leaving when she spotted him looking for her. She ran her hand up the arm of a man who'd been trying to get her attention all night and asked him to dance.

The weight of Dean's stare followed her, watched her, as she wiggled her hips, and didn't brush away the stranger's hand when he spread his palm on her ass.

Dean cut in, damn near taking the other man's arm off at his shoulder. Katie stormed away and Dean followed.

Outside the club, Dean lit into her. "What the fuck, Katie?"

"What's the problem, Dean?"

His face was red with fury, his fists clutched at his side. "What are you doing?"

"I'm dancing, what does it look like?" She trembled, hating the look on his face.

"You shouldn't be here."

"And where should I be? Home? Alone?"

"No, you should be with me."

"Why? I'm not pregnant. You're off the hook."

"Our baby was never a hook!" he yelled.

"Maybe not to you."

His eyes turned to steel. She couldn't have shocked him more with a slap across the face. "When are you going to grow up?" he asked through clenched teeth.

"Whenever I damn well please."

Dean swore under his breath, turned, and walked out of her life.

Now, a year and a half later...he was strolling back in.

Chapter Seven

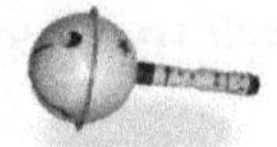

The hard hat Dean had been reduced to wearing now sported a bright pink stripe over the brim. A prank from his men. The day before he'd found a pair of high heeled women's shoes on his desk with small metal plates covering the toes. Someone had taken some time to construct those.

Every day it was something new and Katie hadn't shown her face on the site since that first day.

He dangled the hard hat off his finger and walked to the door of his office. Jo was busy typing something into the computer and barely acknowledged him. "I need another hat," he told her.

A hint of a smile lifted the side of Jo's lips. Her eyes never left the monitor. "You'll have to find one out there. The spares are all being used."

Well, damn, wasn't that convenient. "Of course they are."

Jo chuckled as he ducked back into his office.

He made a couple of phone calls and reviewed the latest purchase order on the roofing supplies. The clock on the wall told him it was ten and still there wasn't any sign of Katie. Maybe she'd changed her mind about the job.

He tapped his fingers along the side of the pink striped hat and gave in. He dialed the hotel and asked for Katie's suite. He told himself he was checking up on her. As Jack had asked him to.

Just a friend.

"I need the family suite," Dean said the moment the receptionist picked up the call. The staff knew when someone called asking about "the family suite" that the caller was a friend.

"I'm sorry, sir, but Miss Morrison isn't in. Can I take a message for her?"

Not in? It was ten in the morning and she wasn't at work. "When do you expect her?"

"I couldn't be sure, sir."

Something in the pit of his stomach soured.

"Sir?"

"I'll call her cell phone." He wouldn't, but leaving a message wasn't an option.

"Very good, sir. And thank you for calling The Morrison."

He disconnected the call and started to dial Monica's number. His finger hesitated over the seventh number and he hung up. Women had a way of talking, and it appeared to him that Monica and Katie had sparked a friendship. If he called Monica asking about Katie, and if Katie was keeping company with a man…

Dean squeezed his eyes shut and ignored the familiar burn in his stomach. The burn that fired up every damn time he'd seen Katie on the cover of a tabloid. There was always some muscled and tanned pretty boy on her arm and rumors about Katie's love life.

She was a bee that wasn't ready to make a hive and nest yet.

It shouldn't bother him that she was probably out doing the same thing she always did, but he'd hoped that maybe she'd grown up a little. Taking the job with Jack felt like a step in that direction for Dean.

Perhaps he was wrong.

He pushed away from his desk, and the urge to call around town checking up on Katie, and left his office.

He passed groups of workers and suffered their snickers and remarks about his hat before he found his plumbing foreman. "Hey, Steve."

Steve Bowman wore a blue-collared shirt with *Bowman Plumbing* written on the left breast pocket. The two of them had worked on several projects over the past couple of years and took the time to ride dirt bikes in the desert on occasion to blow off steam.

Steve stuck his hand out to shake Dean's and glanced at his hat. "Nice hat, princess."

"Zip it."

"And give up the chance of razzing you? Not a chance. Looks like the boys have a sense of humor. Why the pink?"

Dean could mark Steve off as the pink painting culprit. Steve crossed his arms over his chest and chuckled.

"Someone's idea of a joke."

"It's funny."

"No, it's not."

"Maybe not from where you're standing, but where I'm standing, it's this side of hilarious. Pink brings out your eyes, cowboy."

"Do I pay you to deliver shit, or get rid of it?"

Steve pounded him on the back with a good-natured swat and the two of them walked into what would be the main kitchen on the ground floor. "I consulted with the chef over at The Morrison like you suggested and he agreed we should have a second dishwashing station on the opposite end of the kitchens."

The station was the size of a small house. Dean couldn't imagine why they'd need two. "There's already going to be two industrial washers in here. Why the overkill?"

"When one of the washers needs repair, the backup is there, but the repairman get in the way of the work. Makes mealtime impossible."

Dean hadn't thought of that. "Why not shrink the size of this station and add a twin to the other side?"

Steve shrugged. "We could. But with round-the-clock room service, you might reconsider that suggestion."

Dean rubbed his chin. "Do we need to pull another permit?"

The two of them leaned over the blueprints and discussed the physical changes that would have to take place in the space to make the additional washers work.

The noise of the job site hummed all around them. Hammers slammed against wood, table saws buzzed with activity, and at least one radio blared music from a local rock station.

One by one, those background noises faded until Dean heard the click of something delicate, and persistent, approaching from behind him. He glanced over to see Steve smiling over his shoulder.

"Now that's something you don't see *here* every day."

Dean swiveled to find Katie, high heeled and short skirted, striding their way.

His hard hat sat on her head and covered her hair. Her makeup was a little heavy and attempted to cover dark circles under her eyes. Dean saw through it, but chances were no one else would. He remembered once, after a particularly active night in her bed, Katie talked about how makeup was God's gift to women so they could hide their sins. Seeing her painted up reminded him of his phone call to the hotel earlier. Where had she been and whom had she been with?

And why did he care?

"Why is there Sheetrock going up in the halls?" Not a hello, not a *How ya doing*. Just a strange question spilling from Katelyn's pouty lips.

"Excuse me?"

Her shoe caught on something and she needed to tug her foot to set it free. She kept talking as if they were the only two in the room, oblivious to the stares of all the men surrounding them.

"The Sheetrock? That is what they call it, right?"

"Drywall, Sheetrock, same thing."

She came to a stop in front of him and glanced over to Steve. "Hi," she managed to say before swinging her gaze at Dean.

"So why is it going up? I thought we were weeks away from that."

"Things move fast, Katelyn."

"But I thought—"

"Wrong. You thought wrong. Steven Bowman, this is Katelyn Morrison. Jack's sister and misguided interior designer for the hotel."

"A pleasure," she said with a nod.

"The pleasure is mine." Steve lifted his hat with one finger and let it fall back on his head. His eyes soaked her in like a starving man.

Dean had to squelch the desire to shield Katelyn from Steve's gaze.

"I thought Jo said you were weeks away from sheet-wall, or whatever you call it."

"For the complete job, yes, but not in that part of the hotel. Why are you so worked up?"

She waved papers in her hands and rambled. "Niches. I want niches along the main hall and in the main lobby. Those need to be framed into the structure."

Which was true, but the plans didn't call for them.

"Steve, will you please excuse us for a minute. I need to..."

"Go."

"Thank you, Mr. Bowman. Nice meeting you."

Dean stepped around the table he'd been standing in front of and led Katelyn out of the room.

"Back to work," he told his men who had all stopped to witness Katie's appearance and subsequent tirade.

Katelyn forced air into her lungs at a slower rate. She knew she was worked up about the niches...or lack thereof, but she'd had a bitch of a night. Her plan for a night of sleep or better yet, for Savannah's night of sleep, was a bust. The crying began at ten, then again at twelve…somewhere around two a.m., Savannah thought it would be fun to stay awake and try to smile. Which if Katelyn had had half an eye open, she would have probably enjoyed, but she ended up dozing off while Savannah played next to her on the bed and then woke to a nice little puddle from a leaky diaper. How so much came out of such a sweet little thing, Katie would never know.

Savannah finally managed to get back to sleep after four a.m.. Katie overslept and jumped out of bed when Monica lightly knocked on the door after eight and told her she was late.

A trip to the hotel for a refresher was out of the question. Considering the amount of drywall that would have to come down, it was a good thing she didn't delay her arrival.

"See," she said pointing out the drywall that already covered the walls of the main hall. "This is what I'm talking about. I need niches large enough to hold art with spotlighting above each one."

"This isn't your father's hotel. Art isn't something budget-minded patrons are looking for."

"That's crap. While I agree that those staying at The Morrison will stop to reflect on some of the art there, while here, they'll simply enjoy it as they pass by. The niches will preserve the art from being touched as people walk by."

Dean grunted and stared down the long hallway. "You couldn't have told me this earlier this week?"

"I've only been here that long."

"Right. And you couldn't be bothered to dent your social life to come in until today."

Social life? Oh, OK…she got it. Dean thought she was out partying and not taking her job seriously.

"I've been shopping."

Dean rolled his eyes. "Great, like you need more shoes."

"For the hotel. Designing color palettes and finding furniture that works takes time. Time I can't spend here making sure this stuff isn't going up."

"Drywall. It's called drywall."

"Dry whatever! It needs to come down. Or some of it anyway so I can have my niches."

"Fine!" Dean scowled and his gaze wouldn't meet hers. "How many niches are you planning?"

She brushed past him and pointed. "The first one will go here." She found a construction pencil on top of workbench and placed a small *X* on the wall. "Then we can evenly space them so we have ten down each hall."

Dean leaned over and grabbed the pencil from her hand and marked the wall with an *X* the size of a toddler.

Katie crossed her arms over her chest and moved out of his way. He counted to himself as he looked down the hall and shook his head. "You can have five."

"I can have five what?"

"Niches."

"Why only five?"

"Each niche has to be framed, each soffit wired for a light. That increases cost. You can have five on the halls down here."

"What about upstairs?"

He shook his head. "Not in the budget."

"Then increase the budget." Her design was slipping away before her eyes.

"It doesn't work that way."

"But—"

"This isn't a closet remodel, Katie…this is a hotel. You can't make designs that require construction and expect it not to cost money. Working within a budget might be novel for you, but I'm sure you can do it."

He spoke as if she were a child and it was starting to piss her off. The lack of sleep the night before wasn't helping either. "Then give me a budget."

His eyes narrowed and his pissed look slid into amusement. "You're serious."

"Do I look like I'm joking?"

Dean's head started to nod, slowly at first, then faster. "OK…I'll do that on one condition."

A lock of hair had come loose under the stupid hard hat so Katie thrust it behind her ear in frustration. She knew she looked ridiculous. And tired. Lord, just arguing with him was wearing her out.

"Well don't keep me in suspense. Name your price, cowboy."

He lifted his index finger and spoke slower. "I'll give you a budget and you will not argue, debate, or ask for more. I'll give you a workable budget any experienced designer would make work."

"But I'm not experienced—"

"Ah! No excuses! Do we have a deal?"

"And if that doesn't work for me?"

"Then you walk away now. Go home to Texas and take your niches with you."

She tilted her head and took him in. His determined chin and eyes set in stone made her wonder…made her question exactly why he didn't want her around. Then she finally noticed the stripe on his hat. Maybe he didn't like the distraction or the hazing he was obviously getting with the men.

Or maybe it was her.

"Deal." She shoved her hand in front of him and waited.

He hesitated, then his warm palm met hers. Sparks radiated up her arm and raised gooseflesh despite the dry heat filling the room.

She let go quickly and hoped he didn't see her skin flush. "I expect my budget by the end of the day."

Dean mumbled something under his breath as she walked away.

"Oh, and, Dean?"

"Yeah?"

"Nice hat."

Chapter Eight

Patrick Nelson's appearance somehow met, if not exceeded, every preconceived thought in Katelyn's brain about how a private eye should look. He had to be six two, nearly as tall as Dean. He looked thicker than a longhorn stud in a pen. Roped muscle filled in his black short jacket under a buttoned-up dress shirt. This man probably owned one suit and wore it only when he had to.

He screamed retired marine or ex-cop. His dark hair was peppered with gray and his brown eyes had a way of looking through you. If he were fifteen years younger, Katie might have found him attractive. Actually, he was attractive, but she wasn't interested.

She met with him in her room to avoid anyone overhearing their conversation.

They discussed Savannah's sudden appearance in Katelyn's life in depth. They were on a second cup of coffee before he turned the conversation toward her personal life.

He leaned back on the sofa of the penthouse family suite and wrote notes in the small pad of paper he'd pulled from his pocket.

"Who are you dating?"

The question struck her as strange and she hesitated to answer it. "Excuse me?"

"Dating…sleeping with? Who do you spend your time with on a romantic level?"

"I'm not sure what that has to do with Savannah ending up on my doorstep."

"Everything about you is relevant as to why this infant ended up in your arms. Someone knew things about you they couldn't have known by reading the papers."

She shook her head. "I'm not seeing anyone."

"You were on the third page of a Houston tabloid three weeks ago on the arm of a blond in a bar."

"I was?" She didn't know the picture he was referring to. She'd stopped concerning herself with the paparazzi pictures over a year and a half earlier. About the time she and Dean stopped seeing each other.

"You were. Club Zen I think it was."

Oh, that's right. She remembered going to meet a friend who had broken up with her latest. They managed to get through a round before several acquaintances surrounded them. Katelyn had a vague memory of someone taking pictures but didn't think more about it. "I know the club but couldn't tell you a thing about the picture. I wasn't involved with anyone in that crowd that night."

"The magazine said you were lovers."

"The magazine doesn't fact check."

Patrick made a note and continued.

"There's no one in your life?"

"No."

"Who are your girlfriends? Who do you confide in?"

Monica's name came to her lips with ease. "I already told you that Monica was with me the night Savannah showed up." Katie gave him a couple of names of people she considered close friends.

"Do they know about Savannah?"

"No. Only you and Monica know about her."

He scratched his chin in thought. "You wouldn't be the first celebrity, or woman of means, who has had a child dumped on their doorstep. Did it occur to you that this might not be personal?"

"Yeah. But it doesn't change anything. I still don't know who the mom is, and I won't be comfortable until I know Savannah is legally mine. I'm hiring you to find the mom and do the necessary check on this paperwork."

A corner of Patrick's mouth quivered. "I'll find the mom. Not to worry. The speed in which I do it will be the question. I'm going to need access to your suite in Houston."

She nodded. "No one can know you're a private investigator."

"Hence the word 'private.'" He wrote something on a separate sheet of paper and tore it off to give it to her.

It was a name. "Who is Ben Sanderson?"

"Me. That's the name you'll give the hotel. I'll tap into the surveillance and see what I can find."

"What should I tell them about you?"

"Tell them I'm your lover, friend…makes no difference to me. Just make it easy for me to get into the hotel and keep the staff from poking around. I'll do the rest."

She could do that. It wouldn't be the first time she'd told the staff to look the other way to a man's presence.

A loud knock sounded from the door to her suite. She looked at the clock on the wall and thought maybe room service was early. She stood and started for the door. "I ordered dinner. They're early. I can get you something if you like."

Patrick stood and tucked the notebook into his jacket pocket. "I have enough for now. I'll call you in a couple of days to update you on my progress."

He walked behind her as she opened the door.

The smile she'd placed on her lips to greet the hotel staff slid the moment the door opened.

"Dean?" The desire to shut the door and keep him from seeing Patrick made her arm shake. "What are you doing here?" And how had he managed to get up the elevator without a call from the receptionist letting her know he was there?

"You said you wanted a—" His words drifted off as his gaze fell behind her.

Katelyn found her smile and turned toward the man she'd hired. She sent a quick prayer to anyone listening that Patrick was as good as his résumé said. He needed to slip from the room without Dean questioning who he was.

Patrick moved a little closer to the door and placed a hand on her arm. "He doesn't look like room service."

"He's not." Katie twisted toward Dean and felt the air chill.

Dean stepped into the suite, his eyes narrowed to daggers. "Dean Prescott," Dean said, waiting for Patrick to say something.

Patrick lifted a hand for Dean to shake. "Ben Sanderson."

"Dean and I work together at my brother's hotel," she explained.

Patrick nodded and finished shaking Dean's hand.

"The one under construction?"

"That's right."

Patrick nodded and turned his attention on Katie. "I'll call you. Dean, a pleasure."

And then he disappeared leaving Katie to explain his presence.

Yet as she was closing the door behind Patrick, she realized she didn't owe Dean anything. He was the one showing up unexpectedly. The best offense was to put Dean on the defense. Or distract him. Good thing Katie knew how to do both.

"How did you get up here?"

Dean stepped farther into the suite and looked around as if he were trying to figure out what she'd been doing. "I used to sneak up to your suite all the time."

Like she could ever forget. "There's no need to sneak any longer."

"So who was that?"

Avoidance…she would have earned A's in school if there had been a class. "Do you have my budget?"

"Is his name really Ben?"

She froze.

"Who names their kid Ben?"

She crossed her arms over her chest and let Dean make his own conclusions about Patrick. "What's the matter, Dean, jealous?"

He turned on her like a snake coiled up and ready to strike. Whatever he wanted to say died on his lips. "Jack asked me to keep an eye on you while he's away."

"Jack isn't in charge of me, Dean. We both know that."

"You need someone watching out for you."

"Now why do you think that?"

He looked up and down her body with a quick scan. "You look like you've not slept in days and, if I had to guess, you've lost weight since the wedding. And you don't have any to spare, darlin'."

She despised the fact he read her so well.

"Do you have my budget or what?"

Before he could answer, someone knocked on the door again.

"Oh, for Pete's sake. Who is it now?" She swung on the door and ripped it open. "What?"

"I'm sorry, Miss Morrison. I was told to bring your dinner. I can come back."

Good God, she was tired. Snapping at the staff wasn't how she'd been raised and she was instantly sorry. Poor Manny looked like he wanted to crawl away. "Oh, no. Please forgive me. It's been a long day. Bring it in here." She opened the door wider and let the young waiter wheel the cart filled with silver-domed dishes into the room.

"Would you like it in the dining room?"

"That would be fine, Manny." She'd grown used to eating over the sink at Monica's, and shoving bites in between her shower and changing clothes at the hotel. This was the night Monica was going to stay with Savannah so Katie could convince the hotel staff that she actually slept there once in a while. It was all a ruse to keep anyone from asking questions about where she spent her nights.

Maybe it was a good thing Dean had shown up when he did. Him finding her at the hotel would ease any suspicions. Or so she hoped.

She walked around Dean, found her purse, and waited for the waiter to finish. He raised the lid off the salad she'd ordered and looked at her. "Shall I open these now?"

"That won't be—"

"Salad? That's all you're eating?" Dean shoved in behind her and glared at her dinner.

"I like salad."

"So do rabbits. Gaylord always has Texas prime beef on the menu, if I'm not mistaken."

"Yeah, so?"

Dean shrugged out of his jacket and placed it on the back of the chair. "How about two rib eyes, Manny, medium rare with baked potatoes filled with the works. We'll start with the salad."

"I don't remember inviting you to stay."

Manny kept moving his head back and forth, taking in their conversation.

"And yet I'm not going until I've seen you eat and know you're not going to fall over the next time you're at work. It's bad enough you defy gravity with those damn shoes. You don't need to add a lack of nutrition making you weak."

She wanted to argue in the worst way but that took energy. The truth was, she could eat more than a salad and getting Dean to back off without a scene wouldn't be easy. The sooner they ate, the sooner she could move him along.

"Miss Morrison?"

"Medium rare is fine with me," she told Manny.

"And a couple of beers," Dean called after the waiter.

Katie walked Manny out of the room and pressed ten dollars into his palm.

Eat dinner. Placate Dean. Go to sleep. That was her plan.

He wanted to ask. Lord knew it kept every ounce of his dignity not to question.

Ben? Who the hell?

Not to mention the man was far too old for Katie. Could be her father if Dean had to guess.

OK, maybe that was going too far, but the man was older than her by at least ten years, if not more.

Katie excused herself to her room and returned wearing a large pullover cotton shirt and Capri pants. Dean identified the outfit as "Katie casual," the clothes she wore at the end of her day before she went to bed.

Very few people saw her in these clothes and even fewer saw her out of them.

The fact she changed while he was waiting for their steaks to arrive made him smile. At least they hadn't lost that intimacy…not yet anyway.

Dean let Manny back in a short time later and tipped the kid before he left.

"I haven't had a good steak since Texas. This smells amazing."

Katie pushed in, sat at the small dinette, and uncovered her plate. "I thought you liked to grill."

"When I'm camping. Haven't done that in a while." Dean sat across from her and removed the other lids over their food. A crush of pepper, garlic, and herbs arrested his senses as the aroma of the beef met his nose. His stomach rumbled and his mouth watered.

"Why not?"

"Why not what?"

"Why haven't you camped? You like camping."

Dean shrugged and placed a large dollop of butter on Katie's potato before doing the same to his. "No time."

Katie cocked her head to the side.

He picked up his fork and knife and started to dig into his steak. Katie sat motionless, poised as if waiting for him to say something.

"What?"

She shook her head. "Nothing."

She didn't buy his "no time" excuse but he didn't want to make her privy to his thoughts.

He waited until she filled her mouth with the first chunk of pure Angus beef before he asked. "So, who is Ben?"

Her jaw hesitated midchew but she continued and swallowed before she picked up another bite on her fork.

"A friend."

She didn't meet his eyes. Her left eye twitched.

"A lover?" Dammit! Why had those words escaped his tongue? He shouldn't care, and wished he didn't.

Her cheeks grew red. Dean wasn't sure if it was embarrassment or anger that fueled her reaction.

Instead of answering, Katie played with the butter on the edge of her fork before popping a bite of potato into her mouth.

"What makes you think I owe you any explanation about who you find in my suite?"

Now it was his time to squirm. He bit into his food, barely tasting the smoky flavor of the beef. She didn't owe him anything. Not anymore. But damn, it killed him thinking of her with anyone other than him.

"I'd like to think we're still friends," Dean said.

Which was true.

"Friends?" she asked. The question was innocent enough.

"Yeah. We've known each other since we were both kids. Regardless of what has happened between us, we should be friends."

A corner of her mouth lifted as she chewed on another bite of her steak.

A fine film of heat pearled into small beads of sweat on the back of Dean's neck.

"Girlfriends like details, Dean. Do you want details about Ben? Private details?" She drew out the word *private* and made him regret he'd asked.

He dropped his fork and pulled hard from his beer.

"Do you want to give me details about Maggie?"

He lifted the beer again and finished it. The hell he would give her anything about Maggie. Maggie had called off their wedding and Dean thought at the time he wouldn't survive. Now he knew their union would have been a disaster. He'd met Maggie shortly after he and Katie had gone their separate ways. His emotions at the time were a jumbled, hot mess. He had been ready to move to the next phase in his life. A wife, children…a house with a white fucking picket fence.

But then Katie called it off…wait, no, Maggie had called it off.

Dean shook his head and opened the second beer.

Although not knowing who Ben was to Katie burned a hole in his gut, Dean steered the conversation into safer waters. "I have your budget."

Katie sucked in her lower lip and dropped her gaze. "Which is?"

He told her a number, knowing it was probably lower than what she expected. In reality, he knew budgets had a ten percent margin of error, usually ending up higher than expected. Considering she hadn't done this type of work before, she would probably push that percentage close to twenty.

Dean lifted his eyes to hers, expecting to see her temper.

"Fine."

"No argument?"

"I agreed not to argue."

"That never stopped you before."

"What can I say? It's the new me." She finished the last of her steak and placed her napkin on the table.

Dean sat there and stared. *New me?* He supposed there was something new about her. The desire to work, which God knew was cutting edge in Katelyn's world. He attributed her casual clothes to a product of their time together…their intimate time together. Knowing she felt at ease enough to dress down for him brought on a swell of warm comfort. The pretense of being perfectly polished all the time was what she did for others. Yet she hadn't dressed down for Ben.

He smiled. Working out in his mind that even if she and Ben were close, they weren't as comfortable with each other as the two of them were.

Dean finished his second beer and pushed his chair back. "I'm having the walls redone tomorrow morning. You might want to be around to consult with if you want it done your way."

"What time should I be there?"

"Eight."

She rolled her head on her shoulders and tried to hide a yawn.

"I guess that's my cue to leave," he said.

"I don't remember asking you to stay," she quipped.

He chuckled. "You didn't insist I leave either, darlin'." He wondered why that was.

"In case you haven't noticed, I'm tired. Fighting with you would have taken more energy than I have to spend. Now that you know I'm fed and obviously ready for bed." She glanced at her outfit and tossed her hands to her sides. "You can leave."

He passed her en route to the front door. She didn't see him out. "G'night, Katie. See you in the morning."

She waved him off. "Yeah, yeah…eight o'clock."

Chapter Nine

Katelyn jolted out of bed at just after two thirty in the morning. Her heart pounded in her chest like that of a marathon runner on the twenty-second mile.

Something was wrong.

She'd slept too long.

Savannah!

The quiet room of the hotel suite confused and disoriented her. The memories of the events of the past evening reminded her of where she was.

She fell back on her pillows with a sigh. Savannah was with Monica and, although Katie knew Monica was taking care of the baby, she still worried.

She flipped the pillow over, finding its cool surface, and curled up on her side. But no matter how hard she tried, sleep eluded her. The funny thing was, she wasn't all that tired. Shortly after Dean had left, she forced herself to shower and crawl into bed. That was before eight. Before Savannah, six hours of sleep wouldn't have been enough. But apparently that had changed.

After thirty minutes of tossing and turning, Katelyn gave up, showered, and dressed.

As quietly as she could, she let herself into Monica's apartment at just before four. Inside Monica's room, Savannah slept in the bassinette. Just seeing her precious face and the rise and fall of her belly as she breathed instantly calmed every ounce of anxiety inside Katelyn's heart.

She didn't dare risk moving the baby and waking either of them. Instead, Katie tiptoed away and turned on her laptop to see if she could get some work done.

"You just couldn't do it." Monica's words startled her. She had drifted off to sleep, her head pillowed on her arms.

"Did I wake you?"

"No, but it looks like I woke you. How long have you been here?"

Katelyn glanced at the clock on the stove. "A couple of hours."

Monica padded toward the coffeemaker. "You lasted longer than I thought you would."

"What do you mean?"

"Very few new mothers leave their infants with someone else overnight."

Katie shook the fog from her head. "But I'm not a mother."

Monica sent her a weary look. "Yeah, yeah you are."

Savannah's tiny cry sounded from the other room and brought Katelyn to her feet. Once her arms circled around the back of Savannah's head and cooing noises spilled from her mouth in an effort to calm her, Katie thought maybe Monica was right.

"I want to be your mommy. Is that OK with you?" Katie whispered. A wave of unexpected tears welled in her eyes. *Please, God… let me be her mommy.*

Savannah blinked a couple of times and attempted a smile as one tear dropped from Katie's eye.

She wiped the moisture away, refusing to think about someone, anyone, taking Savannah away from her.

An hour and a half later Katie turned over the care of Savannah to the sitter, gathered her purse, and drove to work.

—

"Hey, princess." Steve Bowman waved at Katelyn from his truck. One of the construction workers who barely spoke English had called her princess about a week ago and everyone on the job site took up the nickname and used it.

She wasn't sure if she should be flattered or annoyed.

Princesses were kept women who preened all day long and waited for their princes to give them a purpose in life. Katelyn supposed the title somehow exemplified her before she had taken the job at the hotel, but it didn't completely fit now. It was hard to ignore that she was one of the only women on the site, and certainly the only one who dressed in high heels and short skirts.

There was one thing going for the nickname that she couldn't deny. The men on the site treated her like their queen. A testosterone-dominated workplace would normally result in catcalls and unwanted leering. Katie didn't find that to be the case here. For that, she was grateful.

"Hi, Steve." She placed the now familiar hard hat on her head and retrieved her purse from her car. She noticed a pacifier on the floor and brushed it under the seat and out of sight.

"I was told you wanted to talk to me," Steve said, walking up behind her.

"Right." She shut the door to the car, turned, and smiled at the plumber. "I have an idea for a water feature in the courtyard and wanted to get your opinion."

"Water feature?"

"A dancing fountain…you know, like the one they have on City Walk? The kind kids run in and out of when it's hot?"

Recognition filled Steve's eyes and he nodded. "Where did you have in mind?"

Katelyn motioned toward the construction trailer where an air conditioner ran and they could be more comfortable looking over the plans.

The two of them made their way inside. Jo sat behind her desk and typed feverishly. It appeared that Dean hadn't arrived yet.

"Hi, Jo."

Jo barely spared a glance. "Hey."

Katelyn would have felt slighted if Jo wasn't known for ignoring most everyone when her head was in her work.

"Hello, Josephine."

Jo stopped typing and sent Steve a menacing look. "No one calls me that, *Steven*."

Steve chuckled and winked.

Katie watched the two of them as obvious sparks snapped between them.

That deserves some thought. Steve and Jo…Jo and Steve? Hmmm… something's going on there!

In the conference room, Katie opened up the master plans of the site and tapped her finger in the center courtyard. "This looks like a fountain."

"It is."

A large fountain circled by plants and meandering paths between the main hotel and the bungalows dominated the page.

"Fountains have bases that fill with water."

"This one isn't designed like that. It's more of a tower with the first pool well above kid level. That way they can't climb in," Steve told her.

"Kids love water," she said. "Why not give them something fun?" The swimming pool was already designed for kid play, complete with slides and shallow ends. Katie wanted more. She'd spent part of her weekend over at Universal City Walk. Pulsating water shot up from jets and kids of all ages squealed and splashed in the fountain. Although Savannah was entirely too young to enjoy the water, it wasn't difficult picturing her there when she became a toddler.

"There's a big difference in setting up a fountain and what you have in mind. Have you run this past Dean?"

"Not yet. I wanted to get an idea of cost first."

"How big are you thinking?"

They talked about the space needed and Steve opened a notebook and jotted down a few things.

He was laughing over her shoulder when the door to the small trailer opened and Jo said hello to Dean.

Katie had hoped that Dean wouldn't be around during this brief meeting with Steve. She knew he would scrutinize her ideas. Her budget was hers, however, and she wouldn't let him talk her out of the fountain.

"Hey, Steve."

The men shook hands and Katelyn glanced at Dean before covering the plans she and Steve were looking over. Although she wasn't watching him, Dean dominated the small space and the pine scent of his skin floated toward her.

"I'm going to check on the convention rooms before I leave." She'd only just arrived, but Savannah had her first doctor's appointment at ten.

"I'll get back to you on the quote," Steve told her.

Dean squinted. "What quote?"

Katie offered a smile and pushed away from the desk. "A redesign for the courtyard fountain." More like a redo, but Dean didn't need to know that until she could figure out a way to work it into her budget. His budget.

"Redesign?"

"Yeah, no biggie." Katie brushed off the discussion and moved around the men in the small space.

The weight of Dean's stare followed her as she placed her hard hat on and opened the door to the trailer.

"By the way, Katie, I talked to Jack. He and Jessie will be back next week."

She stalled. Her heart did a full stop in her chest before she turned toward Dean. "I thought they were going back to Houston."

"They are…well, Jessie and Danny anyway. Jack will be here for a few days before returning to Texas."

She refrained from blowing out a breath. Jessie would want to visit Monica, but Jack would probably stay at the hotel. Which would work to her advantage. She would tell her brother that she was staying with a friend and avoid the constant running between both spaces.

"Are they having a good time?"

"He sounded relaxed."

"Good." Hopefully he'd be in his own marital bliss and not notice anything out of sorts with her.

"I'll check in tomorrow. Bye, Dean, Steve…Jo."

Dean smiled, Steve waved, and Jo grunted behind her computer monitor.

Outside the trailer, the dry heat wrapped around her. The path to the main site had several pieces of plywood covering the ground. A rare thunderstorm had come through the day before, wetting the dirt and making the site a mess. Katelyn was busy shoving papers under her arm and didn't notice the warp in the wood below her feet. Her heel found the swollen board and caught. Her tight mini kept her from catching herself and before she knew it, she landed flat on her ass, mud all over her skirt, and her ankle screaming in protest.

She sat there for a moment, stunned that she was sitting on the ground. The papers she was attempting to hold were scattered at her feet. Luckily, no one saw her tumble.

With as much dignity as she could muster, she pushed herself up, ignored her throbbing ankle, and picked up her papers.

Dirt rode high on her thigh and ruined the hem of her silk skirt. Even the hard hat sat in a puddle of mud.

"OK, Grace," she chastised herself.

After wiggling her shoe back on her foot, she attempted to stand. *Attempted* being the key word.

"Dammit."

Pain shot up her leg and nearly had her on the ground a second time. She bit her lip and took another step.

Not so bad. Not good…but not bad.

She made it to her car but decided the trip was all she could take in four-inch heels. The convention hall would have to wait.

Dean's voice and words followed her back to Monica's apartment. "*You're defying gravity in those shoes…This is a construction site, not a dance floor.*" He'd been harping at her daily to get out of her shoes and she had refused.

By the time she managed to pull into the parking spot at Monica's, her ankle was twice the size it should have been and ibuprofen wasn't going to cut it for the pain. She gave up on the shoes and carried them with one hand when she walked in the door.

Mrs. Hoyt clicked her tongue the moment she saw Katie limping. "What did you do?"

"Nothing. I'm OK."

Mrs. Hoyt was the perfect plump grandmother who lived to take care of people. "You need ice." She was already at the freezer by the time Katie set her purse on the counter. Once she managed to sit, a sigh of relief left her lips.

"Damn, shit…" she cursed under her breath. The last thing she needed was a stupid turned ankle to slow her pace, and God knew she hated being wrong.

It killed her that Dean had known this would happen… eventually.

Mrs. Hoyt returned with the ice and gently placed it on Katie's swollen ankle.

"Thanks."

"Hard hats and stilettos don't mix," her babysitter chided.

"Don't remind me."

Mrs. Hoyt raised an eyebrow, but left the rest of her lecture behind her lips.

"Your daughter is sleeping."

Katie attempted a smile and glanced toward the hall. They had an hour before the doctor's appointment.

"Do you want me to stay?"

"I'll be OK." She hopped deeper in the room. "Thanks."

Alone with a sleeping baby in the apartment, Katelyn cursed her ankle again. After a hobble to the bathroom, she found some Motrin and chased it with a glass of milk. It was a good thing Dean hadn't seen her fall. Chances were he would have insisted on a trip to the doctor. Maybe even picked her up and carried her against her will.

The memory of his arms around her, of how safe he once made her feel, squeezed something inside her chest and started to hurt. He'd always made her feel secure, wanted. With Dean she never had to put on airs.

"Makeup is for ugly women. Your skin is perfect," he told her, holding her face in his hands and running his thumb over her lower lip.

"A lady never leaves home without her makeup, Dean Prescott. You have sisters, you know this."

"We're not going anywhere tonight."

They didn't leave that night. And wearing makeup when it was only the two of them became a thing of the past.

But that was well over a year ago, and best forgotten.

Chapter Ten

Dean stretched out his legs on his chaise lounge on his back patio. Mike sat across from him sipping a beer. "How's the hotel?"

Dean hadn't seen Mike since Jack's wedding. When Mikey had called earlier in the day to suggest they get together, he jumped at the opportunity. Outside of work obligations, Dean hadn't had a social life since his breakup with Maggie. At first, he avoided his friends. Not that they let him sulk for long. Jack and Mike had found him up in Big Bear and assisted him with getting good and drunk. He'd spent an entire weekend brooding and cursing anything in a skirt before returning to his life. And even then he did so slowly...if at all.

Jack and Mike saw him through the hard time, and went on to support him ever since. Although they didn't talk about his ex, Dean knew his friends watched him. Whenever they got together, one of them would ask if he was seeing anyone. Checking to see if he was climbing back on the horse, so to speak. In truth, he hadn't. Not because of an undying love for Maggie, but because of how done he was with the whole dating scene. Maggie was a perfect case of "If you can't be with the one you love, love the one you're with." He knew that now. After.

He supposed Maggie had picked up on his feelings and that was why she had broken off their engagement. Being dumped weeks before your wedding sucked. Being married to the wrong person would have sucked more.

"Coming along. No major setbacks."

"Is Katelyn actually showing up to work?"

An instant picture of Katie's blonde hair poking out from under *his* hard hat surfaced. "She is. I'll be the first to admit how shocked I am at how seriously she has taken this job."

"I didn't think she'd last a week. Of course her real work won't come until the hotel is nearly finished...right?"

Dean twisted the top off his beer and shook his head. "She's taken great pride in pointing out design issues in the construction phase. Niches that need electrical and framing. Separate meeting areas outside of conference halls for kids and adults. She even snuck behind my back to talk with my plumber about one of those fancy fountains that shoot water out of the ground for kids to play in."

"What does all that have to do with sofas and wall color?"

"Nothing. I'm gonna grill Jack when he gets back."

"You think he knew how involved she wanted to be?" Mike brushed a fly off his arm as he spoke.

"I think Jack was too busy doing all that sappy married crap before he left to pay Katie much attention. Katie is all kinds of resourceful. Probably snuck in a limited amount of details and had him saying yes without realizing what he was doing." Dean could picture the conversation easily. Chances were Katie cornered Jack with Jessie across the room. *C'mon, Jack. You know I'm a born decorator. No need to hire someone to do the job.*

That's all that would have needed to be said to land the position. And it wasn't as if she was getting paid. How could Jack say no?

"She's busting your budget I'll bet."

"That's just it, she's not."

"What?" Mike sounded as surprised as Dean felt.

"I gave her a budget, a low one thinking she'd balk at it, and so far she's staying within it. I even heard her haggling with a vendor over paint prices."

"No shit?"

"No shit!" Dean took a pull off his beer.

"So Jack was right. Katie isn't acting herself."

Dean shrugged. "Not completely. The work thing is new. I keep expecting her to burn out. I've called the hotel a few times but it doesn't seem she spends a lot of time there." And that was classic Katie behavior.

"Is there a guy?"

Dean thought of that Ben guy and ignored the twist in his gut. "Probably."

"That's good." Mike relaxed with that information.

"Why is that *good*?" Dean didn't think so. Ben was too old for Katie.

"Think about it, Dean. If Katie cut away from her normal life of partying, traveling, and appearing in the tabloids every other week so she could work full-time and stay at the hotel at night watching movies, then we'd all know something wasn't right. So she started to work, find meaning in her life. I get that. Even actors work on occasion. No one gives up everything in their life without a reason. It's like when you gave up camping and riding your bike."

Mike had him up until he started talking about camping. "What does that have to do with anything?"

"Don't get defensive. You know what I'm talking about."

"No. I don't."

"When you were with Maggie, you cut out the things that make you tick. I couldn't get you to go camping all last year. And it wasn't until after Maggie skipped out that you found your bike again. Maggie was your reason for strange behavior."

"Sometimes we do things for the people in our lives."

Mikey sat forward and met Dean's eyes. "If falling in love and getting married means I have to give up everything I like doin', then count me out."

"I didn't give up everything."

Mike snorted.

"I didn't." Dean winced, knowing he sounded like a five-year-old. "OK, maybe I did. I was messed up back then."

"That's my point, buddy. If Katie wasn't acting at all normal, we'd know she was messed up. That something had gone down that none of us knew about. And as much as we might hate it sometimes, we all like to keep tabs on each other. Be there for each other."

Mike was right.

They changed the subject to a local baseball team and grilled a couple of steaks. Katie was never far from Dean's mind. He couldn't shake the feeling that he was missing something...something big.

Dean wasn't sure why Katelyn insisted on showing up to the job site before him, but for the fourth time in a week he pulled alongside her rental car and shook his head.

The top of the convertible was down and he glanced in the backseat. A bright pink pacifier stuck out like a bald man in a hair salon. He reached in and picked it up. Maybe the pacifier was hidden under the seat, and the person who rented it before Katie had lost it.

Still, the presence of the infant toy sparked a moment of recognition much like déjà vu, and didn't let go.

He cupped the plastic binky into his palm and made his way inside.

Jo greeted him and gave him his messages. The light in the conference room was on, and he could hear Katelyn talking on the phone. After the conversation with Mike the day before, and his own nagging feeling that something wasn't quite right, Dean had decided to poke a little more into Katie's mind.

"Mornin', Katelyn," he called from across the room when he heard her say good-bye on the phone.

"Hey, Dean."

Without bothering to enter the conference room, he asked, "Would you mind coming in here for a few minutes?" Dean walked into his office and waited for Katie to follow.

The space in the trailer was tight; barely enough space for the three rooms.

He sat behind his desk and looked over his messages.

"What do you need?"

Dean looked up, somewhat startled. The sound of high heels, which usually accompanied Katie wherever she went, wasn't there. When he glanced over her frame, a pair of designer jeans hugged her slim hips and sneakers adorned her feet.

He didn't know she owned a pair of sneakers.

"Come in, sit down."

She cocked her head to the side. "Am I in trouble, boss?"

When it came to Katie, Dean never felt like the boss. "Should you be?"

She stepped forward and closed the door.

The snarky smile on his face fell. "You're limping." And attempting not to show it by walking slowly and with calculated ease.

When she sat in the chair across from him, she huffed out a breath. "Stubbed my toe," she told him.

He was out of his chair and at her side in an instant. "Liar. You're wearing running shoes." And from what he could tell, only a little bit of that black stuff women wear on their eyes and lip gloss. Mike's words hung in the air. *If Katie wasn't acting at all normal, we'd know she was messed up.*

He knelt down and placed a hand on the foot she was favoring.

"I'm OK." She pulled away.

He dropped his hand to her side and met her gaze. Just a glimpse of her always knocked the wind out of his lungs. Her porcelain skin and pink lips were more tempting than any he'd ever seen. He remembered those lips on his, the feel…the taste.

"Let me look." He lowered his voice. "Please."

Katie rolled her eyes and lifted her leg. "It's not a big deal. Just a sprain."

Her ankle was swollen and wrapped in a bandage, her shoe loosely tied. "When did this happen?"

"Yesterday."

"Here?"

"I'm fine, Dean, really."

"Dammit, Katie. Those shoes—"

"I've heard the lecture already. Monica thinks I sprained it. No big deal."

He narrowed his eyes. "Monica?"

Katie hesitated. "She *is* a nurse."

"But not a doctor. Did you see a doctor? Have an X-ray?"

"I don't need a doctor. It's already feeling better. I'm sure you didn't make me walk in here if you knew I had hurt myself. What did you need?"

Dean forced himself to stand. "No more high heels, Katie. I mean it."

"Whatever."

"I mean it."

She glared at him now. "I don't hear you telling anyone else around here what they can and can't wear."

"No one else tries to walk on heels the size of a number two pencil."

She sat forward, but didn't stand.

Feeling better, my ass.

"Fine, no more stilettos. Now what did you want?"

He fished out the pacifier from his pocket and handed it to her. “I saw this in your car.”

She took to her feet and her face swept of all color. “My car?”

“Yeah, the little red convertible outside? Someone you know have kids?” Like maybe Ben? He thought but didn’t ask.

“Ah, no…er.”

“Maybe the person who rented it before you had kids.”

Katie kept looking at the pacifier in thought. “Yeah…maybe.”

*If Katie wasn’t acting at all normal…*Mike’s voice called inside Dean’s head. Katie wasn’t acting normal. She stared at the binky as if it had legs and was crawling up her arm.

“Is this why you called me in here?”

Dean leaned against his desk and crossed his arms over his chest. “I wanted to ask you about this fountain idea you blew past Steve yesterday.”

“Oh, is that all? OK,” she said sitting back down.

“Katelyn, are you all right?”

She shook her head. “I’m fine. The ankle bites a little, but it isn’t that bad.”

“No, not the ankle. I mean…is there anything going on you want to talk about?”

“Like what?” She sent him a puzzled look.

“I don’t know…you tell me. Is something wrong?”

She looked away, her eye twitching. “What could be wrong? I like what I’m doing here, the guys seem to like me. It’s hot out, but not like Texas. Everything’s great.”

“Great.” She did not lie well.

“About the fountain…” Katelyn changed the subject and went on to tell him her ideas. Which he had to admit, he liked. She didn’t ask for a bigger budget, but Dean knew it would triple the cost of what they had previously planned.

“I need to check this with Jack, see if he likes it.”

Katie smiled. "Tell him to ask Danny's opinion."

"That wouldn't be playing fair. He can't say no to that kid."

The grin that played on Katie's face met her eyes and stayed there. How long had it been since he'd seen her that lit up? "Kids have that effect on people." She hesitated and then said, "You should know that. You have a nephew. How is Robert anyway?"

"Getting big," he told her.

"Isn't Syrie pregnant again?"

"Yep. Has a couple more months to go."

Katie was still smiling. Maybe she'd come to terms with the fact that she couldn't have kids of her own. The last time they'd talked about kids, it was right after the doctor had given her the bad news. It was the only time Dean had seen Katie cry.

"Boy, is she gonna have her hands full."

"Our mom plans on staying with them for a couple of weeks after the baby is born. Help her get used to dealing with two."

"Oh, good. She'll need that."

Dean's heart cracked. Obviously the memory of their child, the one that didn't make it past the first trimester, no longer haunted Katie. He still felt the loss like it was yesterday.

Katie stood. "Give them my best when you talk to them."

"I will."

She started for the door and grabbed the back of the chair for support. Dean shot to her side and slid an arm around her waist. "I thought it wasn't that bad."

"Hurts more when I first get up," she said, excusing away his concern.

She leaned into him and let him walk her out. Dean hated the fact that she was hurting, but warmed with her being in his arms.

Only a class A asshole would enjoy this, he told himself.

"You should go back to the hotel, rest your ankle."

Although he took the brunt of her weight, she still sucked in a breath as she tried to walk. "I'm OK."

She stepped again and moaned.

"The hell!" He lifted her in his arms and told her to hold on.

He carried her through the door and barked at Jo. "Get the door. Katie's going home for the day."

Jo jumped up and cleared the path.

"I can walk, Dean."

She rested a hand on his chest but didn't push away.

"Take tomorrow off," he told her as he walked down the steps of the trailer and over to her car. "If it's only a sprain, it should feel better after the weekend."

Her forehead rested beside her hand on his chest and Dean's heart kicked hard. God he missed this. Missed her.

"You win," she told him. "It hurts like a bitch."

He chuckled. "Need me to drive you home?"

"No. I drive with my right foot, not my left."

He gently placed her inside her car. His hand rested on her thigh as he spoke. "Have someone help you up to your room." He didn't like the sound of that. "You know what, I'll go with you."

"No! I'm fine. I think Monica's home. I'll give her a call; find out if there's a doctor I can see."

The thought of him tucking her into bed dissipated. "Good idea."

"Here's your purse, Katelyn," Jo said from behind Dean.

When he stood, he felt the loss of Katie's heat. She tucked her purse beside her and buckled her seat belt.

"I'll call you," he told her.

"You don't have to do that."

No, he didn't. But he wanted to.

"Use my cell," she said. "In case I'm at the doctor's."

The dust from the road kicked up behind her car as she drove away.

I should have gone with her.

Chapter Eleven

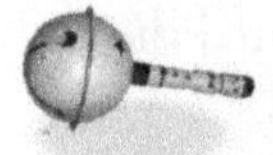

As sure as the sun would rise tomorrow, Katie knew that Dean was going to check up on her over the weekend. The only way to avoid it was to get his nosy ass out of town. And for that, Mike was key.

Talking to Mike was quick and easy.

Work has been stressful. Jack will be back in town next week and Dean could use some downtime. You two should go camping.

Mike fell in line and agreed to push Dean to go with him. As soon as she was off the phone with him, she'd called Dean.

"The doctor said it's a sprain. Ice, elevate, compress. He wants to see me in two weeks." He also told her to wear flat shoes for six weeks. Not that she intended to follow that advice.

"You could have easily broken it in those heels."

"I know," she agreed with him…hoping to make him feel good about the conversation. "Monica agreed to help me out over the weekend. I shouldn't have any problem coming in on Monday." She cast the line and hoped he'd take the bait.

"You sure? I could—"

"I appreciate that you care, Dean, but Monica is the nurse. She's beat me up over my shoes more than you have."

"Remind me to kiss her when I see her again." *And the bait is in the mouth.*

"I saw the schedule for next week. You could use a real weekend off."

Dean's voice wavered. "Maybe."

"I'll see you on Monday, Dean."

"Take care," he said before hanging up.

An hour later Mike sent her a text and let her know that he and Dean were on their way to the desert with their dirt bikes.

Katie leaned back on Monica's sofa with Savannah sleeping at her side and relaxed for the first time since she'd arrived in California.

Monica picked up the phone on the first ring, praying it didn't wake up the baby.

"Hello?" she practically whispered.

"Mo! I'm back!"

Monica jumped up from the couch, moved to the large sliding glass door, and opened it up. "Oh, Jessie, it's so great to hear your voice." Monica needed a good sister chat in the worst way. After brushing off the leaves that had collected on a patio chair, Monica sat down and kept an ear out for Savannah.

"We had such an amazing time."

"I doubt you even made it out of the hotel room."

Jessie laughed. "We did stay an extra night in Florida before we did the island hopping."

Monica could feel her sister's smile over the phone. She deserved happiness and Jack was the perfect man for her. "Is married sex better than single sex?"

"You're going to laugh at me if I answer that."

"No, I won't."

Jessie hesitated. "OK, then. Yes, it is. It's hard to explain why."

"Well try," Monica insisted. "Because you telling me about your sex life will be the closest I've come to having sex in a while."

"I don't know, Mo, it's like every doubt I've ever had, any insecurities leftover from my life before marriage were swiped clean when we said 'I do.' It's just better. Perfect."

"Does all his Texas lovin' mean you guys are going to give Danny a brother or sister soon?"

"Oh, lord, not you, too. Do you have any idea how many people have asked me that since we got back to Texas?"

She could only imagine. "Is Gaylord harping?"

"Him, the housekeeper, Jack's aunt. I'm not opposed to having more kids, but could they lay off for a month at least? Let someone else in the family bring babies into the world."

Monica's eyes traveled to the open door to the apartment. Now would be the perfect time to tell Jessie about Savannah, but she couldn't do that to Katie. "Don't look at me. You have to have sex to have babies and sadly, I'm not."

Jessie laughed. "I'm going to miss you, Mo."

"You'll be too busy decorating that new house and having perfect sex with Jack. Besides, you can climb on that fancy jet and visit whenever you want."

"Jack told me that today before he left."

"Oh, that's right. Katelyn told me he was coming in today."

"You and Katie really hit it off, didn't you?"

Monica thought she heard a noise from Savannah's room. She poked her head inside but didn't hear anything other than the air conditioner turning on and off. "Yeah, we did."

"Jack was worried about her working with him. Has she said anything about the hotel?"

Monica bit her lip. If Jessie thought Katie was living with her, more questions would be asked and it would be hard to keep Savannah out of the conversation.

"Actually, she slept over this weekend. She sprained her ankle at work last week."

"Is she OK?"

"Just a sprain. And if you ask me, a deserving injury. She was wearing four-inch heels, for crying out loud. I told her she needed to wear flats, or tennis shoes. But Miss Fashion wouldn't even buy a pair until last Friday."

"She's lucky it's not worse."

"I know—" Savannah's cry filled the small apartment and made Monica's heart jump inside her chest. "Oh, no."

"What's that?"

"I'm…er, babysitting."

"Babysitting? You?"

"I know…strange. But a friend was in a bind. Can I call you back later?" Monica stepped into the apartment and closed the door behind her.

"Sure. Call when you can. Love you, sis."

"Love you, too." Monica hung up the phone and tossed it on the couch.

"Oh, Vanna…what's the big deal?" After a quick diaper change, Monica moved Savannah to a baby carrier while she prepared a bottle. It took a little while for the baby to calm down. She'd been fussy all night from what she'd heard. When Katie had gone to work that morning, she looked like a zombie. The pace of keeping Savannah a secret was tiresome. It was only a matter of time before someone figured out that they were hiding a baby.

Monica hoped the investigator Katie had hired would come up with something soon. Now that Jessie was back, the last thing Monica wanted to do was lie to her sister.

Dean walked into a quiet office. Jo had called to tell him she had the flu, the icky stomach variety that would spread. She'd offered to come in, but Dean wanted nothing to do with getting ill.

The light on the phone blinked, letting him know there were messages, and the air-conditioning was already on. His office was dark but light under the conference room door ran along the floor.

A weekend with Mike reminded him of how much he'd given up since he'd met Maggie. It wasn't until the second night, while sitting under a blanket of stars, that Mike had told him that Katie had suggested the guys' weekend.

Damn if that didn't warm him just about everywhere. "Katie said you needed a break," Mike had told him.

Here Dean had worried about Katie not getting around on her bum foot, and she was pushing their mutual friend to help Dean relax.

He called himself all kinds of foolish for dreaming about her, but he couldn't help it. Every time he closed his eyes, she was there. Even now, as he stood outside the conference room where he assumed he'd find her, he couldn't stop the fast beat of his heart. Would she be wearing heels? Would she smile when he walked in the room?

Could he get through the day without touching her?

Turning around, he moved away from the door and went to his office. He fired up his computer and tossed his car keys on the desk.

Still, not a sound came from the other room.

He pried the blinds apart over his window and peered outside. The main entrance of the hotel had several workers milling about. But no Katie.

It took less than thirty seconds of his ass in his chair before he shot out of it.

Outside the conference room, he didn't hear a thing. He slowly turned the handle and popped his head in.

His jaw dropped and something inside him melted.

Katie's blonde head rested over one of her arms while the other one was curled up under her chin. Her eyes were closed and her lips were open as she slept. She wore a simple buttoned-up shirt and slacks. Dean glanced under the table and noticed a pair of flat shoes.

She didn't hear him approach so he knelt beside her and lost his brief battle with touching her. A strand of hair fell into her eyes and he swept it behind her ear. He could watch her sleep forever. If she weren't huddled over a desk, he would have left her alone.

"Hey, darlin'," he whispered. He trailed his fingers over her hair and rested his palm on her shoulder. "Katie?"

"Hmm?" she murmured and sighed.

"Time to wake up," he coaxed.

She smiled as she slept. "Dean?"

His stomach twisted and other parts stirred. The memory of her uttering his name, like she was now, gripped him.

She blinked a few times and focused on his face. A spark inside her leapt toward him in that brief moment and told him something that her lips never would. Katie closed her eyes, and shook her head.

But Dean had seen her desire…seen her soften. And he wanted to see it again.

"You're sleeping in the office," he said.

Keeping his hand on her arm, he leaned back, hardly realizing how close his face was to hers.

"Oh, lord." She rubbed her eyes…eyes clean of her usual mask of makeup.

He'd ponder that later.

"It's OK. I'm the only one here."

He forced his hand off her and stood.

"I didn't sleep well this weekend." She glanced at him, and then to the papers she'd been working with before she'd dozed off.

"How's the ankle?"

She looked confused for a minute. "Better. Hurts at night, though."

"You could have taken another day off."

"Too much to do. Besides, Jack will be here today. I don't want him to think it was a mistake letting me help."

Dean crossed his arms over his chest and leaned against the table. "I'd vouch for you, Katie. No one can accuse you of slackin'."

One side of her lips lifted in a grin. "You're probably the only boss who's caught someone sleeping on the job that said that."

"I'm not your boss," he reminded her.

"You're bossy."

"Not the same thing."

"It is from where I'm sitting."

He wanted to sit there, make conversation with her. But that would be obvious. He'd made an art form of being subtle when he pursued her the first time. Now he'd have to be stealthy. The realization that he intended to pursue her again hit him.

The thought didn't disturb him…it did the opposite. For the first time in a long time he looked forward to waking…to going to work…to really living. He still wanted Katelyn Morrison.

"Jack called me this morning. He has a meeting in LA at lunch but will be here before four. You still gonna be here?"

She nodded. "Like I said, I have some things to do."

"Good. Would you mind picking up the phone if you're in the office? Jo's out sick."

"That's funny. One of Bowman's men flagged me down when I came in. Steve is sick, too."

"I hope it isn't going around."

"Do you have any of those bottles of hand sanitizer around here?"

He shook his head. "Don't think so."

Katie pushed away from the table. "I'll run to the store and get some. Maybe some of those Lysol wipes. We can't be too careful."

Dean frowned. "Since when are you a germ-a-phobe?"

"I've spent the whole weekend with a nurse. Monica washes her hands more than anyone I know."

He'd forgotten about that. The fact that Katie was quick with where she'd spent her weekend made him think it wasn't with the much-too-old Ben guy. He smiled.

"Good idea. Grab the big bottles. We'll spread them around and let everyone know to be careful."

She grabbed her purse and limped, albeit not as much as the last time he'd seen her, to the door. "And you say you're not the boss."

He snorted a laugh and watched her leave.

The only reason he kept smiling was because he knew she'd be back.

Chapter Twelve

The heat outside was well over one hundred degrees. Staying inside the construction trailer wasn't a chore for Katelyn.

Dean had offered to pick up lunch and the majority of the job site was quiet. Without Jo in the office, it was actually relaxing. Even the phone didn't bother ringing all that often.

The door slammed, announcing the arrival of lunch.

"I know how fond you are of salad," Dean said as he walked into the room with two huge bags. From the smell traveling to her nose, there was more than lettuce for lunch.

"Yeah."

He set the bags on the edge of the conference table, swooped up several plans, and tucked them to the side. "I got you a salad."

The rich aroma of barbeque teased her stomach and the thought of salad left her hungry. "Ah, thanks."

"You don't want salad?"

"Salad's fine. Great." *Boring.*

Dean removed a clear plastic container of garlic dinner rolls. Next came a slab of ribs smothered in sauce.

Katie licked her lips.

"I, on the other hand, am hungry. Mike suggested a takeout barbeque place down the street. The place was lined up out the door." Out popped an order of baked beans…followed by mashed potatoes.

Out of a second bag, Dean slowly removed a small plastic container with her salad. There wasn't a smell from her container at all.

"It smells amazing, doesn't it?"

"Yeah."

"Here ya go." He set the salad in front of her and smiled.

"Thanks."

The full force of the food hit her senses when he opened the last container and started loading up a paper plate. There was enough food for three people. Katie glanced at her salad and tried to think of it as appetizing.

All she saw was an appetizer and a paltry one at that.

Her stomach rumbled.

Dean tore off one of the ribs and sank his teeth into the meat. "Oh, wow. This is amazing."

Katie opened her salad and stuck a fork into the lettuce.

"Oh, my God. This is better than Mac's. You know that one off the frontage road on the way to your daddy's ranch. So. Good." Dean smacked his lips together and hummed as he chewed.

He ripped off another rib and Katie couldn't stand it anymore. She shot her hand out and stopped him from devouring it.

He sent her a cocky grin and lifted the rib toward her. "Did you want a bite?"

Instead of answering, she leaned forward and bit into the food. Her taste buds sang and her stomach did a happy dance. The smoky sauce hit the back of her tongue and she closed her eyes with the pleasure of it.

"Can I have my hand back?"

She licked her lips as Dean watched. "Not unless you dish me up a plate."

Dean stroked away sauce from her lower lip. Her skin prickled with his touch. Why did he have to be so damn handsome?

"No problem, darlin'." *Darlin'* rolled off his tongue with such a smooth tone she felt him sliding back into her system. It wasn't often Dean used his Texan charm, but when he did, a woman was helpless not to fall under his spell.

Get a grip, Katie.

She forced her gaze away from his and divided the salad.

"Remember the time we went to Mac's after the Halloween party at the high school?"

"I remember you chasing after Sally Richfield who was dressed like a pornographic cat."

Dean chuckled. "Remember the librarian? What was her name?"

"Mrs. Leon."

"That's right. She made Sally wear a lab coat all night. It was only after we all left and went into Mac's that anyone saw her costume."

Katie rolled her eyes back as the garlic from the bread saturated her tongue. "And you were right there sniffing up her skirt."

"Leotard."

"You *would* remember."

Dean talked around his food. "I had to chase her to get my mind off of you."

Katie stopped chewing. "You never took notice of me in high school. I was two years younger."

"I didn't want to notice you in high school. You were Jack's sister and he'd have busted my balls if I made a move toward you."

"No, he wouldn't—OK, yeah, he would have. You never let on."

"You had so many boys tripping over themselves, you wouldn't have noticed if I looked twice."

Katie washed down a forkful of beans with her diet soda. "Since we're playing the honesty game, I guess I should let you know you're wrong. Remember the outfit I wore on my sixteenth birthday?"

A slow Southern smile spread over his lips and he wiggled his eyebrows. “Red plaid mini, black boots, and that skintight tank top with the spaghetti straps. Oh, yeah. I remember.”

Katie sucked in her bottom lip and made a mental note to see if she could find that skirt when she went home. “You'd just started dating that girl from the Catholic school and I wanted to compete.” And when Dean hadn't made a move, Katie decided to keep wearing short skirts and provocative clothing to make him.

He never did...well, not until much later.

“I don't even remember what the girl's name was.”

“Nina.”

“Nina,” he sighed as he said her name.

She tossed a napkin in his general direction. “You, Dean Prescott, were a player back then. Hell, you all were.”

“You did a fair amount of playin'.”

“More show than go.”

“Gaylord yelled at Jack constantly to find you and drag your skinny ass back home.”

She was wild back then. It didn't help that the media followed her around to the point where she couldn't burp without someone writing a story about it. A fabricated bullshit story. After her mother had walked away from them...all of them...Katie searched out attention.

Katie didn't need two-hundred-dollar sessions on a psychiatric couch to understand why she acted out. Her mother had left her when she needed her the most. “Daddy was clueless about raising a teenage daughter.”

“You had your aunt.”

“Not the same.”

Dean's fingertips brushed over the back of her hand. “Do you think of her...your mom?”

It was surreal how Dean knew her thoughts. “Sometimes.” More since Savannah had entered her life. How her mother could birth her children, raise them for so many years, then walk away, Katie couldn't fathom.

"You were a great kid and a beautiful woman. She's the one who's missing out."

Thinking about her mother hadn't made her want to cry since she was a teen, but Dean's calm, understanding words knotted the back of her throat and made her miss a woman who gave her up. Would Savannah think like this one day? Would she wonder why or even blame herself?

Katie pulled her hand away from Dean and lifted her napkin to her lips. She hoped he couldn't see the pain behind her eyes. She attempted a smile and dropped her napkin. Instead of hitting her lap, it fell to the floor. As she bent over to pick it up, Dean did the same.

They both stopped midway and looked at each other. His eyes searched hers and time simply stopped. No, it went in reverse. He placed his palm on the side of her face and drew her in. His lips brushed over hers in soft, even sweeps.

"Oh," she murmured as she reached and glided her hands over his chest. The thick feel of him under her palms felt right, familiar. He teased her lips open and pushed inside. His taste and scent flooded her, bringing back every wonderful memory of their brief, passionate time together. Unlike the fire and impulse they had before, this kiss was one of calm warmth and desire.

Warning bells screamed inside her mind. She'd barely survived him the first time. Playing emotional roulette with him now was dangerous. Even if it felt damn good to be in his arms again.

Dean must have read her thoughts and slowly ended their kiss. He left her light-headed and dizzy. "I can't stop thinking about you, Katie." He dropped his forehead to hers and spoke in hushed tones.

"This isn't smart," she said. She had a baby at home. One who needed to stay hidden until she located Savannah's mother. Diving back into Dean's arms, no matter how warm they were, could jeopardize everything. "We shouldn't do this…for so many reasons."

"Like what?"

"We work together."

He kissed her again, briefly. "You're fired," he teased.

"You can't fire me. You don't pay me."

He reached for her lips again, and she pulled away.

He dropped his arms from her shoulders and let her go. "I won't push," he told her.

She looked past him and drew in a deep breath. "Thank you."

As he picked up their lunch mess, he said, "If you want to kiss me again, my office is right in there…and the door is always open."

He could always make her laugh. "I'll keep that in mind."

"You do that."

Dean kept out of her way for the rest of the day. The task was easy when he could still taste her on his lips. She'd responded to his kiss. Kissed him back, even. The act thrust him into the past to the first time he'd ever touched her. Like this time, she'd met his lips and didn't pull away. They were all limbs and flying clothes back then. Years of pent-up want exploded until they were both spent and staring at the ceiling. It had been glorious.

Although Dean wanted glorious again, this time things were going to be different. Slower.

"Dean!" He heard a familiar voice yelling from across the shell of the hotel lobby and turned to greet his best friend.

"Jack, you son of a bitch."

"No denying that," Jack said. They shook hands and followed it up with a man-hug.

"You look good." Tanned, rested, and Dean needed to add, sexed.

"*Good* doesn't cut it."

"How's the ole ball and chain?"

"Jessie's bound to tie you to your chair with duct tape if she hears you calling her that."

Dean wiggled his eyebrows. "Oh, bondage. Didn't think you did the kink, cowboy."

Jack punched Dean's arm. "Jessie's good. She missed Danny, though. Next time he comes with us."

"Honeymoons aren't supposed to include kids."

"I hear ya." Jack turned full circle and took in the room. It had changed a lot in the weeks he'd been enjoying his bride. "Looks like everything is coming along."

"Only a few small setbacks. The roof isn't complete and that's holding up some of the construction on the west end. Most of the exterior walls are going up. I think we're about a week, maybe two, away from all the plumbing and electrical to finish up. On the inside at least."

"Good, good." Jack's vision of a more family friendly hotel to add to the empire his father had already built was brilliant. Where The Morrison was a five star vision of opulence, Jack's hotel would be a five star vision of family affordable opulence.

The project had been in the early planning stages and ground breaking about the time Maggie had left him, which gave him what he needed to get over her. He'd thrust himself into his work and quickly through his messed up personal life.

"I noticed a convertible in the lot. Katie's?"

"Yeah. She's been in the office all day."

"How's she doing?"

Dean licked his lips, tasted her again. "Good. She's had some innovative ideas, ones I think you're going to like."

Jack stood closer and lowered his voice. "How is she really? I mean, she wasn't acting herself before the wedding."

Dean rubbed his chin. "I'm not sure what's going on, and I understand why you're worried, but she seems fine to me."

"You know her better than most so I'll take your word for it." Jack started to walk toward the door. Dean stopped him.

"Jack, wait up." If things were going to be different with Katie this time, then it started here...with her brother.

"Yeah?"

"About Katie..."

Jack narrowed his eyes. "What about her?"

Oh, hell! This would be so much easier with beer. He glanced around the room and decided they didn't need an audience. "Let's go in and say hi, then go grab a beer."

Jack tilted his head to the side. "There something you need to tell me?"

Dean nodded. "Yeah, but trust me. We need beer."

Chapter Thirteen

In Jack's defense, he waited until the both of them were sitting behind a booth in a bar and halfway through a beer before he asked. "Are you going to tell me what's up with Katie, or are you going to make me guess?"

Dean followed the condensation along the side of his glass with his finger. "You and I have been friends a long time."

"Yes, we have."

"I'd never do anything to jeopardize our friendship." Yet even as Dean uttered these words, he knew that wasn't completely true.

"Why do I get the feeling that you're about to say the word 'but'?"

Dean debated how much he should tell Jack, how much Katie's brother needed to know to understand where he was coming from. The truth was, he was tired of hiding…of lying to his best friend about something as important as Katie.

"I'm going to date your sister," he said. His voice firm.

Jack's jaw dropped.

"Again," Dean added.

Jack picked up his beer, finished it, and signaled for the waiter. "Another round and bring me a shot of whiskey."

"Did you want—"

Jack's eyes never left Dean's. "Doesn't matter. Whatever's on the top shelf is fine."

The waiter left the table and Dean opened his mouth. "I need to—"

Jack held up his hand. "Wait."

Dean took another swig of his drink and contemplated what was going on in Jack's head. How would Dean have reacted if Tom or Mikey wanted to date one of his sisters? Syrie was married, but Ella was twenty-four and beautiful.

After replenishing their drinks, Jack tipped back the shot glass and closed his eyes. "OK…I'm ready."

"You sure you don't want another one?" Dean teased.

"Do I *need* another one?"

"You might."

"You're stalling."

Yes, he was. "I have feelings for your sister. And I think she has them for me, too."

"You think?"

"I know she does. She might not want to, but she does." He thought of their kiss, the way she melted in his arms. "I need to see if we have a chance, Jack. Only this time I need you to know about it."

"This time?"

It was Dean's turn to finish his beer. "Yeah. You see, a year ago…over a year ago actually, Katie and I…we, uh…"

"Do I want to hear this?"

"Probably not. Let's just say we figured out that we were attracted to each other. We both decided to keep our relationship under wraps. No need to involve you or our friends. We snuck around, which was fun for a while." Dean smiled at the memory but Jack was frowning into his beer.

Dean stopped grinning.

"What happened?"

Dean knew he was blowing his agreement with Katie talking to Jack about their past, but he figured if everything worked out, Jack would eventually find out. Telling his best friend the extent of what had happened between him and Katie, however, wasn't necessary.

"Katie wasn't willing to move forward." Which wasn't a lie. Dean had suggested after they learned of her inability to have a baby that they stop hiding and let their families know they were seeing each other. Her response to that was to get close and personal with someone other than him, and to say he was "off the hook" when it came to her.

"What makes you think she's any more ready now?"

That was a good question. "You saw her today. She's settling into a job she loves. We both know she doesn't have to work but she's doing it anyway. She's grounded in a way I've not seen before." She wasn't with the same group of friends, wasn't playing at night in the clubs…at least not that he knew. Her face hadn't been in a tabloid in months.

Jack nodded and sat back in the booth. "Maybe Katie is growing up."

"She's all grown up, Jack. It's not like we're kids."

"She's still my kid sister."

"And I'm your best friend."

"My best friend who seven months ago was ready to marry someone else. I remember the bachelor party, Dean. All the nauseating *Maggie is the best thing that ever happened to me* crap! Then I nursed your sorry ass after a weekend binge when she left you. If you cared about my sister so much, why were you ready to commit to someone else?"

Dean glanced at the TV across the bar showing the local baseball game. "I've had a lot of time to think about that."

"And?"

"I met Maggie after Katie all but dumped me. I hate to say she was a rebound chick, but there's no other way to put it. I cared about Maggie, don't get me wrong. When she broke off our engagement…I don't know, it was a blow to my ego, my manhood. I'm a class A asshole for saying that, but it's true. I didn't want her back after that."

"But that's changed with Katie. You want her back?"

Dean met Jack's eyes and held them. "Yeah. I do. I can't do that sneaking around or pretending I don't care about her. I wanted to do the noble thing and ask your permission…but fuck that. It's Katie's permission I need, not yours. I do, however, want your support, Jack."

"And if it doesn't work out?"

Dean hated the thought of that. It left him cold again. The way he'd felt since she walked away the first time. "We're all adults. We'll figure it out."

They sat in silence for a few minutes, drinking their beers.

"You have my support," Jack finally said.

Dean started to smile.

"I'll kick your ass if you hurt her."

"Wouldn't expect anything less."

"I mean it, Dean. Emergency room ass kicking."

Dean stopped the waiter and asked for another round and a menu. "Now that we're done talking about our *feelings*, like we're fucking women or something, I need you to do me a favor."

Jack shot him a killer look. "I haven't done enough?"

"I need you to keep quiet about this with Katie. If she thinks I've blabbed all of this to you, she's gonna start off pissed with me. I don't need that."

"Well, shit, Dean."

"C'mon. It won't be for long. I'm not willing to date her privately this time. If she wants to keep us hidden, then we won't stand a chance anyway. Just for a little while, Jack. When the time is right, I'll tell her we talked."

"Keeping secrets from each other backfires." Jack had kept the fact he was a rich man from Jessie when they first started dating.

All because Jessie refused to date him because she assumed he was dirt-poor. When she found out he was a millionaire, she ran away. Apparently, trust was more important than money. Jack had to do some serious groveling to win her back.

"Just for a while."

"You're testing our friendship," Jack warned with a smile on his face.

"We've been through worse."

"No, we haven't."

Dean relaxed. *This is good.*

The waiter returned and took their order. As he left, Jack said. "Manhood. You said manhood."

"Fuck you."

Jack popped some peanuts into his mouth. "You're not my type."

It's all good.

"He kissed me."

Monica shifted her attention away from the TV. "Dean?"

"Of course, Dean." Katie closed the door to the apartment and tossed her purse on the kitchen counter. Unlike the first time Dean had made moves on her, this time Katie had a close enough friend to talk to. There was only so much room for secrets inside her head anyway and Savannah was taking up the entire secret room.

Monica turned off the set. "Ooh la la…please tell."

"We were eating lunch. There was barbeque sauce. He kissed me. Oh, Monica, this is awful."

Monica closed her eyes and shook her head. "Excuse me? Why is this awful? Dean is yummy with a capital *Y.* How can *him* kissing *you* be anything but amazing?"

Katie motioned toward the bedroom where she assumed Savannah was sleeping. "Baby. Hellooo? Kissing leads to more kissing, then there's stroking, and hand holding. Phone calls and then midnight booty calls. I can't let this happen again."

"OK, I get it. You're scared he'll find out about Savannah. It's only a matter of time before he does anyway."

She knew that. "Not now. I still don't know who her mother is. He's not going to understand."

"You don't know that."

"I do. He's fiercely loyal to his brother and sisters. Family means everything to him. If he thinks I'm remotely responsible for Savannah not being with her real mom, he'd be…"

"He'd be what?"

"I don't know. He'd be something. Not a good something. His timing sucks."

Monica snickered.

"What?"

"Is his timing the only thing bothering you?"

"Yes. No. I don't know." His kiss haunted her all day. When Jack had arrived, Katie swore she blushed like a virgin being caught kissing a boy in church. Yet there was no way Jack could have known that she and Dean had shared a brief, intimate moment.

"If Dean would have pursued you before Savannah, or months from now…would you run away?"

"There were reasons we didn't work the first time, Monica. Good reasons."

"You didn't care for him?"

"We've been friends forever. Of course I care for him."

Monica rolled her eyes. "I'm not talking about a platonic caring and you know it."

"I cared."

"So you broke it off because he wanted kids. A family. And you couldn't give that to him."

"I still can't." That hadn't changed.

"Bullshit. Look in that room and tell me you can't be a mom."

Katie's jaw snapped shut.

"You have a stronger backbone than most, Katelyn. Don't short-change yourself because your uterus isn't perfect. Lots of women can't have kids."

"Dean wants his own."

"Really? You asked him that? He told you he didn't want you because you can't have his babies?" Monica bit out her questions and scowled.

Katie ground her back teeth together. No. They never had that conversation. She knew she wouldn't survive it so she broke it off. Didn't change the fact that Dean wanted to be a father. A father to his own children.

Monica approached her and lowered her voice. "Think about this, Katelyn Morrison. Three people in this world know you can't have kids. You, Dean, and me. If Dean's making moves on you, then apparently he's not thinking about your infertility."

"Maybe he's just horny."

"Men who want to scratch an itch don't do it with their best friend's sister. Did he push you to jump in the sack today?"

"No." *I won't push.*

"Were you interrupted by someone?"

"No."

"Did he say he was sorry for kissing you? That it shouldn't have happened?"

"No." Those had been her words. Yet she didn't stop him.

"He's into you, Katie. What you need to ask yourself is, if you're into him."

"Ah! God, I haven't been so indecisive my entire life. What the hell is wrong with me?"

Monica patted her on the shoulder before walking away. "You're a mom now. You have to think about someone else and that isn't easy. I watched Jessie do it for years. You think you're indecisive? Jessie was downright manic at times. You wouldn't believe the conversations we had about your brother."

"She thought my brother was a drifter and a broke one at that."

"Yet she fell in love with him anyway. You know Dean isn't a loser. If he's daddy material, then I don't see the problem."

But it did matter. What if she allowed him into her life and Savannah's mom showed up and took her away? If Dean abandoned her then…

"I can't risk it. Not now. Not yet."

"It's your decision."

The expression on Monica's face wasn't resolved.

"But?"

"But I don't think he's gonna back off."

Katie didn't think so either.

An hour later, the phone rang and Monica answered it.

"Hey, Jack. Jessie told me you were coming back."

Katie looked at Monica with wide eyes. She shook her head and mouthed the words *I'm not here.*

"Ah, huh? Yeah."

She listened to one side of the conversation and fished her cell phone out of her purse. Sure enough, there was a missed call from Jack's cell.

"Ah, no. She's not here. I told her she could stay here to keep out of your hair, but I haven't seen her."

Oh, good. Monica remembered to keep the men guessing about where Katie was staying. The last thing they needed was Jack or Dean showing up at Monica's.

Monica and Jack chatted for a few minutes before she hung up.

"Now you have your brother *and* Dean checking up on you. This is gonna get sticky in a heartbeat," Monica pledged.

"In college I dated three guys and one of my teachers and none knew about the other. I can handle two."

"That's because three of them were probably dating your roommate."

"Probably."

"A teacher…really?"

"He was super hot and fresh out of college himself."

"Can't complain about überhot."

"What about you, Monica? How come you're not dating? There's got to be some hot doctors at the hospital."

Monica curled her legs under her on the couch. It was late and they were watching a sitcom and eating popcorn. Savannah was awake and playful…sucking on her fist.

"I'm not all that interested. I don't mind some hot, meaningless sex once in a while. But relationships? Naw. Not for me."

"Not even a date?"

"Dating is harder than sex."

She couldn't dispute that.

"And before you ask…no. There wasn't someone who screwed up men for me."

"Oh, then what did? I know you don't like girls."

Monica tossed back her head and laughed.

Savannah jumped.

"Maybe I do."

"Oh, hon…if you were into women, you wouldn't be able to keep your hands off this." Katie ran a hand down the castoff T-shirt she'd borrowed from Monica's closet after Savannah had spit up half her dinner. There were bags under her eyes for the first time in *ever* and she could use a trip to the salon. She looked like hell.

"You're one confident broad."

"Yes, I am." They both laughed. "Really, why swear off men?"

"Have you met my mom?"

"You know I have."

"We don't get along. She's dragged one man after the other into our lives. She's never happy unless she's shacking up with someone to give her life meaning."

"It doesn't have to be that way with you."

"I know. The way I figure it…if you don't get close, they can't screw you up. I need to take care of myself financially and emotionally. I don't want a man messing that up for me."

"It doesn't have to be that bleak."

"Oh, yeah…have you forgotten our earlier conversation? If Dean were just a booty call, as you put it, then you wouldn't be torn right now. It's a problem because you care. I choose not to care. People at work are starting to call me the Ice Queen. I figure, what the hell, I'll go with it."

"Careful, Monica. That's the path to being alone with a house full of cats when you're seventy."

"No, that means I'm in the red hat club with weekends in Vegas."

Katie picked up a rattle and wiggled it in front of Savannah's face. "What about kids?"

"I'm too young for my biological clock to tick."

"Doesn't mean it won't…someday."

"Someday isn't today. Even then, you and Jessie have shown me you don't need a man to be a mom."

Katie's thoughts turned to Dean.

No, but it would help.

Chapter Fourteen

"I'm flying home tomorrow," Jack told her. "And I haven't seen you here this entire week." They were standing in the living room of the suite at the hotel. She'd made a point of showing up on what she knew was his last day in California.

Katelyn almost felt guilty for deceiving her brother…almost. "What's the matter, Jack? Miss your kid sister hanging around and getting in your way?"

"It hasn't been that way with us in years."

"That's because we don't live under the same roof. If I was here cramping your style, you'd hate me within three days."

"I'm a married man. You can't cramp my style if my wife isn't here."

Katie lifted her hand. "Let me rephrase then, you'd cramp *my* style."

The entire week had gone without a hitch. Jack had arrived and intervened between her and Dean at every turn. Each day she would make an appearance at the job site and then go back to the hotel long enough to pick up clothes and drop off dirties. Every night was spent at Monica's with Savannah. So far, her brother and anyone else watching were clueless.

"I'm just saying that you don't have to find another place to stay if you wanna come home."

She pictured Savannah. "Home isn't a hotel, Jack. I know it's been like that for both of us most of our lives, but is that really any way to live? There's something to be said for preparing your own meals and making your own bed."

Jack regarded her with narrow eyes. "Is that what you're doing? Preparing your own meals and making your own bed?"

She didn't meet his eyes. "In a way."

"Where?"

"Excuse me?"

"Where? Where are you doing this? Cuz I've not seen the backside of you walking out the door all week and I don't think you've bought a house."

Oh, no...this isn't good. "I have friends."

"Male friends?"

She hadn't seen that coming. "Maybe. What's this about, Jack? Since when do you dig into my personal life?"

"Dammit, Katie, you know I care. You dug into my personal life not too long ago and I couldn't be happier for it. I want to see you find the same happiness."

She'd talked with Monica for the first time when Jack had gotten pissing drunk after he'd asked Jessie to marry him and she'd refused. It was comical, really. Jack had posed as a waiter...a broke waiter working at The Morrison and not the son of *the* Morrison. As a single mom, Jessie wanted nothing to do with dating or marrying a man who had no bigger aspirations than waiting tables. And Jack, the fool, posed as a broke loser because he was tired of women going after him for his money. The two of them had nearly lost their future together because they hadn't been honest with each other. Sure, Jessie might have been honest about not wanting to fall in love with Jack...but she was in love. It took Monica and Katie working together to hook them up to make it all *happily ever after* in the end.

"I'm going through a few changes right now, Jack. I'm going to be fine."

Jack rubbed his chin. "You'd tell me if you're in any trouble… have anything you need help with?"

She walked over to him and placed a hand on his shoulder. "If I'm ever in a position where I don't know what to do…or my options are washed up, I'd call you."

"People care about you."

"I know that."

"You can always call on Dean if I'm not here."

Her gaze shot to his.

He didn't flinch.

What do you know? "Or Mikey. They're both nearby."

Jack nodded. "Right. Dean is closer. You work with him."

"He reminds me who the boss is every chance he gets."

Jack let one corner of his mouth lift up. "Promise me you'll call if you need me."

She rolled her eyes.

"Promise me!"

"OK, OK…I promise to call if I *need* you." Right now she was doing fine on her own. She had a PI working day and night to find Savannah's birth mom and Katelyn was juggling living in two places at once. She didn't *need* anything other than a good night's sleep.

Katie leaned against one of the finished walls in the huge open space that would eventually be the lobby of the hotel. Beside her, Jo sipped a beer and focused on what her boss was saying.

Dean stood in front of at least three dozen workers, all of them with drinks in their hands, and thanked them for all their hard work.

"Does he always do this?" Katie asked Jo.

"Every time we hit this phase and then again when the project is complete. It's his way of keeping the employees and subs happy."

"Paying them makes them happy."

Jo snorted. "Yeah, but blowing off steam and sharing a beer builds loyalty. At least that's what Dean says."

Katie looked around the room and the smiling faces and men listening attentively to their boss. She couldn't argue with his approach to loyalty. Work had come to a halt just after noon and a large grill was set up outside. A caterer had arrived with tables, chairs, food, and drinks. Not only was Dean springing for the party, everyone on site was getting paid a full day's wages to drink with the boss.

No, Katie couldn't argue with Dean's approach.

She sipped her champagne, thankful that Dean had the good sense to make sure a couple of bottles were available. Beer wasn't her drink of choice.

"I know I say this every time, but I couldn't do this without all of you," Dean told the crowd. "You're dependable and skilled…the best damn crew I've ever worked with."

"We're the only crew you've ever worked with," someone shouted.

Several men laughed.

"Not true," Dean corrected him. "Five years ago I went through a group of framers who couldn't be counted on to save my life. Then there was that excuse for an electrician…no, you guys are what gives Prescott Construction its good name."

"And a few good women!" Jo yelled across the room.

Katie smiled at Jo, lifted her glass in salute to the statement.

"Even if one of them steals the boss's hat and never gives it back." The comment came from inside the crowd and all eyes were on Katie. She still wore Dean's hard hat while his had gone through a number of pranks. First was the strip of pink paint then came a few rhinestones glued into the brim. Dean switched the hat out once the words "I'm so pretty" were printed on the back.

Yet he never asked for *his* hat back.

And Katie never offered it.

That, she knew, was their way of teasing each other. Even after Jack had flown back to Texas and she'd had a brief but firm conversation with Dean saying that she wasn't ready to have him kissing her right now.

She couldn't come out and tell him she *never* wanted him kissing her, because that would have been a lie.

"He can afford another one," Katie told the men.

Dean caught her eye and spoke directly to her. "Miss Morrison is hard to say no to."

"Ha! Then why are there only five niches down the halls and not ten?"

Laughter erupted from the men.

Someone hissed like a cat.

"Touché."

Dean turned back to his crew and continued his pep talk. He spoke about the next phase and his desire to have the hotel completed before the holidays. He finished up quickly and encouraged everyone to eat.

Music filled the room from an impressive portable player and work was completely forgotten.

Dean snagged an open bottle of sparkling wine from a bucket of ice as he walked toward her. "Looks like you could use a refill."

Katie lifted her glass.

"Oh, is it *Wait on the help* day? I could use another beer, boss," Jo said.

Dean chuckled and turned to get her one.

Steve was a step ahead of Dean and handed Jo a beer with a wink. "Here ya go, Jo."

Jo's face turned beet red and her gaze drifted to the floor. "Thanks."

Looked like things had gotten interesting between these two. At last count, Jo had been snarky and standoffish and now there was a coy smile and knowing blush. Katie sipped her wine and watched.

"Nice speech, Dean," Steve commented.

"I meant every word. I have a great crew."

"You make it easy for them. It's hard to get work in this economy."

"Even when work wasn't this hard to get, these men rose above the average. You know it. I know it."

Steve nodded and lifted his beer. "For many more projects to come."

Dean toasted and turned his attention back to Katie. "What about you, Katie? You think you'll want to do this again after Jack's hotel is finished?"

She'd asked herself that question a few times. The job itself had thus far served its goal. It gave her direction and purpose. Then again, so did Savannah. Juggling the secret and the job…and Dean.

"I think that's a no," Jo said.

"No. I'd do it again. Will do it again."

"But?" Dean watched her intently.

"I think I'll take this to a new level. Manage others to do what I do."

"More than a worker bee."

"Is that what I am?"

"Hardly," Jo said over her beer. "Oh, c'mon," she replied when all three of them stared at her. "Worker bees don't set their own hours and come and go as they please."

Katie couldn't help but see that Jo didn't think very well of her. For some reason she wanted Jo's approval.

"You're right. Bosses are the ones who work beyond nine to five and come in on the weekends," Dean defended her. "Katie has worked hard on this project."

"We all have." Jo didn't seem affected by his words or his rising anger.

Katie stepped in. "I realize that, unlike anyone else here, I'm the only one who hasn't had to work to afford to live. I can't alter the fact that I was born to money, which I wouldn't change for the world. My father worked hard to make his fortune and Jack is doing the same. I'm just trying to figure out where I fit, Jo. I know I am the boss's daughter, or in this case, sister, and it would be damn hard for Dean to fire me, but that doesn't make me a slacker."

Jo's face had gone blank. "I didn't call you a slacker."

"Ya kinda did, Josephine," Steve said under his breath.

"Oh, hell…I didn't mean to. Sorry, Katie."

"It's OK."

"No, it's not. I've been a little edgy lately, not that that's an excuse. My mother would slap my butt if she knew I'd been so rude."

Jo simply vocalized what so many others thought. And that was refreshing…rude, but refreshing.

"No worries."

Dean and Steve let the women work it out while they drank their beer. Steve broke the tension with a laugh. "*Slap your butt.* I'd like to see that."

Jo swiveled on him. "I'll bet you would. And *don't* call me Josephine!"

Steve's eyes grew wide. "Put your claws away, woman. Maybe food is the medicine you need." He drew her in the direction of the food line leaving Dean and Katie alone.

"Wonder what has her all fired up?"

Katie thought of her own little bundle of *fired up* and shrugged. "Who knows? Let it go."

"Still…"

"People have judged me every day of my life, Dean. That isn't going to change. The truth is, I've never had to work and you *can't* fire me."

"Seems to me you've made up for that by working harder, darlin'."

"I'm working harder because I don't know what the hell I'm doing half the time."

"Could have fooled me."

"Oh, please. Everything is a learning curve. And my boss's budget is as tight as an ant's ass."

Dean gifted her with his signature smile complete with the cleft in his chin and sparkle in his gray eyes. "I could put in a word with your boss, get a bigger budget."

"Don't you dare!"

"OK, OK…put *your* claws away, woman," he repeated Steve's words. "C'mon, you need food, too." Dean slung an arm over her shoulders and shoved her toward the buffet.

The same barbeque they had shared when he'd kissed her over two weeks ago.

Patrick sauntered into The Morrison in Houston as if he owned the place.

He glanced behind the front desk and noted an elderly woman who probably claimed at least eight grandchildren as her own.

Miss May, he said to himself.

He offered a friendly smile and walked straight for the elevators.

The second set. Katelyn had told him the first ones didn't access the penthouse level and the passkey wouldn't work.

Guests shuffled by with suitcases in hand. There were plenty of Stetsons and cowboy boots. So many that he thought maybe he should be wearing one or the other to fit in. He didn't have time to think on it long before the elevator made a resounding *ding* and the doors opened.

A few guests stepped into the elevator beside him and pressed the buttons for their floors.

He stepped in and waved a mechanical key over an invisible sensor that would push the elevator to the top floor.

He stared at the numbers as the elevator ascended, completely aware of the coy glances he was given as he rode the elevator with strangers.

Twice the elevator stopped and guests stepped out. Each one turned to take a second look his way.

Their actions told him one of two things: Whoever had dropped a baby off at Katelyn's didn't have a passkey. Or if they did, they certainly didn't catch the elevator with another hotel guest or someone would have seen something.

Patrick had stayed in a few fancy hotels in his time, but he hadn't yet had the privilege of sleeping in a penthouse.

Katelyn had mentioned that people noticed her when she walked by, but he thought it was because of her striking appearance and larger-than-life presence when she walked into a room. Patrick was none of those things and he'd been seen by a half dozen people, including one employee within minutes of walking in the door.

The elevator opened to a short hallway with rooms only on two sides. One suite took up the west end of the hotel, the other took the east.

Katelyn's was number one.

Fitting.

The same key that let him on the elevator flashed a green light over the hotel door so he could enter Katelyn's personal space without so much as a hello.

He opened the door and at the same time removed a small notebook from the inside pocket of his jacket.

Who makes the electronic keys?

Who has access to the codes to Katelyn's suite?

He made a few more notes about housekeeping and room service. All of whom would be able to get up into the suite without detection.

Much like the hotel he'd first met Katelyn in, this one was packed full of opulence and the evidence of money. Big money.

Marble tile floors were a softer hue than the one in California, the decor feminine. There were fresh flowers in the vase by the door, which struck him as funny since Katelyn wasn't expected to return to Houston anytime soon.

He flipped on a switch and the room lit up. The sun was setting in Houston and the lights of the city were twinkling on the horizon. Patrick lost himself in the view for a moment.

Did the mother of the child know what a privilege it would be to have her child grow up with enough money to afford this view in whatever city they lived? Did they know flowers would greet the baby every day?

Did that play into the decision to give up Savannah?

Patrick moved into the room and noticed a small light above his head turn red.

Motion detector.

Before continuing his perusal of Katelyn's personal space, he opened the outside door once again and looked in the small corridor. Above the elevator, a motion detector turned red.

He scribbled more notes in his notebook. *Who was in charge of watching the detectors? When did they go off and alert the authorities?*

Patrick removed his jacket, hung it on the back of a chair, and noted the time on his watch. He sat on the large white sofa and crossed a leg over his opposite knee before picking up a magazine. Any security worth their salt would be at the door in less than two…

Click!

Make that thirty seconds.

Patrick turned the page of the magazine and glanced up when two men wearing suits, but who certainly were armed, stepped into the room.

"Miss Morrison?" they called out.

"She's not here," Patrick told them.

One of the men moved into the doorway but kept his left hip toward the hall. The other had a hand on a radio.

"You would be who?" the large man in the doorway asked.

Patrick stood and moved slowly to the man, extending his hand. "Ben Sanderson. Katie told me I could crash here tonight. I had an unexpected layover. Damn airline lost my luggage."

The security guard straightened and looked around the room. "She didn't call ahead."

"She said she'd try...but she was with friends...out. Well, you know Katie. Call her, she'll vouch for me." He removed the key from his pocket and waved it in the air. "She gave me her key. I'll be back in LA with her next week."

The guards exchanged a glance and proceeded to relax.

"We'll check with Miss Morrison."

"Suit yourself." Patrick moved back into the room and picked up the phone. "Is the kitchen still open? Damn domestic flights don't even serve peanuts anymore."

If there was one thing Patrick had learned in all his years of being a PI, it was that when you acted as if you belonged, people seldom questioned if you did.

"Yeah, the kitchen's still open."

"Thank God. I'm starved." Ben allowed the kitchen to patch through the line and proceeded to order the chef's special. He glanced around the room, noticed a bar, and knew he could pour himself a drink.

The guards talked among themselves before they excused themselves, apologizing for their presence, and left. Patrick knew the guards would be back if Katie hadn't dropped his name with someone in power at the hotel.

Patrick kicked off his shoes after they were gone in case the place held hidden cameras. Best to act like he'd just gotten off an airplane.

He poured himself two fingers of Crown Royal and brought the whiskey to his lips.

The TV provided background noise while he waited for room service to arrive.

Patrick noted the large cart in which the food arrived. One that could easily conceal an infant seat.

He scribbled a note.

He ate. Made himself at home.

Enjoyed the opulence of high-rise and high-dollar living.

Only after he'd forced himself from the room, under the guise of needing a cigarette and considering the home owner, he sauntered outside after dark and "accidently" got lost in the far reaches of the hotel.

There were plenty of his assignments that left him cold, hungry, and tired.

This wasn't one of them.

I'm drunk.

OK…maybe not drunk in the truest sense, but tipsy beyond anything Katelyn had been in the past several months.

Many of the employees had stuck around long past five. They cranked up the music and kept drinking until the caterers had left and Dean pulled the plug. He called a series of cabs that arrived to take his more inebriated employees home.

Such a thoughtful boss.

Katie couldn't bring herself to stand, let alone even consider driving home. And this was the one night a week that she spent at the hotel…alone.

"Ready to go, darlin'?" Dean walked around the massive room turning off the work lights. Most of the mess had been cleaned up and what wasn't would be picked up by the early morning workers over the weekend.

"I think you should call me a cab, too, Dean. I haven't drank that much since the wedding." The wedding that changed her life in the most unexpected way.

"Jack would have my ass if I poured you into a cab. Give me a minute and I'll lock up the office before I see you home."

Dean walked from the room with all his Texan swagger and Katie had to close her eyes to help her focus. She hadn't drunk that much but, on the legs of a lack of sleep, the alcohol must have shot straight to her head.

She rested her eyes for a few seconds and waited for Dean to return.

"Wake up, darlin'. Don't want the staff to think I'm a schmuck taking advantage of the queen bee around here."

Katie woke with a start. She was in Dean's truck with a seat belt over her lap. The bright lights of the hotel parking lot illuminated the truck and made her blink. "How did I get here?"

"You were out. I managed to get you in here without waking you."

"Oh, my word." She shook the fog from her brain and glanced at the clock. At least an hour had passed. "Look what time it is."

"Like I said, you were gone. I thought about taking you to my place but I didn't want to scare you off."

She rubbed a hand over her face, completely ignoring her makeup. "What makes you think I'd scare that easily?"

Dean fixed her with a stare. "You pass out at work and wake up in my bed…you don't think that would cause you to freak?"

Well when he put it that way.

"I—I trust you."

He shook his head before getting out of the truck. "That makes one of us."

A grin settled over her lips and warmth spread throughout her body as he walked around the front of the truck before opening her door.

"Steady enough to walk?" he asked.

"Yeah." She'd been more tired than drunk. Sure her head still swam a little, but there wasn't a dense fog over her eyes shading her vision.

His arm snaked around her waist even though she didn't need it. Part of her wanted to push him away, but the other part…the woman who enjoyed the deep heat of his hand resting on her hip and the masculine scent of his skin as it reached her nose…that part wanted to snuggle up and enjoy the cocoon of his arms.

Huddled close, they walked to the lit drive of the hotel. A valet opened the door for them as they walked through and addressed Katie by name.

"Good evening, Miss Morrison," the receptionist said as they walked by. "Did you want your messages?"

She waved the woman off. "In the morning."

"Yes, Miss Morrison. Have a nice evening."

Dean walked her through the lobby and to the bank of elevators. "Do you have your key?" he asked as his fingers skimmed over her arms. Shivers ran down her skin despite the warm temperature of the California summer evening.

She dug into her purse and removed the elevator key. They stepped inside, alone, and she waved the card over the lock. The key accessed the penthouse level and bypassed anyone going up along the way. It was a small measure of security she had living in a hotel with often hundreds of strangers.

They arrived on the top floor without saying anything to each other.

It wasn't until they were inside her hotel room that she managed to say, "I don't even feel tipsy anymore. You don't have to keep holding me up."

Dean didn't let go.

She didn't wiggle out of his arms.

He did, however, remove her purse from her fingers and toss the bag on a nearby table.

"Not tipsy?" he asked.

"No. Tired, but not drunk."

He let a grin spread on his lips and he returned his hand to her arm. They were face to face, and his body heat warmed her skin.

"Good. I don't want you thinking I've taken advantage of you."

She narrowed her eyes and stared at his lips. Lips she'd kissed more times than she could possibly count. "Taken advantage of what?"

"Of this."

Those perfect lips slid over hers and the room around them disappeared.

Chapter Fifteen

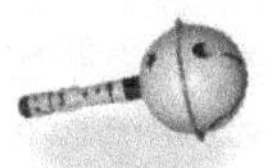

Dean held her in his arms and kissed her so completely, hours could have slid by. He'd stared at her lips all night wanting a taste. Katie may have told him she wasn't ready to see him romantically again, but she hadn't stopped watching him. In fact, since Jack had returned to Texas, Katie managed to set his blood on fire almost hourly with the nibbling on her lips as she watched him working…or the hunger in her gaze when he roamed the job site with her in tow.

Katie might have said she wasn't ready, but her body screamed for him to risk kissing her again.

She released a tiny hum, one he vividly remembered from their past as she tilted her head back and opened to him.

Dean held her tight enough to tell her he wanted her, but loose enough so she could escape if she truly wanted to.

Please don't want to.

Her breasts pushed up against his chest and her arms circled the back of his neck. He smiled under her kiss and followed the lovely curve of her hip with his hand. Katie lifted her leg into his touch. The heat of her center made direct contact with his growing erection and he moaned.

She nipped at his lips and broke their kiss. "This is such a bad idea." Her breathless words would have alarmed him if Katie's soft fingers weren't tugging at his shirt.

Dean kissed her neck and the sensitive lobe of her ear.

"God that feels good."

"We always feel good together," he reminded her. He'd never forgotten the feel of her body over his, the taste of her skin. The globe of her butt met his palm and he brought her closer. Her hips buckled along with her knees.

She wanted him; there was no doubt in Dean's mind. But he was a Southern gentleman and he'd never seduce an unwilling woman. As much as it would kill him walking away now, he'd force himself to.

Lifting his lips from her neck, he waited until her hooded gaze met his. Soft, warm desire spoke to him in silence.

"I want to hold you, make slow sweet love to you until your body is draped over mine like silk, and both of us are too weak to open our eyes." His words were delivered in a hoarse whisper.

The pulse in her throat moved faster as she swallowed with his words.

He lifted a hand to her cheek and stroked her swollen lips with his thumb. "If you're going to ask that I leave, have mercy, and do it now."

Katie drowned in the depth of his gray eyes. He had the perfect amount of Southern drawl lacing his words. She'd never forgotten how in sync they were together, how well they fit. The image of them naked and rolling around on satin sheets was intoxicating. The sad truth was she'd not so much as kissed a man since she and Dean had broken apart. It wasn't that she'd closed herself off from men, she simply didn't feel a big enough spark to dive into that pool again.

With Dean the fireworks were a given.

Another harsh reality reminded her that, with Dean, she could be herself. There was no pretense or expectations other than what they were both willing to give. She'd not shared that with anyone ever…except with Dean.

"I don't want to lose you as a friend," she whispered.

"That's never going to happen."

He kissed her again, hot indecent kisses that scattered all coherent thought. He lifted her in his strong, capable arms and walked them both to her bedroom.

They tumbled onto the bed, their lips fused in a way that left them gasping for air.

She kicked her shoes to the floor and reached under Dean's shirt. What had started out as somewhat lazy and familiar switched into combustible. The need to feel his naked skin on hers made her push him away. She unbuttoned his shirt, fumbling as she went.

He quickly became frustrated with her clothing and started pulling it over her head.

"What happened to slow and sweet?" she asked, chuckling.

His eyes glossed over as her breasts peeked out from under the lacy pink bra he found beneath her clothing. "Next time. I promise."

Dean's lips found the tender flesh between her breasts and he licked her through her bra. Her nipples pebbled and ached. Katie fell back to the bed and enveloped herself in the feel of him touching her, kissing her. "So good." It had always been so good.

He pulled her bra aside and filled his mouth with her breast. Deep inside, her belly tightened.

His knee wedged between her thighs and she shamelessly pushed against him, her skirt riding high, and her panties moist with desire.

He kissed a path down her flat stomach. "Anxious, darlin'?" he chuckled.

More than he could ever possibly know.

"I want fireworks, Dean." She'd never refrained from telling him what she wanted in bed. *I'm not starting now.*

He tugged at the zipper of her skirt, then tugged again, and removed it from her hips.

Dean drew in a deep breath through his nose and rolled his eyes back. "You're killing me, Katie. I'd sit in my office..." He leaned down and dragged his tongue along the dainty fabric that passed for her panties. "And wonder if you still wore lingerie."

"Most women wear underwear."

"Not like you, Katie. Never like you. It's like Christmas every time I unwrap you. You've made me hard just wondering what color, what shape, was hidden under your clothes."

Pure feminine bliss rolled over her. He'd thought about her, wondered about her long before now.

He kissed the crease between her thigh and her hip. "What color did you wear at the wedding?" he asked.

Hot air forced from his mouth threatened her ability to speak. "G-gold and white s-satin."

Dean growled.

He pushed her panties aside and placed his lips where the cloth had been. He was there, in exactly the right place, rolling his tongue in delightful swirls as if tasting the perfect ice cream from a tiny cone.

She couldn't breathe. Dean found her pleasure and didn't relent until she called his name and rode out the first orgasm she'd had in what felt like forever.

"How are those fireworks, darlin'?"

She smiled, laughed even as she ran her hands over his shoulders. "Bright and shiny," she said. "Wanna see 'em?"

Dean crawled up her body and dropped an elbow on each side of her head. He kissed the tip of her nose. "Oh, yeah."

She wrapped one limber leg over his hips and shoved on his chest. "Where did your pants go, cowboy? I don't remember taking them off." He wore only boxer briefs that were losing the battle of containing his excitement.

"Too binding," he said.

"These need to go, too." His boxers met the floor and she ran her hands up his legs until she cupped him fully. She leaned forward to taste and Dean stopped her. "One lick and I'm toast. Condom, Katie, back pocket of my pants."

"Don't you want—"

"Oh, yeah…I want. But first I need you."

She believed him. His need for her.

Katie scrambled off the bed and tossed his pants to him.

He tore open his wallet, found the condom, and covered himself in seconds.

"C'mere," he beckoned.

Their lips met with wet kisses filled with promises. His arms were everywhere, as if he'd forgotten what she felt like and was starved to rediscover her.

Dean lifted her easily, guiding her over his impressive length, until she felt him slowly push deep inside. Even with her on top of him, he held the control. And she liked giving it to him here, when they were intimate. Not once had he taken that power to a scary place, and because of that, her trust in him never faltered.

"So tight," he hissed between his lips. "Sweet Jesus, Katie, you're killing me."

He opened her slowly and completely, like only a big man could, until they were both holding their breaths and her hips were flush with his. She smiled into his neck and savored the feel of him. She'd missed him, terribly. Never did she think she would be in his arms again when she'd told him good-bye the first time.

She swiped away the awful memory and thought only of now. Of this moment in his arms. Her hips rolled onto his once… twice. Dean's fingers squeezed her waist and within a heartbeat she was under him. Skin to skin they found a frantic pace that suited them both. The confession of wanting him, needing him, and missing him sat on the tip of her tongue as her body responded to his.

She bit her lip, refusing to say anything but meaningless moans that encouraged every move he made. Those confessions would place her heart exactly where her body was now, wrapped around Dean.

He tilted her hips and plunged even deeper. "Now you're killing me," she told him.

Dean slowed down. "Too much?"

"God, no. Please."

He locked eyes with her and slid in her with delicious friction, keeping the pace until neither of them could hold their eyes open. One second she was warming up to her orgasm and then it exploded over her, long shuddering spasms that wrung her out.

"Oh, Katie," Dean muttered as he reached his release. The expression of bliss on his face was one she'd put there and that felt damn good.

He collapsed on top of her with a sigh. "Oh, baby. I missed you."

She stilled. His words hung there, waiting for a response. "We were always good in bed."

Dean shifted his weight and pulled her with him onto their sides. "*Good* is such a paltry word. Magnificent, spectacular."

She liked that. The emotions mixed up with missing him drifted away as they enjoyed a little pillow talk. "No one does it better." Katie had told him that in their past. She meant it then and even more now.

"Like a Bond film…the music from the movie. *Makes me feel bad for the rest.*" He stroked the side of her face as they talked.

"Are you going to serenade me, cowboy?"

"I might."

"Aren't you supposed to do that before we hit the sheets?" The length of him slid from her body. She regretted the loss.

"Before, during…after. I'll sing if your ears can handle it."

Katie snuggled into her pillow and curled one arm under her head. "I've stood beside you a time or two in church. You have a nice voice." A rich baritone she hadn't expected the first time she'd heard it.

"We just had the most sinfully amazing sex this side of the equator and you had to go and mention church."

"I never understood how something so good could be considered so bad," she told him. "If touching heaven is a sin, then sign me up."

"Keep danglin' that apple, li'l Eve, and I'll follow."

She poked his chest with her index finger. "Don't even think of not sharing the blame for being here."

His coy look was comical. "Oh, I'll take all the blame...and the credit."

Her heavy eyelids started to fall and took longer to look back up. "Good. Glad that's settled. You take the blame, I take the credit. All is right in my world."

His chest rumbled as he laughed. He tucked her under his chin and sighed. "Go to sleep, Katelyn."

He did not have to tell her twice.

Early morning light winked through the curtains that were being blown around by the air-conditioning vent in the wall. Katie blinked open her eyes and sighed. Her limbs were lax and her mind free of worry. She couldn't remember ever feeling this rested.

Warm images of the night with Dean put a grin on her face. She'd worried if she'd regret their night by the time morning arrived. She didn't. She couldn't. Everything about them felt complete and, even if she needed to be less than honest with him about how she felt, she wouldn't lie to herself.

Katie rolled to her side expecting to see him there and found nothing. Her heart lurched. Had he left in the night? Was he upset they were sharing a bed again? Though she didn't want that, she also knew she couldn't keep up the pace they'd had before with Savannah in her life. Not with the infant hidden anyway.

Pushing the covers aside, she padded across the plush carpet to the bathroom. She took care of her needs and ran a brush through her hair. What little makeup she'd worn the day before was smudged on her face, but she left it there. If Dean was somewhere in the massive penthouse suite, he'd appreciate that she didn't gussy up for him. She covered up with the white terry cloth bathrobe that hung on the back of the bathroom door and made her way into the living room.

Richly brewed coffee met her nose as she rounded the corner. Dean sat on the sofa with his feet propped up on the coffee table. He drank his coffee while reading the paper. When he didn't notice her walk in, she cleared her throat.

He dropped the paper and looked up with an instant smile. His gaze traveled her body and his smile fell.

"What? I don't look as good in the morning?" she teased.

"No." He set his coffee down and walked to her side. "You look even better."

It was so easy fishing for compliments with Dean. "You're full of shit, Dean Prescott. I have mascara smudged under my eyes and eye shadow on my forehead. I look like day old bread."

He grasped her slim waist and pulled her into his arms. "I like day old bread. A little hard on the outside with the insides still soft and tender. Warm it up, and butter melts on it all the same."

She couldn't stop smiling. "That's one heck of a line. Might need to write it down and blog about it."

"You blog?"

"No." But she'd thought about it after visiting several in the last month. Between designer blogs and mommy blogs, Katie had opened up an entire world of cyber information she couldn't find in books. "But I might wanna."

Dean brushed his lips over hers. "Good mornin', darlin'."

Katie sighed. "Good morning."

He turned toward the service and poured her a cup of coffee with cream and sugar, just the way she liked it.

"Thanks."

"I took the liberty of ordering a few things. I know you're not big on breakfast, but—"

"You are," she finished for him.

"Right."

The first sip of coffee opened her eyes even wider. It felt wonderful to have a morning of relaxation. A tiny bit of guilt pulled at the back of her brain. Monica would expect her there by ten. Which meant Katie would have to find a way to have Dean leave without any questions.

"You got up early," Katie said. It was Saturday and neither one of them would go to work.

"Couldn't avoid it. My cell phone started chiming thirty minutes ago."

"Is everything OK?"

"Probably. I need to go by the site. The Santa Ana winds started up last night and there's a mess at the hotel."

Katie looked out the window and noticed a haze. Being on the top floor of the hotel, she didn't see any trees blowing around and the thick windows didn't allow any wind noise. "Jack said the winds here can be nasty."

"The gusts can reach hurricane speeds. They knock down power lines, semitrucks. Out here, they kick up dust and topple trees. Leaves quite a mess most of the time."

She sipped her coffee. Well, at least she wouldn't have to push him out the door.

Dean topped off his coffee and brought a plate of fruit and toast over to her.

"You don't have to wait on me."

"It's my way of assuring you're going to eat since I can't stay here and watch."

"I don't forget to eat." Actually, she had forgotten to eat…more than once in the past month.

"I'm sorry I have to run off. I'd rather we spend the day together and talk about us."

She bit into the dry toast to hide her expression. What could she say to hold him off on pushing "us" right then?

"You know, Dean. It might be good for us to *think* about the *us* part before we *talk* about it. I wasn't exactly expecting this."

He sat beside her, his face blank. "You don't look like a woman filled with remorse."

"That's because I'm not." She didn't want to lead him on or shove him away. Patrick was due to call her over the weekend to update the baby status. If Katie could hold off Dean until Savannah was out of the closet…

"I'm not either."

"I need to think. And I can't do that with you by my side."

"All right. I can accept that."

Good. One hurdle down.

"There's just one thing I want you to do when you're *thinking*," he said.

"Oh, yeah…what's that?"

He took her lips with his and tilted her head back. The taste of coffee and jam laced his tongue as it took its sweet time playing with hers. Katie's eyes fluttered closed and thoughts of *thinking* drifted away.

Their slow morning kiss ended too soon. "*Think* of that."

Dean sure knew how to stack the cards in his favor. It would be impossible to close her eyes and not think of him.

"Go to work, cowboy."

He winked, kissed her forehead, and sauntered to the door. Yep, he'd certainly developed a certain swagger since the last time he'd shared her bed.

She liked it.

"Have a beautiful day, darlin'."

Katie kissed her finger and waved in his direction. "'Bye."

She took her time finishing her coffee and eating her toast.

And she thought.

Denying her attraction, her emotions, when it came to Dean felt like a waste of energy. She didn't have a deep reserve of energy.

She'd walked away from him, and everything he wanted in life when she found out she couldn't have children. Yet here she was with a child counting on her every single day.

No. There had to be a better reason to stay away from Dean than a dysfunctional…no, the doctor had called it an *inhospitable* uterus.

There was always the question if Dean could accept Savannah and what he would do when he found out about her.

"I'll have to think about everything later," she told herself.

After a quick shower and packing a small bag with fresh clothes, Katie made her way out of the hotel. She stopped at the reception desk. Naomi had a younger woman beside her watching every move she made.

"Hi, Naomi."

"Miss Morrison, hello. Have you met Tammy? She's new with us."

Katie put on her most congenial smile. Most new employees tripped over themselves when they found out she was a Morrison. Katie always did her best to be as unassuming as possible. "Hi, Tammy. How are you liking it here?"

"I love it. Thanks for asking."

"Good, good. Listen, Naomi, I need you to be alert to any phone calls coming in for me."

Naomi picked up a pen and waited for Katie to continue.

"If Patrick Nelson or a Ben Sanderson call, have them call my cell. Oh, and Dean Prescott."

"I can do that."

"Good."

"Tell housekeeping I left my laundry in the bedroom closet and be sure and send the red dress to the dry cleaners."

"Will we expect you this evening?"

Katie glanced at the time on the clock behind the desk. "No. I will check in tomorrow."

"Very good. Have a nice day, Miss Morrison."

"You, too, Naomi. Nice meeting you, Tammy."

The women said good-bye and Katie left the hotel with a smile on her face. Between the amazing sex and a good night's sleep, she couldn't wait to spend the day playing with Savannah. She missed her daughter.

Chapter Sixteen

He sent flowers. Two dozen long-stem pink roses. Roses that would match the frilly bra and panties Katie had worn last night.

Flowers had been off limits before…when they'd met in secret.

Not this time.

Dean wasn't going to hide…this time.

He smiled after getting off the phone with the florist. Dean escaped into the mess of his day but didn't mind any of it. The temporary power pole had gone down and sparked a small fire. Luckily, he had a security guard on site at night who had managed to take down the flames with a fire extinguisher. The power company and the fire department then needed to repair and sign off on the broken pole, which took the whole morning.

One full pallet of roofing material escaped its binding and blew all over the site. Dirt covered every surface. Even three of the Porta-potties had tipped over. Now that was a mess. Two windows, one standard and one bay, broke when some kind of debris flew through them.

He called in a couple of guys and lent a hand securing the material that might be a problem again overnight. The forecast of Santa Ana winds and red flag warnings wasn't going to be lifted until early Monday morning. Outside of the immediate issues, Dean saw no need to fix everything until after the wind stopped. He called the portable john guys and asked them to come by and upright the toilets.

Feeling gritty from working in the dust-coated wind all day, Dean made his way home while singing along with the radio. Damn he felt good.

At home he checked his messages and heard only the men from the job site when they'd attempted to get a hold of him that morning. Nothing from Katie.

Did she like the flowers?

Of course she did. She might not admit it, but she'd enjoy them anyway.

Don't most women call and thank a man for flowers after they arrive?

Then again, she wanted time to think. Thinking didn't include talking to him about flowers sent just hours after he left.

Dean took a long, hot shower and scrubbed the dirt from his hair. Hair that needed some quality time with a pair of scissors. After his shower, he made himself a simple sandwich and chased it with a beer.

It was nearly seven.

He needed to see her. He wouldn't stay long. Just long enough to know that she wasn't sitting in a pile of regret after last night.

He shoved into his cowboy boots and found a hat. On the weekends, he tried to capture his Texan side, a side Katie liked and he would exploit at every turn.

The ride to The Morrison was short despite the wind blowing sand across the roads like blizzards blow snow.

Determined strides took him through the doors and to the elevators. He didn't have a key to the penthouse level so he turned toward the stairs. Then he stopped.

No. He'd used the back way up in the past. Thinking of that left a bad taste in his mouth.

Behind the reception desk stood a girl no older than twenty-two. She smiled easily and asked to help him.

Dean looked at her name tag and used it. "Hi, Tammy. Would you be kind enough to let Miss Morrison know that I'm on my way up?"

Tammy's eyes grew wide. "Miss Morrison…right…" She flipped through some papers on the desk. "Ah, are you Patrick Nelson?"

Dean felt his happy disposition slip. *Who the hell is he?* "No."

Tammy's smile started to fade.

"Ben Sanderson?"

The old guy? What the hell? "No!"

"Oh, um, Dean Prescott?"

Finally, his name made the short list. "Bingo."

Tammy grinned, entirely pleased she'd gotten the name right. "Oh, good."

Dean turned toward the elevators with his fists gripped at his sides. What in the depths of hell was Katie doing?

"Mr. Prescott," Tammy called behind him.

He turned and barked at the girl. "What?"

"Um, Miss Morrison isn't here. She asked if you or any of the others called, to have you call her cell phone."

He glared at the elevators. *Not home? That explains the lack of phone call about the flowers.* Hard to say thank you if you haven't seen them yet.

"Did she say when she'd be back?"

"Tomorrow…I think. Yeah, tomorrow."

"Tomorrow?" So where the hell was she sleeping tonight? And with whom?

"Savannah's sleeping and you've had a glass of wine. I'll go." Katie moved about the apartment and found her purse. "I'll swing by the grocery store and pick up more formula before getting our dinner. Do we need anything else?"

Monica reclined on the couch as Katie shuffled around the room. It was nice having someone there to run simple errands. It didn't suck that Katie was used to eating out so she ordered takeout half the week. *It's a little thing I can do for you letting Savannah and I stay here.* Katie had insisted and Monica wasn't about to refuse. "Might as well get diapers. And get a bigger size. Savannah's growing out of those tiny ones."

Katie paused for a moment and a smile slid over her lips. "She's getting big."

Monica made a swishing motion with her hands. "Go. Before she wakes up."

"Right." Katie shuffled out of the apartment while Monica continued to drink her wine. Even though Jessie and Katelyn were actually sisters-in-law, Monica found the joy in a sister by marriage. There was a huge bonus that they both held very little regard for their mothers—one for having left and the other for staying, yet not really being there for Monica and Jessie. Monica could see how hard Katie was trying to make things right for Savannah, and much of that stemmed from a lack of a mother in Katie's life.

Monica turned the channel to the opening credits for the popular reality show that spun new musical talent. Twenty minutes into the show, a loud knock jarred her from the TV.

She surged off the couch. "Keep it down," she called out. The thought of putting a note on the door about a baby sleeping crossed her mind.

The knock came again, this time louder.

"I'm coming." She grabbed the door and swung it open. "What's the big…Dean?"

Dean's gaze soared over her, his brows pitched together with barely contained fury. His eyes sparked and not in a good way.

"Where's Katelyn?"

"Excuse me?"

He pushed his way into the apartment, did a quick once-over and turned to her again. “Katelyn? Where is she?”

“W-what?” Monica felt a nest of lies start to form on her tongue and wondered just how much she should say. Did he know Katie was staying with her? Had he seen her leave?

“C’mon, Monica, you two have been thick ever since Jack and Jessie hooked up. You know what’s going on with her and we need to talk.” His voice rose, crackling the air with tension.

Monica glanced beyond him toward Katie and Savannah’s room. Dean was going to wake the baby with all his yelling. “She’s not here.”

“But you know where she is, damn it, and you’re going to tell me.”

Monica thrust her hands on her hips and straightened her shoulders. “The big macho *Tell me now or else* routine isn’t going to work with me, Dean. You can take your alpha self and march the hell out of here.”

The wind left Dean’s sails with her words. His shoulders slumped and he lowered his gaze. “Sorry, Monica. I didn’t mean to come off like that. It’s just…” He glanced up and turned away from her. “It’s Katie. I’ve been trying to get a hold of her…” His words trailed off as he looked around the room.

An infant swing sat in the corner. A forgotten pacifier and baby rattle cluttered the kitchen counter.

Monica rushed in front of him and made him focus on her. “Katie’s not here. You might try her cell phone.” She laid a hand on his arm and tried to push him out of the apartment.

“Tried that.” He easily dodged her hand and picked up a baby bottle. “Have a kid when no one was looking?”

“I babysit sometimes.” *Not a lie.*

“Don’t nurses make decent money?”

“Yeah.”

"So you babysit for charity?" Doubt laced his gaze and he moved deeper into the room and made an audible sniff.

"Kinda." She knew if Dean searched hard, he'd find evidence of Katelyn. In fact, a pair of stilettos that defined Katie were carelessly tossed under the coffee table. "You can see that Katie isn't here so you should look for her somewhere else."

Dean's eyes settled on her and she felt the need to fidget. "Why the hurry, Monica?"

"I'm watching my favorite show and you're becoming a pain in my ass. If I wanted company, I'd have invited you over."

"Right." Dean sniffed the air again.

"You sound like a dog. Do you have a cold or something?"

Dean grinned. "Do you know who Tom Ford is?"

Where the hell did that question come from. "Tom who?"

"The designer."

"Why would I know that?"

"He's a fashion designer who created a very unique perfume."

Monica squeezed her eyes shut and shook her head. "I'm not sure what perfume has to do with you sniffing around my apartment like a bloodhound."

Dean smelled the air again and moved toward the hall, closer to where Savannah was sleeping.

Monica's heart thudded in her chest. It was as if a house of cards were standing in the direct path of a cat's swishing tail and she couldn't get to the cat before it knocked the cards over. She scrambled in front of him again, blocking his path to the hall. "I'll call Katie myself. Tell her you're looking for her."

"Black Orchid. I'd know the scent anywhere." He was rambling about perfume and moving around her.

She pushed in front of him again.

He smiled, placed his hands on her shoulders, and moved her to the side. "It's Katie's perfume. I know because I've bought it for her before." Dean lifted his finger and waved it once in front of her face. "Stay!"

She did. She didn't mean to, but she couldn't stop watching the slow-motion action of him opening the door to Katie's room.

She heard him draw in a breath and let it out slowly.

A hundred lies formed. *I'm babysitting for a friend. I have a roommate that wears Katie's perfume.*

Dean sauntered into the bedroom and peeked into the small bassinet.

His gaze shifted from Savannah who was just opening her eyes to the interior of Katie's room. The closet space was limited and Katie's clothes hung on hooks and on the curtain rod. A mountain of shoes took up one corner and another was filled with baby essentials.

"Oh, God!" Katie shrieked behind Monica.

Monica turned to stare at the panicked face of her friend. "I tried to make him leave."

The only sound in the room was that of the breath escaping the occupants.

A storm brewed under the surface of Katie's skin. She met Dean's confused stare and held still.

Her game was up. No explanation large enough would keep him from knowing that she was living with Monica. And why.

No one spoke. No one moved.

Savannah let out a wail and all three of them turned to her.

Katie shoved past Monica and had to step over Dean's foot to get to the baby.

"It's OK, baby girl. I'm here," she cooed. The instant Savannah was in her arms she quieted. Katie flung a burp cloth over her shoulder and positioned Savannah so she was looking over her shoulder.

Savannah hiccupped a few times and Katie rocked. "Shh, it's OK." Gathering her courage, Katie turned toward Dean and met his stare.

They said nothing.

"I think I should go." Monica finally spoke. "Unless you want me to stay, Katie."

"No. It's OK. I'm OK."

Monica sent her a sympathetic smile before turning to Dean. "You behave." She wiggled a finger in front of his face as he had done hers.

Monica slipped from the room and out of the apartment.

Katie moved around the room and prepared to change Savannah's soiled diaper. Dean had backed up to the doorway and watched in complete silence.

Several weeks of practice granted her speed and agility with the task. Within a couple of minutes, Katie had Savannah back in her arms, before she walked past Dean and into the living room. Katie folded Savannah into the swing and turned the knob. Savannah attempted a smile and contentedly enjoyed the rocking motion.

Without explanation, she washed her hands in the sink and moved to prepare a bottle. Just because Savannah wasn't screaming for it, didn't mean she wouldn't ask soon if it was delayed for long. The domestic chores and silence gave Katie a little time to think. Her heart had finally slowed to a normal pace and the situation felt less dire.

"She's yours, isn't she?" Dean asked.

"Yes. No. Well, not quite mine." That had to be the most screwed-up answer to a question ever.

"Which is it?" Dean's question was soft.

Katie placed a plastic liner into a bottle and filled it with formula. A pot was already on the stove to boil so she turned it on. "Legally she's mine. At least as far as we can tell."

"I don't understand. How can you not know?"

"It's complicated, Dean."

Dean turned toward the living room and watched Savannah on the swing. "She's grown. It's Savannah, right?"

"Yeah."

Dean removed his cowboy hat and tossed it on table. It was his way of saying he wasn't leaving any time soon. "I could use a beer."

Katie opened the refrigerator and handed him one.

He finished half of it in one swallow. His shoulders slumped and he blew out a long-suffering sigh. "She's why you've been so worn out, why you're not at the hotel?"

"Yeah. Monica let us stay here until we work things out. I couldn't exactly parade an infant around without everyone knowing about her. Daddy would blow a gasket and Jack…I don't even know what Jack would do."

"I don't get it. You need to start at the beginning, darlin', cuz I'm lost. You have a baby that may or may not be yours. When I looked for you at the hotel, they said you were out…late at night. They rambled off a list of names trying to come up with mine. Is everything a lie?"

I had to lie.

Guilt for her deception made her fidget. "I'll tell you everything, Dean."

"Why do I hear a *but* in your voice?"

"*But* you need to promise me you'll keep this between the two of us. For now anyway."

His eyes narrowed again. "Are you in trouble?"

"No. Nothing like that. Promise me, Dean. Before I tell you anything you have to promise you'll keep silent."

He placed his empty beer bottle on the counter and covered her hand with his. "I promise, now spill. What the hell is going on?"

Chapter Seventeen

The entire time Katelyn told her crazy-ass story she moved about the room fussing and feeding Savannah. She fed, burped, and cleaned up the baby's mess without so much as a frown. Katie didn't even seem to notice the patch of wetness that missed the cloth and soaked into her dress shirt.

Dean watched in utter fascination and attempted to wrap his mind around the story Katie told. Babies left on doorsteps and fabricated documents giving custody of a child to a stranger. The whole thing was out of a soap opera yet it was actually happening to someone he knew. Someone he cared about.

"I've hired a private investigator to locate the real mom. You met him. Patrick Nelson."

"Patrick?" He couldn't remember a man by that name.

"Ben Sanderson. You remember. Older gentleman."

"The old guy. Right." What a relief that was.

"He's not *that* old."

"Too old for you," he told her.

She grinned for the first time since he entered the apartment. "Jealous, Dean?"

"Damn right. So let me get this straight. You've spent every night possible right here with Savannah and Monica and only a handful of nights crashing at the hotel?"

"Yeah."

"No guys. You're not seeing anyone?"

Katie rolled her eyes. "Like I have time. Oh, wait…this *is* a jealous thing. You were worried I'd been sleeping around?"

"That's what you *wanted* everyone to believe." He certainly had. Considering their past…her past, the lie was easily believed. Yet somehow, someway, he knew something was wrong, and Jack had been one hundred percent correct. Katie hadn't been acting normal because nothing about her life was normal. The party girl everyone knew was at home playing house. Alone.

"I wasn't," she said plainly. "Well, except last night…with you." She paused. "Listen, about last night—"

Dean held up a hand and stopped her. "No *About last night* conversations yet. We're not done with this one. So you hired a PI and you've found out what?"

"Nearly nothing. I'm expecting a call from Patrick any day. We're baffled. You and my doctors were the only ones to know about my inability to conceive so Patrick is digging into anyone who works in the doctor's office. I'm not the first rich woman who's had a baby left on her doorstep I'm sure. But this felt personal. Like the woman knew me."

"But you don't know her?"

"Not a clue."

"Wow." He was equally relieved and concerned. Relieved that Katie wasn't sleeping around with another man, not to mention she had a damn good explanation for her odd behavior. He was concerned that the baby's mother would show up and take Savannah away. Or worse, accuse Katie of taking her.

"Wow. It's a lot to take in."

"Tell me about it." Katie glanced down at Savannah who was content to sit in her lap playing with a colorful rattle she could hardly hold.

Katie leaned down and kissed Savannah's nose. "You're the most precious thing ever. Aren't you?"

Dean swallowed hard. He didn't consider himself an emotional sap but seeing a woman with her baby made his heart swell. He'd thought of this moment well over a year ago when they'd learned of Katie's pregnancy.

Then after the miscarriage, Katie acted distant…broke off everything between them. Watching her now, he asked himself if maybe everything Katie did then was a defense mechanism. Her way of coping with the loss. Here he thought she'd been a selfish child when clearly that wasn't the case.

There was no mistaking the bond between Katie and Savannah. Deep in his heart he'd believed that, all those months ago, Katie was as into becoming a mother as he was about being a dad. Seeing her like this, with a child in her lap, made him remember their quiet moments, their honest moments.

"You'll never let her go, will you?" Dean asked.

Katie shook her head. "Not without a fight."

"So why look for the mother at all?"

Katie met his eyes and blew out a breath. "Wouldn't you? If someone left a child on your doorstep, wouldn't you wonder who the parents were? Not to mention the legal reasons."

"If someone left a child on my doorstep, darlin', I'd know the baby was mine. Or at least have a quick paternity test to figure it out."

Katie rolled her eyes again. "You know what I mean. If you were a woman and didn't know…wouldn't you question?"

He never considered the female position…didn't think it was possible for a man. "Yeah. I'd wonder."

"So I'm looking. I owe it to Savannah and me. I don't know what drove her biological mother to give her away and I can't rest until I do."

Dean scooted closer to her on the couch and Savannah turned her head in his direction. Her tiny hand lifted up and Dean offered her a finger. She clasped it and gripped him hard. There was no stopping the smile on his lips.

"What if you don't find her?"

"I'll cross that road when I come to it. No reason to invite trouble. That's what Aunt Bea always says. I get it now. Savannah and I will figure it out together. And when the day comes that she asks about her real mom, I'll be able to tell her I tried to find her."

Dean knew more than most how much Katie missed having her mother. He rested his head on Katie's shoulder and stared down at the tiny blue-eyed bundle. Savannah still gripped his finger and something even deeper inside of him.

"What can I do to help?"

Beside him, Katie released a deep breath. "Just keep her existence quiet for a little longer. Once Patrick has exhausted his search for the mom, I'll contact a lawyer and make damn sure I can keep her. Then I'll tell my family."

Dean couldn't remember a time in his life when he heard Katie so convicted. There was no kidding around, no unsure tone in her voice. Something told him that, if anyone shoved, she'd take the baby with a wad of money and split.

Mothers protect their children and all that.

Now that Dean knew about Savannah, Katie found a much more comfortable pace in life. She gave up pretending to stay in the hotel altogether and moved most of her things into Monica's small apartment.

"Are you sure it's OK that we're still here?" Katie asked Monica a few nights after Dean found out her secret.

Dressed in scrubs, Monica shrugged Katie's concerns away. "When I was in nursing school, Jessie took care of everything for me. Yeah, I worked on the side to help, but the money I brought in didn't amount to a whole lot. She never complained and, from what

I could tell, never had a need to. You're like a sister to me, Katie, and I wouldn't want you to have to go through any of this alone. You and Savannah are welcome here for as long as you need to be."

"It makes all the difference in the world to have someone who understands what's going on."

"How is Dean taking it?"

"Good, I guess."

"You guess?"

"He's anxious, I think. You know, like you and I were in the beginning. He asks if I've heard from Patrick every day."

"Have you…heard from Patrick?"

Katie shook her head. "I'd have told you if he'd called. What if we never find the mother, Mo? What if we do find her and she wants Savannah back?"

"Stop! Seriously, Katie, you're going to talk yourself crazy with the 'what ifs.' Savannah is nearly two months old and you've not heard one word from a biological mother wanting an update. Instead of vacillating between thoughts of *What if you find the mother* and *What if she wants her back*, you might want to think about how you're going to tell Jack, Jessie, and your dad that you have a baby."

Her skin itched to tell her family about Savannah. The dozens and dozens of pictures she'd taken of her sat in a memory card just waiting to be shared. "How I tell them anything will depend on what I find out about the mother."

"And if you never find out about the mother?"

"Then I'll just tell them all the truth. It's not like I can keep it a secret forever."

Monica gripped her hands together. "Why not tell them now? Seems Dean took the information well. My guess is your dad and brother might do the same."

Katie laughed. "You don't know my dad. He's as subtle as a Saint Bernard in a china shop. He'd bulldoze his way into hospitals, into medical records…into people's lives to get what he wants. If I told him about Savannah, we'd probably find the mother sooner, but I might lose everything in the process. The last thing I want is a media circus or a police investigation of any kind. Savannah is going to grow up knowing I wanted her from the beginning. If her biological mother had some kind of secret or need to keep Savannah away from her, the last thing I want to do is blow that up in the woman's face. She left Savannah to me for a reason and I aim to find out what that reason is…quietly. My dad isn't quiet!"

"What about Jack?"

"Jack would take it better. But he'd want the answers just as much as my dad."

"If he found out, would he keep things quiet?"

Katie rubbed her hands over her face. "I think so. For a while. But the more people that know, the harder it becomes to keep the secret."

Monica turned away and cast her eyes to the floor.

The hair on Katie's arms stood up. "Do you think Jack suspects something?"

"I think Jessie is suspicious. I've managed to keep my sister from knowing what's going on this long but, now that they are back from the honeymoon, she wants me to come and visit. I've put her off, Katie, but the longer I do that, the more Jessie is going to wonder."

Just when Katie thought she could relax a little, concerns and drama piled up. "It shouldn't be much longer."

"I hope so. Jessie and I are close. It would be hard to keep this inside me if she was here and I don't think she'd keep the information from Jack. I couldn't ask her to."

Katie placed a hand on top of Monica's. "I know this isn't the easiest secret to keep. I won't blame you if something slips out. Just promise me you'll let me know if it does, so I can work on damage control before word spreads."

Monica lent her a smile. "I will. Now I've got to go. We've been shorthanded in the ER with a stupid summer flu going around."

Savannah slept while Katie finished getting ready for work. She sent a quick text to Patrick and told him she needed an update today.

He had to know something by now...

Monica slid onto the worn-out sofa in the break room and ignored her heart rate that she felt reverberating all the way to her toes. She'd hit the ER running. A five-car pileup on the interstate with two full traumas and one full arrest met her before she could manage half a cup of coffee. The emergency room overflowed with patients sick with the flu, the typical accidents that resulted in broken bones and a need for stitches, and the elderly with every medical issue under the sun. But all of those could wait. The traumas pumped her blood and forced her to think fast.

She loved it.

The adrenaline, the pace. Everything about it.

The petty shit choking up the ER tended to piss her off when the serious crap went down. It didn't help that the department was short staffed and she had to do the work of two nurses and hope to hell no one fell through the cracks.

She helped stabilize one patient and get him to surgery within that golden hour and then was able to comfort a grieving family when they learned their loved one didn't make it.

In truth, that part sucked. But she had been told when she took the job that, in order to work the ER, she needed to get in and make a difference by helping or get the hell out of the way.

She chose to make a difference.

The alarm of the radio went off announcing another ambulance call. Although she wasn't the lead nurse on the radio, she forced herself up and out of the break room to find out what was coming in.

Mark, a fellow nurse, sat in the radio room talking to the paramedics in the field. Monica squeezed in the door to look over his shoulder.

"Another car accident?" she whispered to herself.

The medic on the line spoke quickly, rattling off vital signs. The mic on the radio room worked one way at a time. Mark multitasked by writing down what the medic told him and talking to Monica at the same time. "It's another trauma. Female, late twenties, rollover in a convertible. Head trauma. Five minutes out."

Monica froze.

Working without emotion was fine, until you knew the patient.

"Go tell Dr. Eddy we have another one coming in," Mark said.

Monica nodded and left the room. She pulled her cell phone from her pocket and sent a quick text to Katie.

Are you OK?

She paused hoping Katie replied.

It's not Katie. Lots of people drive convertibles in California.

"We have another one," Monica told Dr. Eddy. She turned to Alice who manned the phones. "Call a code trauma and call Neuro."

Alice already had the phone to her ear.

As the code was being called, Monica's phone signaled a text.

Katie.

I'm good. What's up?

Relief swelled Monica's chest.

Nothing...just checking in.

Hours later when Monica was finishing some paperwork, Dr. Eddy plopped down beside her. "What a bitch of a day."

"You can say that again. The only thing that didn't come through that door was an MI," she said with a curt laugh. A heart attack victim was the last thing this day needed.

Dr. Eddy, or Walt, as most of them referred to him, had worked the ER for eight years. He was a good-looking man with short brown hair and chocolate brown eyes. He was known to date many women, but hadn't yet settled down. No wonder, he was always working and when the ER didn't call him in, he volunteered his time with Borderless Doctors. "I'm still on for three more hours. Don't jinx me."

Monica laughed. "Sorry."

He rubbed the back of his neck as he spoke. "Listen, I wondered if you'd be interested in signing up with BNs."

"BNs? What's that?"

"Borderless Nurses. The same program for Borderless Doctors only for nurses. We can always use the help. You're young, smart, energetic. It helps that you don't have a family or kids."

Monica sat back and considered his words. "I might be interested."

"I work with the disaster team. We go in after nature screws up an area, stay for a week or two at a time, and pull out."

"How would that work here? I know the doctors' group gives you the time off, but I'm not sure the hospital feels the same about the nurses."

"Are you kidding me? The hospital loves the publicity. Besides, there's a clause in the nurses' union contract mandating that the hospital allows you two weeks off on a moment's notice for emergencies you volunteer to help with. They won't fire you, if that's what you're worried about."

Monica didn't know about the contract. In fact, she often tried to ignore the fact that she even belonged to a union. Sadly, she didn't have a choice if she wanted to work where she did.

"I don't know."

"I have to be honest. The hours are hard, you don't sleep, and they don't pay."

"Why do you do it?"

"Sanity. There's something about helping the truly helpless that energizes me to come in here every day. The hours are crazy insane when you're out there. You see shit you'll wish you hadn't, but when it's all over, you're damn happy you helped. Not everyone can be a part of a relief effort outside of giving money. Doctors and nurses…search and rescue…we have skills that money can't buy."

Walt put in a good pitch.

Hell, helping people was what she did.

"What do I need to do?"

Walt let his grin spread. "I have some paperwork in my locker and there's a training session in Florida this weekend. They pay for the flight, hotel, and food. All you have to do is show up."

"I'll have to check my schedule," she told him.

"You're off. I already checked."

Monica crossed her arms over her chest. "You checked?"

He nodded. "I like working with nurses I trust. Out there, trust is everything. So, yeah, I checked."

The training was more than a weekend, it was a full week. But it only took a couple of swaps on the schedule to give her the time off she needed.

That night when Monica was eating dinner and talking with Katie, she knew she'd made the right decision.

"I'll be gone a week. Which is perfect. Jessie won't think I'm snubbing her and the chances of me having a moment to even talk to her are slim. You'll have the place to yourself."

"What brought this on?" Katie asked.

"I don't know. It was a crazy day at work. Lots of accidents. When one of the doctors suggested I sign up, I thought, *What the hell?* There will probably be a day that I can't do this. I might as well do it now."

"Sounds like you'll be going into war zones. Earthquakes, tornados, floods…I don't know how you handle the things you see locally, let alone something on a disaster scale."

Monica shrugged and forked in another bite. "Who knows if I can cut it," she said around her food. "I won't know until I try. Besides, you've paid my rent for the whole year so why not?"

They had argued about the rent thing but, in the end, Katie won.

It was as if something bigger than Monica was leading her in the direction of helping others.

"I'll support you any way I can."

"Just water the plants," Monica said laughing. "Oh, and I was thinking today…maybe it's time you bought a bigger car to drive. Convertibles aren't the safest cars to be driving out there, especially with kids in the passenger seat."

Nothing like a little bit of manipulation to make things right in her world.

Dr. Eddy had taught her that earlier.

Chapter Eighteen

"I'm buying a car and I don't have a clue where to start."

Dean shook his head and stared at Katie across his desk. "A car?"

"Yeah. I've driven plenty. But I realized that I've never bought one before. Yeah, my dad picked out the little black number I drove around in high school…but…"

She didn't have to continue that story. She'd ditched it in a waterless aqueduct while showing off to her friends before her eighteenth birthday. After that, Gaylord paid a driver most of the time. Then she started renting cars. Convertibles, sport cars…anything flashy to get noticed.

Now Dean watched the girl turn into a responsible woman…a mother before his eyes. She waved several brochures at him like a flag. "Safety and reliability are paramount. I can't have Savannah flying out a window or through a soft top because some asshole pulls out in front of us."

Dean sat back in his chair, smug in his thoughts. "Where did this come from?"

Katie waved him off as if he hadn't said a thing. "Monica. She suggested it before she left."

"Monica left?"

"Yeah, some nurses without borders thing. She'll be back in a week or so."

Dean's smug smile fell. "You're alone at her apartment?"

Katie rolled her eyes. "I'm not alone. Savannah is there."

"Oh, that makes me feel *so* much better. Nothing like a dirty diaper to deter unwanted guests."

"Are you suggesting I can't take care of myself?"

"No." *Yes.*

"Yes, you are!"

"No, I'm not." *Yes*, he was. Damn…and Katie saw right through him. The daggers sprang from her eyes with sparks of anger. He diverted her attention. "So Monica's gone and she suggested you buy a car before leaving, to where exactly?"

"Florida." Apparently, Katie's grudge wasn't going to last long. As was expected when her mind was centered on something else. Dean scooted forward when she moved around the desk and placed the brochures in front of him. "My first thought was one of those big numbers. You know, an old Lincoln or Escalade. They hold up in a crash…right?"

"They do."

"But I've never driven one of those. They're big."

"Very big."

She leaned forward letting her tight silk top gape in just the right place, reminding him of the creamy skin he'd find underneath if given the chance.

"Are they hard to drive?"

He licked his lips. "Not hard."

"There are smaller cars, more agile."

Dean pushed lust from his brain and attempted to concentrate on Katie's words. "You need to test-drive the bigger cars…see if you're comfortable with them. Did you drive a truck on the ranch?"

"Dusty two lane roads with only one car…yeah, but it's been years."

"You're not old enough for it to have been years."

"You know exactly how old I am. C'mon, Dean. I need direction here and I'm not afraid to ask for it. I'd ask Jessie, if she knew about Savannah. But she doesn't, so I'm asking you."

Dean concentrated on the pamphlets on his desk. "Keep it American," he said as he tossed two brochures in the trash. "Your daddy would kick your butt if you arrived in anything made outside of Detroit."

"He never said a thing about the Italian cars I drove home."

"You rented those. Doesn't count. Let's look up crash reports on these models." He narrowed his search to midsize SUVs, something he thought Katie could drive without worry of crashing into guardrails.

"Oh, look…that has a TV in the back. Savannah will love it."

"Savannah's what?…Two months old? I don't think she's thinking of a TV."

"But she will, someday."

Dean smiled and pushed away from his desk. "Let's go."

"Go? We have work to do."

He grabbed his keys and tucked his cell phone into his pocket. "Perks of being the boss. C'mon. Let's shop."

"Are you sure?"

It tickled him that Katie contemplated staying at work instead of shopping for a car. He leaned in and surprised her with a kiss. A simple pass of his lips over hers…and it felt entirely too right. "I'm sure."

He walked through his office and told Jo to call him if there was fire or blood on the site and to take messages for everything else.

Katelyn's sparkling new Cadillac crossover fully loaded was sleek, sexy, powerful, and American.

For some reason Dean wasn't quite clear about, Katie sent a picture text to Monica who was apparently in the air en route to Florida.

Katie had grown up somewhere when Dean wasn't looking.

He liked it.

The hotel loomed in front of him. His gazed settled on the people milling in and out of the hot, moist Texas heat completely oblivious to anyone around them. When called on to act as a witness, no one would be able to give any distinct identification about him at all, which was part of his problem. He'd found no one, not one soul, who'd seen a woman or man walk into the hotel where Katelyn lived, and drop off a baby.

Patrick had sent word to Katelyn about his progress. She was understandably unhappy that he didn't have a name yet. The mother had done a very good job at hiding who she was. Not that he wouldn't find her out…but these things did take time.

He'd been unsuccessful at infiltrating the hospital records where Savannah was born. Although he was working on a hack to find the information anyway, he didn't want to go to jail to determine who the birth mother was. The best option was to get back into the hotel and attempt to access Katelyn's room without a key to the elevator or her room.

He cased the outside of the hotel like a thief. He watched a pair of window washers with a shrug. A new mother wouldn't dare that route. But a fire escape wasn't unthinkable. Twenty-four floors might be a little much for a new mom. But then who said the mother dropped off the baby? It could have been someone hired to do the job.

Patrick's gut said differently.

This mom, the one who took so much care leaving Savannah outside a door without any chance she'd be left there for long, had been close by when Katelyn and Monica stumbled upon Savannah.

This mom wouldn't have given someone else the chance to fuck that up.

But how?

That was what he struggled with.

There were service workers moving in and out of the hotel without notice. Food service, linen service, florists, and the occasional man or woman that appeared anticipated. The ebb and flow of the hotel was like water flowing through a river, expected and sometimes forceful.

Patrick made a note: *Mom could have easily penetrated the building through service entrance if dressed appropriately.*

Inside the hotel lobby, he moved to an arrangement of chairs and sat with his cell phone in his hands. No one bothered him, noticed him…spoke to him.

After thirty minutes of sitting, he picked himself up and moved to a coffeehouse inside the hotel and ordered a simple coffee, black.

He noticed a service hallway alongside the restaurant, a passage he'd found the first time he'd spent time wandering the hotel, and walked toward it. The cell phone in his pocket made noise right on time and he lifted it to his ear.

In the receiver was nothing but static. He walked through the service door talking into his phone and acting distracted. The plain tile floors of a back corridor, which none of the hotel guests ever saw, met his feet as he marched down one hall to another. Soon there were extra folding beds lining the halls and carts used to carry any number of things throughout the building.

"I thought you were meeting me here!" he all but hollered into the phone to no one. "I'm at the hotel now." He twisted down another corridor and found two elevators.

Service elevators.

He turned in a circle and looked around him, acting confused. "What the fuck?" he said aloud in case there were cameras with audio watching. He punched the up button on the elevator and talked into the phone. "Upstairs? Where?"

The deserted hall wasn't surprising. It wasn't check in, check out, or mealtime. If there was a quiet time in a hotel, it was now. The service elevator made a noise and opened. He acted as if he were still talking on his phone and stepped inside. He pressed the uppermost floors and took a seamless ride to the top.

He stepped into a similar bare corridor and twisted around until he found a stairwell. The door opened easily and he shuffled up… toward the penthouse.

"Bingo!" he said as he stepped into the short hallway of Katelyn's hotel home.

He tapped his pockets and put his phone away.

The mother didn't make it inside the room. Only the corridor. He once again looked at the adjacent door to the vacant penthouse suite.

The mother could have rented it. Yet according to the online files he'd hacked into, it was vacant the night of Jack and Jessie's wedding.

So where had the mother hid?

In the service hall.

Patrick let himself into Katelyn's suite for a second time in a month.

Fresh flowers met his nose.

But that wasn't all.

There, in the middle of the room, was a man wearing a cowboy hat and a frown.

"Who are you?" The stranger all but yelled the question.

Patrick plastered a smile on his lips and met the somewhat familiar man's hostility with a smile. "A friend of Katelyn's," he said, using the same excuse he'd done before.

The man glared beyond him to the door. "She's not here."

Patrick thought of removing his jacket, but his service revolver was holstered and visible so he simply smiled. "Yeah, I know. She said I could crash here when I'm in town."

The other man pushed up his Texas-issued cowboy hat on his brow and crossed his arms over his chest. "She did, did she?"

"She did. Who are you?" Patrick decided to act like a lover.

The man wasn't dressed as a hotel employee and he acted as if he owned the place. Katelyn had made it clear Patrick wouldn't encounter anyone in her room.

"Who are you?" The question was a shout.

"Ben Sanderson. Who the hell are you?" Best to act the *pissed* lover.

"Jack Morrison. Her brother!"

Oh, fuck!

Chapter Nineteen

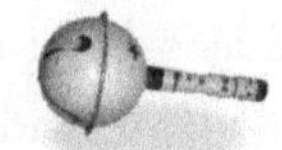

Dean's palms itched. Outside of the office or car hunting, he'd not spent a moment alone with Katelyn since the day he'd learned about Savannah.

That was all about to change. Knowing that Monica wasn't home and he wouldn't be interrupting "girl time," he made a quick stop at home for a shower and a change of clothes after work, then headed straight over to Katelyn's.

He parked his truck in a guest parking spot and walked up the not-so-quiet path to the apartment. Someone in the complex was playing music too loud, and someone else shouted something about taking the trash out.

Apartment living wasn't something he ever had to endure. His parents lived well, invested in sound stocks that didn't crash when Wall Street fell. His father's upbringing was in rural Texas where his grandfather worked on an oil field. Hard work and Prescotts went hand in hand. Somewhere in the chain Dean's father had moved from blue to white collar and passed that on to his children.

Dean knew how to do most of the jobs he expected of his employees, but he managed his staff better by acting as their mentor in the physical work.

Standing outside the apartment building was as foreign to him as it must have been to Katelyn the first time she'd come here.

Yet this was where she chose to stay...at least for now.

Dean knocked on Katie's door and rocked back on his heels.

He rubbed his hands on his jeans and thought maybe he should have something with him, something to offer Katie...food...wine... diapers?

Katie opened the door wearing a pair of sweats—designer sweats, but cotton pants nonetheless—with Savannah on her arm. Katie hesitated and offered him a smile.

"I thought you two ladies might like some company," he said with what he knew was his most boyish smile.

Katie's cheeks turned pink. She glanced down at her little girl and asked, "What do you think, Savannah? Are we accepting strays tonight?"

Savannah lifted her head a fraction and Katie grinned. "Guess you can come in."

He followed her through the door, closed, and locked it behind him.

"I wasn't expecting you."

"Those are the best kinds of visits, don't you think?" Dean moved about the apartment while Katie put Savannah down on a blanket in the middle of the floor.

"Depends on if you like the visitor."

Dean swiveled her way. "I hope I'm in the *like* category."

Katie laughed and moved into the small kitchen. "As if you ever worry about that. Want something to drink?"

While Katie moved around the kitchen, pouring them both glasses of iced sweet tea, Dean kept an eye on Savannah as she played. The tiny wisps of hair were brushed back and bright blue eyes watched him intently.

"She's beautiful, isn't she? I know all moms say that about their children...but she really is."

Dean stretched out and picked up a colorful toy before waving it in front of Savannah's gaze. "She's amazing, Katie."

"You can pick her up. She doesn't bite." Katie sat beside him and pressed her back against the couch.

She was so small. His hand took up half her body as he lifted Savannah onto his lap. He propped her on his bent knees and was blessed with a smile.

Dean's heart kicked in his chest. "You're gonna break hearts with that smile, darlin'. Just like your mommy."

Katie brushed alongside him and stared. "I can watch her for hours. I wonder what she's thinking. Everything around her is so big and she's so helpless on her own."

"My sister says babies only think of food, sleep, and diaper changes."

Katie giggled. "Yeah, there's a lot of that. But like right now… she's staring at you. Listening to your deep voice. What's she thinking?"

Dean kissed the top of Katie's head as she rested it on his shoulder. "I know what I'm thinking. That she's one lucky baby to have ended up on your doorstep. Your love for her is obvious."

"She's easy to love."

Just like you.

Dean tried to push aside his thoughts. Did he really want to visit that pain again? He'd barely survived loving Katie the first time, yet here he was inviting himself back into her life again… only this time she had someone else with her. Someone precious and vulnerable.

Katie played with Savannah's hand, which sat inside Dean's larger one. She traced their fingers together, appeared mesmerized by the difference in size. The girls watched each other, both of them smiling.

Resistance was futile and Dean knew it. Before he'd asked for Jack's blessing, Dean knew he was going to work hard to win Katie back. This time, he had two girls to win.

While keeping hold of Savannah, Dean tucked a finger under Katie's chin and directed her attention to him.

The tiny lines around her eyes that would manifest when she was deep in thought softened as he looked his fill. Without words, Dean leaned forward and met her lips with his.

She sighed and closed her eyes.

She was soft and welcoming…perfect. When Dean moved away, Katie blinked and ran her tongue over her lips. "What was that for?"

"Do I need a reason?" he asked softly.

Katie swallowed, her eyes never leaving his. A flash of fear passed over her. "Are you sure you want this…me, us?"

Dean traced her lips with his thumb. "I'm willing to try if you are."

"We didn't work before."

"We didn't give us a chance before."

Katie dropped her gaze to Savannah and sucked in her bottom lip. Her nod was slow…hesitant. "OK." She smiled. "OK…"

This time when he kissed her, he put fire into it. Well, as much fire as he could with an infant in his lap. Katie caught his cheek with her hand and pressed into his touch.

Savannah let out a tiny cry and broke them apart. Both of them laughed.

"I'm just kissing your mommy, Savannah. You're going to have to get used to that."

Later that night, as he worshiped every inch of Katie's body, reminding them both of how well they fit together, Dean knew he'd already fallen deep.

As he moved within her, and listened to her call his name when she shattered in his arms, he felt his heart open completely.

He was home.

"What the hell is going on?" Monica yelled the frantic question into the phone. Katie pulled the receiver from her ear.

"What are you talking about?"

"Jessie left a message on my cell. She said to call her back ASAP. Said she needed the inside scoop on you and Dean. Did you two go public with your relationship?"

Katie let go of her purse she'd just placed over her shoulder, dropping it to the floor. The trip to the grocery store would have to wait.

"No we've not gone public. You're the only one who knows we're seeing each other."

"You might want to check your facts. Jessie acted as if she knew something was going on."

"How would Jessie know anything?"

"Jack…I think. The message was garbled and, to tell the truth, I don't want to call her back. Seems Jack is worried about his friend Dean because Jack thinks you're hanging on to some guy in Texas."

"There is no one in Texas." Hadn't been in a while.

"Well Jessie seemed to think so."

"There isn't anyone."

"Well someone is telling Jack differently."

Katie rubbed the back of her stiff neck. "Why would Jack care anyway?"

"I don't know…listen, I've got to go. I'm going to pretend the call messed up and I didn't get it."

"How is everything there? Enjoying yourself?"

"I love it, Katie. I can see myself doing this for a long time."

"Be careful."

"I will. See ya next week."

Katie hung up the phone and grabbed her purse a second time.

Her phone rang again.

"Did you forget something?" she asked, assuming it was Monica again.

"I don't think so," the male voice said. "It's Patrick. I take it you were expecting another call."

Katie set her purse down again. "Sorry 'bout that. I'm Miss Popular today."

"You are that. Listen…I need access to the security tapes or files of the hotel for the days leading up to Savannah being left at your door. I think I know how she got up to your room and where she might have been hiding after she dropped Savannah off."

"I'll call and have them available. I looked at some of them the day after and didn't see anything."

"Were you looking for a woman carrying a baby?"

Savannah started to fuss in the infant carrier so Katie picked it up with her free hand and swayed her back and forth, calming her.

"Well, yeah."

"If you were dumping a baby, would you walk in, set the car seat down, and then walk away?"

Katie cringed at the word *dumping.* Savannah wasn't dumped. "No. I guess not."

"Exactly. So, can you get me the files?"

"Yeah…I think so. I'll call the hotel."

"OK. The files should be digital so have them e-mail 'em to you and then you can forward them to me."

"Sure." She jotted down the information he asked for and put a note on top of her laptop. "Anything else?"

"Yeah…one thing. I met your brother yesterday. He wasn't happy to see me."

Katie stopped rocking Savannah and set her down before she dropped her. "My brother?"

"He was at your place. Seemed shocked you had a guy friend visiting. He bought that we were close, but I wouldn't be surprised if he's asked the staff here to look out for me and notify him when I'm around. I'm going to lay low here for a while."

Jessie! So that explained her frantic call. But it wasn't uncommon for Katie to have a lover around. Why would Jack start asking about Dean? Unless…

"Lay low. My brother is a direct link to my dad. And we don't want him onto this…not yet."

"Whatever you say."

"That's what I say…but, Patrick, we're running out of time. The older Savannah gets, the harder it is to hide her. I need answers."

"I know you do. And I'm on the edge of a breakthrough. Hang in there a little longer."

"OK. Good luck."

She bypassed the grocery store and drove directly to Dean's. His modest home sat along the foothills and gave a view of the vast expanse of cities that sat below the San Bernardino Mountains, otherwise known as the Inland Empire.

After carefully unbuckling the car seat, Katie swung the diaper bag and her purse over her arm and marched her sleeping child up the steps of his home.

She rang the doorbell and attempted to calm herself before he opened the door.

He must have said something to Jack about them, or Jack wouldn't be asking about Patrick and butting into her life. The last thing she needed now was her brother poking his nose where it didn't belong.

Dean opened the door, saw her, and beamed a smile.

She frowned, cutting off his smile.

"What a nice surprise."

"Shh, she's asleep." And he might not think seeing them was so nice once she let him know why she was there. Dean let them in out of the heat. Katie brushed past him, into the living room, and placed

Savannah in the middle of the floor. She didn't bother taking her out of the car seat for fear she'd wake.

Dean walked up behind her and whispered. "What's wrong?"

She swung around, hushed him again, then marched out of the room, and out of earshot of the baby. Once she made it to the back of the house, she met Dean's eyes with her hands on her hips. "You told my brother about us. Didn't you?"

Dean blinked twice and kept his lips shut.

"Dammit, Dean."

"I told him I wanted to see you…on a personal level."

"Why?"

"Because I'm not sneaking around this time, Katie. If we're going to give us a shot, and that means seeing each other outside the bedroom."

"Did you stop and think about what I want? The last thing I need right now is my brother sticking his nose in my business. What if he comes around or finds out about Savannah? Did you think of that?" she said in a ragged whisper, keeping her voice low.

Dean's jaw clenched and his arms crossed over his chest. "I didn't know about Savannah when I spoke to Jack. I was only thinking of you and me."

She hadn't considered that. She turned away and stared out the glass doors to the backyard.

Dean moved behind her and placed his hands on her shoulders. She tried to shrug out of them but he held tight. "What happened, Katie?"

"Jessie called Monica asking about us…you and me. She said Jack was worried about who I was spending time with. Jack hasn't asked who I've been with for years. I knew something wasn't right. Then Patrick called, said he ran into Jack at the hotel when he was looking for information on Savannah's real mom. So Jack thinks I'm sleeping with Patrick while his best friend is trying to sleep with me. Great, huh?"

Dean slowly wrapped his arms around her and leaned his chin on the top of her head. "I can call Jack, tell him you're only sleeping with me."

She snorted out a small laugh and tried to find the humor. "It's all becoming so complicated. I just want to find Savannah's birth mom and make damn sure I can keep this little girl. Is that asking too much?"

"No, it's not. We'll find her."

"If Jack finds out about Savannah, my dad will get involved. I want this all figured out before that happens, Dean. My dad thinks I'm as irresponsible as my mother. I don't want to confirm that to him."

She felt Dean stiffen behind her. His words were soft in her ear. "You're not your mother. Nowhere close, darlin'."

Her throat clogged with emotion as she spoke. "When the doctor told me I couldn't have kids…a part of me said, *Well, I'll never have to worry about not wanting them after I have them.*"

"You're not your mother."

Katie relaxed in his arms, took comfort from his broad frame. "Every day I worry that I'm going to look at that precious little girl and want her gone…out of my life. But then the thought frightens me." A tear slid off her cheek and she sniffed. "I love her so much, Dean. I know it's a cliché but I'd move heaven and earth to keep that baby safe. To do right by her."

Dean turned her around to face him, wiped her tears with his thumbs. "You listen to me, Katelyn Morrison. You are not your mother. If you ever doubt your own gene pool, then look to your dad. He stepped up when your mother walked out on all of you and he'd move the state of Texas with his bare hands to keep you safe. That love, that loyalty, stems from his side. So don't second-guess your heart."

"I don't want to disappoint him…I don't want to fail Savannah."

"Wanting to be the perfect daughter, after all the bumps you've given that man in his life, is almost comical, but I get it. If he saw you with your baby girl, he'd be so proud of you…of what you're trying so hard to do. As for being the perfect mother, hon, I haven't yet met a perfect mom. You're going to make mistakes but none of them are going to result in Savannah needing a therapist's couch when she's an adult."

Katie gave him a half-baked smile. "Since when did you become so wise?"

"I've always been wise. You just weren't looking."

She chuckled and let some of the day's tension drift away.

Dean kissed her, slowly, and circled her with his arms. He tilted her head and deepened their kiss. As his tongue slid over hers, her body tingled and her mind went soft.

Savannah.

She stiffened in his arms and ended their kiss. "That has to wait," she told him.

"Oh, why?"

"I was running out the door to pick up more formula before Monica called me. Then Patrick called and I ran here. Savannah is going to wake up anytime and I'm out."

"Want me to go?"

"No. I'll go. Mind if I leave her with you? I'll only be a minute."

Dean winked. "I can handle her. I do have a nephew, you know."

"I remember." Katie gave him a peck of a kiss as she dashed out of the room. She gathered her purse and moved to the front door. "You're sure?"

"Go, worrywart. We'll be fine."

Chapter Twenty

"O.M.Geeee. Katelyn? Is that you?"

Katie swiveled in the baby goods and feminine hygiene aisle to the sound of her name. In her path was one of the last people she'd ever thought she'd see in a grocery store.

"Sasha?"

Sasha Godier lived in New York and occasionally France. *What the hell is she doing here?*

"It is you..." Sasha rushed forward in five-inch heels, which was a task in itself, and threw her arms around Katelyn's shoulders. With heels, Sasha actually met Katelyn's height. It helped that Katie was wearing a flat pair of shoes. And no makeup.

Katie rubbed a hand over her face and hoped her longtime friend...er, acquaintance, didn't notice her lack of polish.

"What on earth are you doing here?" Sasha asked in a rush.

"Helping...er, a friend. My God, it's good to see you." Katie's response was automatic and completely insincere. She expected no less of Sasha.

"You...you look positively...tired." Sasha grasped Katie's hands and offered a most stoic look of alarm. "Oh, God. Tell me your father hasn't cut you off."

She would think that...wouldn't she?

"No. Nothing like that. You caught me at an awkward time. What are *you* doing here?"

Sasha glanced around her and whispered. "I met someone."

"That's great."

Sasha ran a hand down her skirt and stood taller. "It is…he's amazing. Married, but amazing."

Speechless. There was no other response. "Married?"

"He doesn't love her." Sasha tossed a lock of perfectly dyed black hair from her shoulder and released a nervous giggle. "He flies in and sees me. And it's soooo close to LA. Don't you think?"

Katie bit her lip and avoided saying anything controversial. She and Sasha had partied in Vienna, and hit the best clubs in New York. They weren't friends. Just…people who hung out. Plastic people who knew very little about the other. What Katie did know was that Sasha had always been looking for someone rich enough to help her escape her dysfunctional family.

To hear she was hooking up with a married man wasn't surprising.

Actually, it was depressing.

"Very close to the city."

They stood there, taking in the other in silence. "Well, I should go," Katie told her.

"Great seeing you."

"You, too." Sasha kissed both Katie's cheeks and let her swivel away. Out of the corner of Katie's eye, she noticed Sasha grab an early pregnancy test.

Katie peered down at the bottles of formula in her basket and forced herself to continue walking forward.

It's not your business.

Take the baby and run, she wanted to shout at her *could be* friend. But she couldn't do that. Shouldn't do that.

The cashier smiled as she rang up Katelyn's purchases and bagged the formula.

In her car, Katie grasped the wheel and realized her heart was beating too fast. The lie she was living was larger than Sasha's…by a lot.

Something needed to change.

The answers from Patrick were coming too slow for Dean's taste. He'd spent some time researching private detectives and found one who specialized in finding parents of adopted children. Dean took the opportunity of Katie leaving Savannah in his care to snap a couple of pictures with his cell phone. Not that a picture could help that much. She'd grown so much in such a short time, she wouldn't look at all like she did the day she was born. As he saw it, all infants started to look alike.

Savannah could easily be his niece or even Jack's daughter for that matter.

As if hearing his thoughts, Savannah slowly blinked her eyes open.

Dean couldn't stop the grin that spread over his face. She really was amazing.

Without waiting for her to fuss, he unbuckled her from the car seat and lifted her into his arms. She protested with a whine and, with one pat of her bottom, Dean understood her needs. He noticed a diaper bag left on his sofa and attempted to grab it while holding her. He fiddled a little before giving up and setting her down on the floor.

Savannah's shriek filled the room.

"I'm hurrying, darlin'. No need to cry."

But Savannah didn't listen. She went on crying and flailing her arms as if to emphasize her point about his delay.

He found several diapers and a box of those wet wipe things moms used. Dean had seen Katie use a cushion for diaper changes and searched the bag for one.

"OK, baby girl. We'll get you out of that old one and into this new one, but you're going to have to give me a little break. I haven't done this before."

His words seemed to calm her a little. She blinked several times and hiccupped on her tears. He managed to unsnap the outfit and expose the damage.

"Whoa! What is your mama feeding you?"

A dozen wipes later, her tiny behind was clean and she was kicking her legs and smiling. "You like being naked? Is that what you want?"

Savannah kicked at his hand. He laughed and snuck a clean diaper under her. "My carpet won't hold up to the abuse," he told her. "And your mama would tie me up if she came home and you were exposed. We can't have that," he cooed.

It took him twice as long as it should have, but in the end, Savannah was clean and smiling as he talked to her.

He left her safely in the middle of the floor on her back and ran the soiled diaper to the outside trash. When he made it back inside, he found her on her tummy and lifting her head.

"Look at you." He removed his cell phone from his pocket and crawled on the floor with her, taking pictures. "Did you do that all by yourself?"

Savannah smiled, lost the strength in her neck, and bopped her chin on the floor. She cried at the shock. He walked her around the room for a while, but she kept crying. He moved to the backyard and let the early evening air wrap around them.

That was where Katie found them less than twenty minutes later. Dean was pointing out different objects and plants with Savannah propped against him.

"There's your mommy. I told you she'd be back."

Katie stopped in the doorway and stared at the two of them.

"What? Do I have baby powder on my face?" Dean asked.

She shook her head and grinned. "No. It's just…"

"It's just what?"

"I rushed and I didn't need to. Look at you two. It's sweet."

Dean leaned down and brought his lips close to Savannah's ear. "Hear that, I'm sweet. Maybe I can score some points and keep my girls here with me tonight?"

"Her bassinet is at the apartment."

Dean shrugged. "Let's go shopping. She's getting too big for the tiny bed anyway. Might as well get ready for the next phase."

"There isn't room in the apartment for a crib."

"I have plenty of room here." The words popped out of his mouth before he realized what he was saying.

"Excuse me?"

He settled into the thought of Katie and Savannah staying with him. "Stay here. You and Savannah. Move in with me."

Katie's brows pitched together. "That's fast, Dean. I mean, we're just starting over. Moving in is huge."

Dean placed Savannah on his shoulder and walked over to Katie. "What better way to see if this is going to work, with all of us, than to have you stay here."

"I don't know. It's a major step."

"And staying with Monica in an apartment wasn't a big move? C'mon. It doesn't have to be permanent. We'll take it one day at a time. Besides, Savannah rolled over a little while ago. She's growing out of her tiny quarters whether a crib will fit in your space or not."

"She rolled over for you?" Katie's eyes grew large. She reached out and took Savannah in her arms. "You rolled over? Oh, baby… I'm so proud of you." She kissed Savannah several times.

"I take it rolling over is a new thing?"

"It is."

"I took pictures."

"You did?"

Dean moved into the house, shut the door, and fished his phone out of his pocket. He showed Katie the snapshots of Savannah grinning and lifting her head.

"Move in with me," Dean said as he reached out and smoothed her hair with his hand.

"An instant family could be disastrous," she warned him.

"Or it could be perfect. Since when do you shy away from a challenge?"

"You're being manipulative, Dean Prescott."

He chuckled and dropped his hand from her hair. "That's how I get what I want."

She didn't say no…in fact, she looked like she might just be considering his proposal. He suppressed a grin and waited for her to say something.

"I'll think about it."

He chewed the inside of his cheek and rocked back on his heels. *Thinking about it is a start.*

"I can accept that."

"It's not a yes."

He grinned. "No, *I'll think about it* isn't a yes. It's closer to a yes than a no…but it's not a yes."

She squeezed her eyes together. "How do you figure?"

Dean looked to the ceiling and thought back on his childhood. "How often did Gaylord say to you, *I'll think about it, Katelyn*…and he eventually said no?"

She tilted her chin. "If I buttered him up, he never said no."

Dean let a slow, evil grin spread over his face.

Let the buttering begin!

The delivery boy from the local florist must have thought her suitor was crazy. First, there were roses…a dozen pink ones with a big red bow. Alongside the flowers was a package of diapers.

Katie couldn't look at the flowers without laughing. Leave it to Dean to court her with diapers. The next day at work she told him about her strange gifts with a smart-ass comment about someone getting her address mixed up with a nursery.

The next day a bouquet of orchids arrived along with a box of formula.

At work, Dean asked how Savannah was eating. Katie let him know she wouldn't be hungry for weeks.

Then came star lilies with a teddy bear...then sunflowers with a handmade knit blanket.

By the time Monica arrived home from Florida, the apartment looked like a gift shop.

"My God, this place looks like a flower shop threw up in here," Monica said when she walked in.

"Dean."

Monica dropped her duffel bag at the door and sniffed the first bouquet. "Did you fight?"

Katie laughed. "No. He wants me and Savannah to move in with him."

Monica moved to the second set of flowers and sniffed. "All this to convince you to change your address?"

Smiling, Katie said, "Yeah. He sent stuff for Savannah, too."

"Wow." Monica moved into the room and flopped onto the couch. "Hold out for something that won't die or get used up," she told her with a laugh.

Katie reached over and hugged Monica. "It's good to see you. How was it?"

"Amazing. I know it's only training...but the people were crazy-excited about what they do. It's an adrenaline rush like nothing else. There was disaster triage training, figuring out who was beyond saving, and working on those who had a chance."

The thought sickened Katie, but she understood the drama enough through Monica's eyes to be excited for her friend.

"Could you leave someone who was suffering to take care of someone else?"

"I don't know. I have to try. In the ER we're told that one day we might have to make that choice but, as of yet, I've always stayed with a patient until there was nothing left. The thought of getting out there in the thick of something and working day after day to help people…I like it, Katie. Helping people is why I wanted to be a nurse." Monica's green eyes sparkled as she spoke.

"Thank God there are people like you out there. I couldn't do it."

Monica tapped her thigh and moved from the couch to the refrigerator. "Don't sell yourself short. You'd do what you had to if pushed to the wall. I doubt you'd crumble."

Katie shrugged. "If pushed, maybe. But I wouldn't jump in the disaster willingly."

"According to you, you jumped into some crazy crap earlier in life." Monica popped the tab on a soda and drank her fill.

Yeah, she had. But with Savannah, that had all changed. Actually, shortly after Jack and Jessie had hooked up, all that had changed.

No…when she and Dean had broken it off! That was when it had all changed. "Life is different now," she said softly.

"So…ya gonna do it?"

"Do what?"

"Move in with Dean?"

"Should I?"

"Oh, don't put this on me. This is your decision. You two have a huge history. I couldn't give you sound advice if I wanted to."

Fair enough. "I want to. I think I do."

"What's stopping you?"

"What if it doesn't work? How badly will it hurt if I end up leaving?"

Monica drank more soda and smirked. "The *easy* questions," she said. "That's the problems with relationships. You don't know if they are going to work out. There are no guarantees and tons of heartache along the way."

"Some work out great, like Jack and Jessie."

"Some suck, like your parents and mine."

"That's cold, Monica."

Monica looked beyond Katie to a bundle of flowers. "And true, or you'd already be packed."

She had her there. Fear was what kept her from moving her crap and giving in to the flowers and formula.

"Fear is a shitty way to live life."

Monica leveled her gaze with Katie's. "It's when that fear goes away that you know you've found the right person to risk everything for."

Chapter Twenty-One

Monica's words spoke to her all night long...even during the three o'clock feeding and diaper changing of Savannah.

Fear. What did she really fear?

She feared Savannah's biological mom changing her mind.

She feared that her secret would be revealed before Patrick could identify the real mom.

She feared...nothing else. At one point, she'd worried how Dean would react to Savannah. If the last couple of weeks were any indication, Dean was on board the baby express and more than willing to help. The fact that he knew about Savannah helped with the overall hiding of her. None of her family suspected a thing and for that, she was profoundly grateful.

With the lights in her room dimmed and Savannah sucking on her nightly bottle, Katie wrote down the pros and cons of moving in with Dean. Since she'd taken on the job as hotel interior designer, charts and lists had become something she couldn't live without.

"Let's start with the bright side, shall we, Savannah?"

Savannah pulled in her cheeks and blinked.

"Pros...we get to see Dean every day," she whispered. *And I can sleep with him every night.*

"You can have your own room. It's a house and not an apartment." Not that she minded living with Monica, but compared to what she was used to, her current personal space was smaller than her closet back home.

"If Jessie were to drop in to visit Monica, we'd be busted." Katie put a few pluses next to Jessie's name on the paper.

"I can work from Dean's house some days. Oh, and carpool." Not that she'd ever worried about that in the past.

Now for the cons…"We'll miss Monica." Yet even as she jotted Monica's name on the con side of the paper, she had to write it on the plus side, too. Monica would never complain, but Katie had ambushed her into staying with her in the first place. She was young and single. Taking care of a baby after helping her own sister with her nephew couldn't be on top of her list of things she wanted to do. Besides, visiting Monica would be easier and more appreciated if they didn't live together.

"Babysitter?" She wrote the word with a big question mark next to it. Mrs. Hoyt was the only babysitter Savannah knew outside of Monica. Maybe Mrs. Hoyt could be bribed to drive over to sit with Savannah. Katie would have to ask or start her search for a sitter again.

Katie put aside her pen and removed the bottle from Savannah's lips to burp her midway through her meal. After only a few encouraging taps on her back, Savannah belched better than a fan at a baseball game and then settled in to the remainder of her meal.

She tapped her pen on the paper, searching for another con. Everything else she could think of fell under the unknown category.

How would Dean react to being a full-time live-in with an infant? With her? Would they tire of each other? Would their feelings fade?

The question that kept popping up in her head was, would she regret not taking a chance if she didn't move in with him? The answer was a big, huge yes.

Placing her notepad aside, Katie removed the bottle from Savannah's slack lips and carefully lifted her into the bassinet. Then Katie settled back in her bed.

As Katie drifted off to sleep, she lost most of the fear she'd been thinking about all night and replaced it with excitement.

Outside of a weekend engagement, she'd never lived with a man she wasn't related to. There would be challenges, but Dean was right. She confronted life's tests head-on.

Jo typed away at her desk when Katie strode into the office the next day. She glanced up long enough to say a quick, "Hey, Katie." And then kept on typing.

"Hi," she said before glancing beyond Jo and seeing that Dean's desk was empty.

"Where is—"

"Dean's at the back of the site by the parking garage."

"Thanks."

After placing her Prescott hard hat on, she walked out of the office and across the job site to find her soon-to-be roommate.

"Hello, Miss Morrison," one of the painters called from his ladder.

Instead of trying to figure out who it was from her angle, she simply waved and greeted the man. "Hey. It looks good."

"I try," he said with a wave.

Katie kept walking and greeted no less than four more people in her path. She remembered two names and scolded herself for not knowing the others. She told herself it was easy for them to remember her. She was one of maybe four women who walked around on site. And she was certainly the only one wearing skirts and heels. Although the heels had been less and less as of late.

Her father would be proud. He hated the skintight outfits she'd worn for the greater part of a decade. Oh, she loved her sexy outfits but with a baby, they simply weren't practical.

The two story parking garage was well under way with its construction. Dean stood with his subcontractor talking. Both their backs were to her as she approached.

Behind them, she waited until their conversation had stalled to make her presence known.

They'd made love all night long on Friday. Talked about absolutely nothing and tickled each other's toes while eating ice cream in bed. Saturday morning she packed herself and Savannah up and left for Monica's to think. She'd told Dean she wanted the rest of the weekend to consider his offer. It was now Monday.

She wanted more nights of ice cream and tickling.

More nights…more days.

"Hey, Dean…Lou," she said over the noise of the heavy equipment in the yard. Lou turned quickly while Dean took his time to swivel his head her way. When he did, his eyes questioned her. She blinked twice, offered a coy smile, and glanced at Lou.

"Katelyn. I didn't expect to see you today."

"I don't know why. I work here."

Lou shook her hand and smiled.

Funny how handshakes were something she'd grown used to. Used to be it was fake pats on the back of her hand or double kisses to both cheeks from near strangers. The world of silicone and Botox was now filled with tool belts and handshakes.

Who knew?

"What are you doing out here?" Dean asked with a smirk.

She paused, met his eyes. "I'm letting you know I'm not going to be around today."

His smirk flickered. "Oh?"

"Yeah…I'm, uh…" She licked her lips and pulled her bottom lip between her teeth for a moment.

He caught her movements and his eyes clouded over.

"I'm moving today. It might take me a couple of days to get settled. Think you can do without me around here?"

Dean's attention traveled from her lips, and slowly to her eyes. He sat there, deep inside her gaze. The noise around them mellowed into a low hum. "Moving?"

"Across town."

One edge of his lips drew up. He drew in a deep breath and smiled full-on as the meaning behind her words sank in. "Take all the time you need."

"Are you sure?" she teased. "The carpet guys are coming here tomorrow to measure."

"I think we can handle it, Katie."

"Good," she said.

"Moving?" Lou asked. "Aren't you staying at the hotel?"

"I found this great place in the foothills."

Lou had worked with Dean for years. Like most of the people on the site, he assumed she lived at the hotel.

"Better than a hotel, eh?"

"Yeah…you could say that," she said.

"Good seeing you again, Katelyn. Tell your brother I said hello next time you see him," Lou said, as he walked off, giving them a small measure of privacy.

"I will." She smiled at Dean and turned to leave…then swung around. "Oh, I need the keys." She reached her hand out and hesitated.

Dean's gaze never left hers as he reached into his back pocket and he removed a key from the ring. He placed it in her palm and enfolded her hand around it. "Take your time."

"Thanks," she said as she turned and left.

The heat of his stare settled on her back as she walked away. She stood taller, kept her head higher...and, yes, she swung her hips more than God intended.

The smile she held on her lips spread all the way to her brain cells. There were more than a few backward glances as she made her way across the job site. At her car, she tossed her hard hat in the front seat and settled behind the wheel.

She'd already packed a few things...and outside of her wardrobe and the baby things she'd accumulated for Savannah, there wasn't a lot to take over to Dean's house.

Katie couldn't help but wonder how long it would before Dean made an excuse and made his way home.

Mrs. Hoyt wasn't as difficult to convince to babysit across town as Katie had thought. They'd worked out a three day a week schedule. With any luck, Katie wouldn't need her more than that.

Katie filled her "mommy-bus," which was what she nicknamed her SUV, with her clothes and essentials for Savannah before packing Savannah up and driving them both to Dean's. Monica followed with a carload of stuff and helped her unload.

"You're sure about this?" Monica asked as she removed the clothes-filled hangers from the car...followed by the last box filled with diapers and baby powder.

"I know I won't be happy if I don't try. Dean's one of the good guys, Monica. I've known that since I was a kid. Besides...he loves Savannah."

They stood in the living room of the house with all the boxes and stacks of clothes removed from both cars.

"OK," Monica sighed. "But if you ever need to move back, you know where I am."

Katie pulled Monica into a heartwarming hug. "Thank you, Monica. You've been a sister and so much more."

Monica tapped her back a few times and sniffled. "It's crazy. I went from Jessie being around all the time to you being there. I wonder what it's going to feel like to be alone for a while?"

Katie hadn't thought of that. "I'm just a few streets away."

Monica laughed as she pulled away. "A few streets, one freeway, and an entire airport away…but who's drawing a map?"

Katie laughed.

Monica's face grew stoic. "Call me if you need anything!"

"I will. You, too!"

"OK." Monica leaned over and kissed Savannah. "Be good for your mommy. She's the best."

Katie lifted Savannah into her arms, picked up her tiny hand, and waved as Monica drove away.

Alone, she wandered about Dean's home and moved a few of her clothes into his closet. He'd pushed aside some of his clothes as if picturing what it would look like with her clothes in his space.

She smiled at the thought and lined up some of her favorite heels on the floor of the closet next to his shoes.

Dean lived simply. A bachelor in every way. He'd moved to the area shortly after their breakup. Jack had told her it was because work in the area had taken off. She had her doubts. Texas was one of the only states in the union that wasn't as hard hit by the recession depressing the country. California wasn't as fortunate.

Pushing aside the thoughts as to why Dean had moved to a suburb of LA, Katie walked around his home and took note of her surroundings. There was a distinct lack of knickknacks and dust collectors. He had the occasional family photo, but for the most part the place felt like a house and not a home. Maybe together they could make it a home.

Katie stepped into the guest room across the hall from Dean's master bedroom. She pictured a crib where she'd placed a playpen to aid in Savannah's afternoon nap. The room would be close enough to hear Savannah in the middle of the night, but far enough away so she and Dean wouldn't wake with every toss and turn Savannah managed during the night.

All the books Katie had read assured her that she was a typical new mom that jumped to help Savannah with every whine. According to the mommy bloggers, that wasn't always a good thing. Maybe now with a little more space, Savannah would sleep better at night.

And so could she.

A mom could hope.

After putting Savannah down for a nap, Katie set out for the kitchen to take inventory and make shelf room for formula, baby food, plastic bottles, and bowls. Now that Savannah was eating a little solid food, she was growing even bigger. Everything about her was looking less like an infant, and more like a tiny girl.

When most of the unpacking was finished, Katie considered pulling out her spreadsheets and working on the tight budget she'd been given for the hotel, but then decided on a cool drink on the back porch. It had been a long time since she'd enjoyed a quiet veranda moment.

Curling her legs under her, she closed her eyes and enjoyed the warm breeze. It was unseasonably cool for Southern California in late summer. She could picture herself curling up under a blanket with a cup of hot chocolate in the fall.

It wasn't long before her mind drifted to how this new living arrangement was going to work out. Her cooking was marginal at best. Dean obviously hadn't starved as a single man, so maybe he had more hidden talents. They could order out. Hire a cook. But bringing in too many eyes of domestic help could backfire. Although Katie had dodged the media in the past year, they still knew of her. If they found her with a baby, she would make the tabloids and rumors would fly.

Low profile. That's what she had to remember.

The hair on her neck prickled and she turned toward the open door leading into the house.

Dean leaned against the frame, a bouquet of white roses sitting limply in his hand. His eyes were soft, the smile he wore could only be described as dreamy.

"You're home early," she said softly.

Dean unceremoniously dropped the flowers on the table beside her and captured her face in his palms. His lips were warm and welcoming and edged on desperate. Dean brought her to her feet without words, kept her lips locked to his.

She knew how he felt. The enormity of them living together, of their growing feelings for the other…all of that played out as he kissed her. His tongue traveled into her mouth and traced hers. The prickling of her skin she'd experienced as he watched from the doorway started to tingle down her spine.

Her breasts pushed against his chest and she held his waist tightly.

She was breathless when he stopped kissing her long enough to breathe.

"You're really here."

She kissed his chin and drew in his fresh pine scent. "We are."

Dean traced the sides of her face with his thumbs. "Where's Savannah?"

"Guest room. Napping."

He lifted one eyebrow and said, "Good." He tugged her into the house, closed the door, and moved them to the living room before he started kissing her all over again.

His intention was clear and she was more than willing to consummate their new arrangement.

The buttons of her silk shirt were undone, each one with a kiss and a press of Dean's tongue against her skin. When only her baby blue lace bra covered her torso, she repeated Dean's movements and removed his shirt with slow kisses.

The feel of his broad chest and tight abs played at the edges of her fingertips. How many nights had she thought of touching him again, of tasting him? She circled his nipples with her tongue, and laid playful bites when they pebbled. Dean loved foreplay, almost as much as she did. He pressed against her as they stood next to the couch, his erection stiff within his jeans.

He stopped the nipple play by backing her down and covering her half-clothed body with his. "I want to make love to you in every room in this house," he said against her ear.

"Sounds like a challenge."

Dean kissed the portion of her breast not covered by her bra. "We know you like a challenge."

She moaned as he blew hot air through the thin layer of cloth covering her breast. He chuckled quietly, circled his hand around her back, and unclasped her bra. He laved each nipple until they were tight with need and her hips bucked against his.

The couch cushioned one of her legs as Dean moved lower, his tongue dancing across her belly. The desire to tear into his clothes and have him naked and covering her clouded her brain. Equal parts of her wanted to feel him, all of him, deep inside her while her body craved the teasing kisses and scrapes of his teeth.

He wiggled her out of the linen slacks she wore. Her barely-there panties were moist already when he kissed around the straps holding the material together. "I love how you smell," he told her, running his tongue around the edge of her panties. "How you taste."

Her body clenched.

As he moved lower to sample her, she held him away.

"I want to taste you," she told him.

His eyes twitched. "Later," he said.

But she didn't want to wait. Her body was so fired up, he could look at her and she'd explode. It was time to welcome him home.

Katie pushed up and ran her hands down his chest before finding the clasp of his jeans.

"Now."

Dean lifted his hands as if in surrender and helped her relieve him of his clothes.

His thick erection strained against his stomach and her mouth watered. Katie moved so he could lie on the couch before she ran her fingertips along his hip.

The tips of her hair brushed against his penis and he said something under his breath. Katie smiled, kissed his hip, and let her cheek rest against his desire. She teased him as he had done her when they'd made love before.

With only her lips, her tongue, she tasted. His hand fell to her shoulder as he moaned. She smiled around him and took as much as she could manage.

"Fuck."

She giggled. "Not yet."

"Oh, darlin'."

Yeah, she knew the feeling. So she kept going, taking him, and ignoring her own empty body. Dean would take care of her no matter how far he allowed this to go.

A tiny taste splashed on her tongue and Dean pulled her away.

"C'mere," he groaned.

She crawled up his body and kissed him.

Dean pushed her panties off and ran his hand along her butt with a playful squeeze.

His wet kisses stilled long enough to say. "Condom, back pocket…wallet."

Instead of reaching for his jeans, she nudged his legs between hers and opened wide for him. "You of all people know there's no need." They'd already talked about their health, and that wasn't a concern. If moving in wasn't a sign of commitment, Katie wasn't sure what else there was.

"Are you sure?" he asked.

She felt the tip of him slide against her. "I want to feel you…all of you, inside me."

He grinned and she sank onto him.

On top, she set the pace. The small confines of the couch made for different angles and sparks of pleasure from different places.

There was no energy for talking as they both plunged, kissed, and licked their way toward climax.

He was the only man she'd ever felt safe enough with to enjoy making love without a barrier. The heat of him and the feel of him making her slicker deep inside brought on a swift and powerful orgasm. She hardly settled into a pace when he thrust faster and tumbled her over the edge.

The warm gush of his seed filled her and God help her, she peaked again.

Katie lay limply in his arms as the world returned. The deep thud of his heart against his chest met her ear and took its time slowing down.

"We're throwing the condoms away," she told him.

"We are?"

"Yeah…we are."

His chest rumbled and she closed her eyes and simply enjoyed a few quiet moments in his arms.

As it turned out, neither one of them really cooked. Dean had the barbeque thing down. He was down-home Texas that way. But when it came to dishes off the grill, they were painfully dependent on the microwave.

Not that he expected Katie to know her way around a kitchen. He knew the life she'd lived before, and it wasn't full of domestic chores. There had always been a housekeeper at her father's ranch and a cook at the hotel.

Dean didn't care. He happily moved the guest bed out of the extra room and they set up a proper nursery for Savannah. After only a couple of nights in his home, Savannah was sleeping for six solid hours. A blessing according to Katie.

As a welcome home gift to her, he framed a picture he'd taken of Savannah and Katie together and wrapped it in pink paper.

For a woman who understood four-hundred-dollar dinners in five-star restaurants and whose shoe collection alone could feed a small country…it was the small things she was taking pleasure in now.

She loved the gift and set it on his fireplace mantel along with other family photos he had displayed.

"This one was all of you as kids, right?"

He and his siblings had been dragged to plenty of photographers growing up. His mother had given him this particular picture when he moved away. All four of them were under the age of seven, his youngest sister barely old enough to sit on her own. In fact, she leaned against Dean in the picture and the photographer managed to get her smiling.

Dean glanced between the photos and noticed the same round cheeks, and same button nose, between Savannah and Ella.

It was natural to see your own face in that of a child…a child you wanted as your own. At least that's what he told himself.

Unable to stop himself, later that night he dug into an old box of photos and found more childhood memories.

He realized that he and his siblings all had the same nose. Funny how he hadn't noticed it before. Even his nephew had the Prescott button as a baby. He shook aside his thoughts. He'd come to terms with Katie's inability to have his child long ago. He'd give up his ability to have a child who looked like him to keep Katie in his life any day.

Watching Katie with Savannah proved that being a parent had more to do with your heart than it did with DNA.

It was then he realized that he could easily see himself as a full-time dad, a father to Savannah, and not just on a temporary basis.

It was too soon to push Katie into a deeper commitment. And without the private detective determining some answers, she wouldn't want to make any more changes.

"You're rushing, Dean," he scolded himself. The girls had only been living under his roof for a few days and already he was trying to see his face in Savannah's, and Katie's life in his, permanently.

They needed to work through a few things before he could jump to the next level. And hadn't he jumped with Maggie?

No, he'd take this slower. Like the good Southern boy he could be.

When he wanted to.

Chapter Twenty-Two

Patrick called her at work. He was arriving at the hotel and wanted to know if he could meet her there within the hour.

He had information and wanted to deliver it to her in person.

Katie's hands shook as she spoke quietly into the phone. "Do you know who she is?"

"I need confirmation...but I think you may be able to do that for me. Is your suite being used?"

"No. I'll call the hotel and tell them to let you in."

"Good," Patrick said into the phone. "Oh—and, Katie, come alone."

Now the hair on the nape of her neck stood on end. Her first thought was to drag Dean along. They were both waiting for this information. They both wanted to know the answers.

"Why?"

"Because *you're* my client. And I think it's in your best interest to hear the news first. Trust me."

She ran a hand through her hair, something she never did. "OK."

Patrick hung up and her insides pitched in protest. *What does he know? Who is the mom?*

Why did he think she could identify the mother?

There obviously had to be some connection to her and maybe even someone else that Monica or Dean could identify. If that were the case, then Patrick was right in her being alone when they spoke.

Katie took advantage of the fact that Dean was busy with an inspector who would monopolize most of his afternoon.

Thirty minutes after Patrick's phone call, Katie wrote a quick note and posted it on Dean's phone in his office.

Finished here early. I have a few products I want to see before I order. SYAH.

SYAH was their own acronym for "See you at home." So far, no one at work knew they had moved in together. It wasn't a secret that they were seeing each other, but they didn't go around kissing or fondling at work.

Jo had made a few comments about the two of them being much more relaxed than previous weeks. Katie bunted right back with questions about how Steve Bowman was doing. Jo's cheeks had grown red and she busied herself with her work and avoided any further comments.

Jo and Steve were obviously into each other, but Katie wasn't clear if the two of them had even shared a meal outside of the shindig Dean had put on weeks ago. Not that it mattered to her. She and Jo were cordial, but Katie doubted they could be real friends.

Katie drove in silence to the hotel and called ahead to let them know she was coming.

The suite hadn't changed…yet the marble floors felt cold, the colors of the room sterile. Without family pictures or a few misplaced items filtered about the room, it just wasn't home.

Dean's home with its rustic lines and masculine edge made her more comfortable than the finest silk. She wouldn't mind a few extravagant extras…like a cook and a housekeeper. But those things could wait. Dean had actually talked about live-in help once they had everything with Savannah settled.

That day might be today.

She checked the time on the clock and tapped her foot. The receptionist at the front desk was supposed to call her when Patrick arrived.

As the minutes ticked past the hour he was supposed to get there, her pulse sped up and she started to pace the room.

The knock on her door made her jump.

Katie drew in a deep, calming breath and blew it out slowly before opening the door. She painted on a smile and hoped her nerves didn't show.

Only the hall was empty.

A sense of déjà vu swam over her. Her gaze snapped to her feet.

There was a note on the floor that read, *Look up!*

When she did, she noticed a domed camera over her head. A noise drew her attention down the hall. Patrick stood several feet away with his hands tucked into his signature black jacket.

"What's this?" she asked waving the paper.

"It's evidence of a flaw in your hotel security." He pushed away from the wall to join her. "Mind if I come in?"

"Of course not."

Inside the suite, Patrick removed a seven-inch tablet from an inside pocket of his jacket.

Katie noted the gun he had strapped to his side. A gun she assumed he had, but hadn't seen until now. She couldn't help but think he showed it to her now to emphasize his point.

Patrick set the tablet down and picked up the phone on a hall table. He handed her the cordless handset and said, "Call the desk and ask if I've arrived."

Katie's eyes drew together. "Why?"

"Just do it."

Katie waited for the receptionist to answer. When she did, her cheerful voice said, "What can we do for you, Miss Morrison."

"Yes, eh…" She glanced over at Patrick and stuttered, "D-did Mr. Sanderson arrive yet?"

"No. I'm sorry, Miss Morrison. We've not had anyone call on you yet. We'll be sure to let you know when he's on his way up."

Katie frowned. "OK. Thank you." She hung up the phone. "I don't understand."

Patrick sat in one of the chairs and encouraged her to sit as well. "They don't know I'm here. I've already checked into the hotel under an alias."

"So you came up without them knowing."

"Obviously. Which is exactly what Savannah's mother did."

Katie sat and leaned forward. "I'm listening."

Patrick rubbed his hands together with a smile. "The first day I visited your suite in Houston, I walked in like I owned the place. No one stopped or questioned me until I made it to your room. Through normal routes, your security was stellar. Nice to see they weren't flunkies who couldn't make it into the local police detail."

"Good to know."

Patrick turned on his digital device and played a video clip of him walking through the hotel in Houston. He entered and exited an elevator and let himself into Katie's suite without incident. Within seconds, security was at the door. One man had a gun in his hand.

"The clip is spliced together to show how I walked into your room. But notice here…" He paused the clip, showing an empty hall. "And here." He paused it again. "I'm not in range of the camera. The angle I came out of the elevator gave a clear picture of me. Easily identifiable."

"When I looked at the clips of the night Savannah was left, I didn't see anyone come out of an elevator," Katie told him.

"I know. I'll get to that in a minute. Here is another day I went to your suite. This was when I ran into your brother. I went ahead and ran the tape of him coming up and into the room. It's all seamless. Yeah, he pushes in and out of view, but for the most part he's undeniably there."

She mumbled an acknowledgment of his words.

"Now…keep watching."

He fast-forwarded the clip. "I haven't spliced any footage together," he told her. Once he hit a twenty-minute marker, he slowed the clip down to normal speed.

The door to her suite opened and out walked Patrick and Jack…together.

"Were you in there the whole time?"

"No. I surprised your brother after he arrived."

"But I didn't see you go in."

"Exactly."

Katie sat back in her chair. "So how did you get in?"

"Apparently rich people love their privacy nearly as much as they do their security."

Katie nodded. "I can agree with that."

"The angle of the cameras aren't directly on the door to the suite. You've lived in hotels most of your life. I'm sure you've snuck in late at night before."

"Yeah, when I was a kid. We'd hug the wall and slip inside." A friend of hers who was sleeping with a would-be rock star had told her about the hotel cameras. There were nights when she was a teenager that she snuck in, or had someone else sneak in. Katie had stopped hiding from the cameras years ago.

"I snuck into your suite by staying out of direct line with the cameras. The motion detectors inside the room would have triggered, notifying security that someone was in your room, but that didn't happen because Jack was already inside."

"I think there are motion detectors in the halls, too," she told him.

"Yeah, but the only thing security will do once the motion detectors are tripped is look at the video feed. If they don't see anything, or the inside of the room isn't tripped, they'll most likely ignore it. The night the mom left Savannah, you and Monica were home. Security would ignore the motion detectors entirely with the two of you walking in and out.

"OK…so how did the mom get into the foyer? She didn't use the elevator."

"There are usually two penthouse suites in your bigger hotels. The one in Houston across from yours was vacant the night of the wedding. So we know that the mom wasn't in there. There was no footage of a woman with a baby walking the halls of the hotel late at night. But there isn't a multitude of cameras in the staff areas. My first thought was the mom used a fire escape. A stairwell. But they are all locked on the main floors. You can come down a stairwell, in case of a fire, but you can't go up. Chances are there is some kind of trigger on the doors, something electronic, that opens the locks if the fire alarm is screaming."

"There weren't any alarms going off that night. Besides, taking the stairs up twenty-plus floors with an infant is a long hike."

"Right. But if the mother was staying in the hotel…say a few floors below yours…not such a chore, if she could gain entry to the upper floors."

Katie murmured her agreement. She hadn't considered that.

"I don't think she hiked up the stairs at all," Patrick said.

"She didn't?"

"No. She used the staff elevators. A trick you might know something about."

Katie's eyes widened. Yeah. She knew how to get around the hotel without detection. She'd grown up in them. "How would she know where the staff elevators even are? They aren't on a guest map of the hotel and they're not accessible from the inside of the guest halls."

"How she knew about the staff routes I can only assume. Someone told her about them is my guess. Who knows, maybe the mom worked in a hotel at one point. I considered that angle for a while. Thought maybe mom was a maid, someone who knew who you were…left her baby for you to raise."

Katie had considered that scenario as well. "But the letter…a staff member wouldn't know those details about me."

"I agree."

"So the mom befriended a staff member? Learned the lay of the hotel from someone working in Houston?"

Patrick shook his head. "Doubtful. Look, this is what she did. She rented a room at the hotel and arrived a day early. You never saw her arriving or leaving the hotel because she didn't do it on the day you were looking at the videos. There are five hundred thirty-three rooms at the Houston Morrison. She knew you wouldn't look for a single woman registering without a child."

"I didn't even consider that she was a guest. I figured she dropped the baby and ran."

"She obviously brought the baby in later. Somehow, she got her hands on a room service staff uniform. Not very hard to do. The laundry service is seen going in and out of the hotel daily. She could have gotten her hands on one either on site by finding the staff room or by following a truck to where the laundry is washed. Either way, she manages to get a uniform. This tells me a couple things about our girl. She's smart, and very determined to keep her identity a secret."

"Obviously."

"As a guest, she then orders room service. A tray arrives and the waiter leaves the rolling cart in the room to be picked up later. Instead of asking room service to clean up her mess, or leaving the cart in the hall, she keeps the food on the plates and waits. She waits until she knows you're back in your room. She then changes into a uniform and loads up Savannah…under the cart and hidden by the tablecloth…and wheels her down the hall to the service door. She travels the path to your suite in a service elevator and waits outside the penthouse hall door. She hears you and Monica coming home and then tucks in behind the camera angle before knocking on your door and leaving Savannah."

Katie pictured everything Patrick was saying…easily mapping out the woman's path. "So she was hiding behind the service door the whole time Monica and I were standing in my doorway."

"Yep."

"Do we have any footage of her?"

Patrick moved from his chair to the sofa and sat beside her before turning on his tablet. "I do. In one shot, she's wearing what is clearly a wig…in another she's not."

Katie clenched her fists in her lap. She'd waited forever for this moment. "Do I know her"

"You have to tell me."

Patrick played the footage. "I looked through hours of this… hallway footage of room service trays being rolled in and out of rooms. There aren't that many single women checking into the hotel who aren't a part of a convention. There weren't any going on when all of this was happening. I only had to focus on a few floors. Here is the tray being rolled in." Katie watched as guest services arrived at a room and stepped inside. The person who opened the door was out of the frame.

The tape cut and started back up again. "Here it's after midnight."

Sure enough, a woman with dark hair was leaving the room pushing the tray. Her head was down but that didn't stop Katie from squinting her eyes to try and see her features. She was petite…for a new mom. About the same height as her. The woman in the video kept looking around as if she was nervous.

Patrick voiced what she saw. "She's nervous."

"Yeah, I can tell."

She pushed the cart through an unlocked service door. With the exception of the penthouse level, the others weren't locked. If a diplomat visited or a security need arose, they could be, but in Houston that wasn't needed at the time Savannah was being delivered.

The woman hesitated at the service door and looked up.

Patrick froze the image. He zoomed in and the quality started to fade, but her features were still visible.

Katie swallowed hard and her hands started to tingle.

It can't be.

"Do you know her?"

Katie bit her lip. "I need to see another picture. Her hair isn't right."

"Like I said. It's a wig."

Patrick moved the images forward. When the woman was seen again, she was careless about her face. The wig was gone, and she was all but running, holding her stomach, as she made her way back to her room.

Patrick stopped the film again and zoomed in.

There, with tears streaming down her face was a woman Katie had never met but knew a whole lot about.

"It's Maggie. Dean's ex-fiancée."

Her entire body started to tremble.

Patrick turned off the tablet and set it down. "Dean is your boyfriend?"

She nodded wordlessly. "I just moved in with him."

"Did he know Maggie was pregnant?"

Katie blinked a few times. Her mind went numb. "No." He would never have allowed Maggie to have his child without him.

She stood and started to pace off the energy swarming her body.

Savannah was Dean's daughter. His biological daughter.

More his than hers.

"Dean and I dated over a year ago," she found herself explaining to Patrick. "He used to sneak up to my suite during the time we were together. He must have mentioned that to Maggie."

"It did look as if Maggie knew the routine of the hotel. But unless Dean drew her a map, she had to have figured this out by herself."

She thought of the note left with Savannah at the door. "It makes sense now. Dean knew I couldn't have children." It hurt to think he'd told his fiancée about her. She wanted to be angry with him but all she could feel was shock.

"I still don't know why she gave Savannah up. Maggie called off their wedding and didn't give him much of an explanation as to why."

"She was pregnant. Maybe she freaked. Women get emotional when they're pregnant," Patrick said.

"Maybe."

"Or maybe their breakup had more to do with you than it did Dean. Either way, I think we know who the mother is…and in light of the timeline, we know who the daddy is. From what I've discovered, Maggie is living with her aunt just north of Los Angeles."

"How far away?" she asked.

"Hour and a half. Two, tops."

Just yesterday the fabric of her life felt as if it were being sewn at the edges to hold everything together. Dean welcomed her and Savannah into his home and she'd never felt more comfortable in her life.

Outside of her father's home when she was a child, Dean's was home. More than Monica's…more than the suite in a Houston hotel she called her own. The information Patrick delivered dripped acid onto that fabric. The fabric smoldered and left gaping holes.

"What should I do?" she asked almost to herself.

Patrick moved from the couch and placed a supportive hand on her shoulder. "Does he love you?"

Katie's gaze flickered in Patrick's direction. "I—I…we just reunited."

"You're a smart woman, Katelyn. Smarter than many of my clients. Would Maggie deliver her child to you as a tool to get Dean back?"

"She left him," she snapped. "Common knowledge."

"Are you sure?"

"Yeah. My brother and Dean are best friends. Jack and Dean's story of her exit was virtually the same."

She barely noticed him stroking her back in comfort. "You can wait…see if Maggie comes to you."

"Wouldn't she have done that by now?"

Patrick didn't meet her eyes when she looked at him. "If she had a nefarious reason for leaving Savannah with you…and she wanted to avoid any possibility of prosecution of child abandonment, she'll get in touch with you soon."

"How can you know that?"

"Texas laws differ from California. A mother can leave a child with a *responsible adult* for up to six months before the state considers it abandonment."

"We're both in California."

Patrick moved his head to the side. "Doesn't matter. She left Savannah in Texas. The papers for legal guardianship…the birth certificate were drawn up here in California. Maggie was careful in how she executed this entire ordeal. With the lawyers you could afford to hire, she would be hard-pressed to get Savannah back if she wanted to. And after six months, it's all but ironclad. If she'd left Savannah here in California, there would be even less legality she could stand on."

Katie blinked away the moisture in her eyes. "Savannah's nearly three months old."

Patrick offered a sympathetic look. "If it helps…I don't think she's coming back. She meant for you to have this child. I think it will be up to you to confront her."

"And if I don't?"

Patrick shrugged. "After six months you can relax. Even if she came after you for guardianship at that time, any lawyer worth their bar exam could get you custody."

Katie ran both of her hands over her face and turned away from him. "None of this answers the question of why."

"No. You asked for an identity. I told you when we started that I would find out who…how…but I'm not inside the head of this woman and I don't know why she left you her child. It could be that she felt she wasn't ready for parenthood. Or she couldn't raise the child of a man who didn't love her. Women are like that. For those answers you're going to have to ask her."

She cringed at the thought.

How could she talk to the woman Dean had been engaged to, the woman that could give him children…did give him a child?

When Katie had heard of Dean's engagement, a part of her heart, her soul, had shattered.

Katie remembered those first and only days of knowing that, inside her, a life formed. A life created by her and Dean. And then that awful night had come.

At first, there were a few spots. She quickly looked up her symptoms on the Internet and realized that many women spotted during their first trimester.

But it wasn't spotting.

Within an hour, she knew there was a problem.

She called Dean, frantic. Told him to meet her at the hospital.

He held her as the doctor told her she'd lost their child. Something inside her was broken and she knew it. A week later her regular doctor sat beside her and Dean and told them that Katie couldn't carry a child to term. Her inhospitable uterus would reject any pregnancy she could possibly conceive. The fact she already had was no surprise according to the doctor.

Katie had stopped listening at that point.

She would live a life without children.

The man she loved…the man who looked at her deeper than anyone ever had, wanted children. Wanted that life.

Hurting beyond reason, Katie did what she needed to do.

She wove lies and drove Dean away.

Straight into Maggie's arms.

And now Katie was raising their child.

How could she face Dean and not tell him?

His own child was under his roof and Katie was the fraud. The thought of life without Savannah…without Dean, made her sick.

"Do you want my advice?" Patrick asked.

"God, please." She had no idea which way to turn.

"Wait. Irrational decisions are rarely the right ones. Take a few days to digest this information before you do anything."

She turned to him. "I live with Dean. It's not like I can avoid seeing him."

Patrick rolled his eyes. "You're a woman. Plea some womanly issue and keep your distance while you figure out what to do."

Chapter Twenty-Three

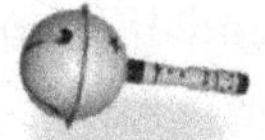

After only a week of living with each other, Dean felt closer to Katie than he ever had before. Their physical relationship was *off the charts* amazing. They talked about nearly everything…up until the day she left work early.

She returned from her day and claimed to be feeling unwell.

Claimed. He didn't think she was sick. Some of the spark had left her face and he couldn't help but think it was him.

While they were both sitting on the couch and watching some mindless television show, Dean lifted her feet in his lap and started rubbing lazy circles with his thumbs. Katie's features lost some of the stress he'd seen behind her eyes.

"God that feels good," she told him.

"Relaxing?"

She offered half a smile and hummed her appreciation.

He waited until her upper body melted into the couch before he asked her, "What's going on, Katie?"

Her eyes popped open. "Going on?"

"Yeah. You've been preoccupied the last couple days. Stressed."

Her throat moved and she blinked. "I am stressed," she told him. "Worried about what Patrick is going to discover…worried he won't find the mom at all."

"She couldn't have just disappeared."

"You never know. The evening news is always talking about people dropping off the face of the earth."

Dean didn't think this mom left the country. A few feet away a mechanical swing clicked as it rocked Savannah back and forth. Her little eyes were losing the battle of staying open. "He'll find her." Dean stroked the arch of her foot as they talked.

"If he does and I know her? What then? Do I approach her?"

He hadn't thought of that. "You can't do anything until you know who she is. When we find out who she is, we'll figure out what to do as a couple."

Katie's eyes instantly filled and Dean's heart wept.

"Oh, baby. Don't worry." He pulled her into his lap and wrapped her in his arms. His action prompted tears to fall and a whimper to escape her throat. "I'm here."

She buried her head against his chest and clutched his shirt. "He could tell me anything, Dean. The mom could be someone I know. What if Savannah is Jack's daughter…or someone he knows?"

Dean stroked her hair. "Jack and Jessie have been exclusive since they met. And I don't think he was seeing anyone for a while before they met."

Katie pulled away and searched his eyes. "But it could be something like that. What then? Damn it. I wish I'd never hired Patrick."

Dean removed a tear with his thumb. "You're letting this eat you up, Katie. We'll find out who the mom is and then move on." He dropped a finger to her lips when she started to ask another question. "And if we don't find out who the mom is…we move on."

He kissed the tip of her nose.

"Thank you…for being here with me," she said. "I don't want to do this alone."

"You're not alone. Is this what's been on your mind?"

She looked away. "Yeah. Sorry I've been so off."

Dean lifted her chin to stare into her eyes. "I know this is going to sound awful of me, but I'm glad it's baby drama and not me. You had me thinking you'd regretted your move here."

Her eyes widened. “What? No! We’re the best thing to happen since Savannah ended up on my doorstep.”

He kissed away the salty tears and she offered a tired smile before settling back into his arms.

Savannah gave in to dreamland and, from the way Katie had relaxed, she wasn’t far behind.

Dean tried to watch the television and remove his thoughts from what Katie had said…but her worry transferred over to him.

What if Savannah was related to one of them…to him?

What if the father showed up demanding her?

What if someone was playing a sick game?

God help anyone who would try anything cruel with the woman he loved and the child brought into their life.

Dean considered himself about as even tempered as they came… but that didn’t mean he wouldn’t come out fighting.

Katie had dodged a bullet. With as much honesty as she could bear, she’d shared her concerns with Dean. Her dishonesty was eating her up. Over and over she told herself it was a simple omission of the truth.

Just because Maggie was the mother…or the woman in the pictures running from the scene of the crime, there were no guarantees Dean was the father. In fact, Maggie might have had an affair and that was why she’d broken off their engagement.

Katie doubted the latter.

With a copy of the letter Maggie had left with Savannah, Katie met with Monica for a “long lunch” and an even longer talk.

They chose a table on an outside patio and suffered the warm temperatures to avoid notice.

Katie’s hands trembled as they sat and kept the talk light until they’d ordered food.

"You didn't ask me here to talk about work, Katie. What's up?"

Katie removed her sunglasses and Monica's gaze opened wide. "You know something."

Swallowing hard, Katie nodded. "Promise me this stays between us."

"Of course—"

"No. Not *of course*. This is huge, Monica. And you're the closest thing I have to a sister. My mother is God-knows-where and I wouldn't trust her with this anyway. Promise me…pinky, blood… or whatever it is you sisters do that makes you take something to the grave if need be."

Monica grasped her hands. "You're worrying me."

"Promise!"

"I promise. I'll take this to the grave if you need me to."

Katie paused and set her sunglasses back on her nose. "I know who the mother is."

"Hookay…"

"I think I know who the father is."

Monica sat perfectly still and waited.

"Patrick found a security tape of Maggie passing herself off as room service in the hotel that night." Saying which night wasn't necessary. They were both there.

Monica squinted, confused. "Maggie? Why does that name sound familiar?"

"She is Dean's ex."

Monica's jaw dropped. "Oh, my God. So you think Dean is…"

Katie nodded. "I think he is."

Monica dropped back in her chair as the information sank in. "Are you sure?"

"I'm not positive about anything." Katie removed a copy of the original note left with Savannah from her purse and flattened the well-worn edges on the table.

"I've been going over this for weeks and now it all makes sense." She cleared her throat and read a passage from the letter. "*Savannah was conceived with love, albeit one-sided, and deserves a mother who can give her everything.* Dean hasn't come out and told me that he didn't love Maggie, but if he did, I don't think he would have let her just walk out on him. Jack told me a couple times that he didn't think Maggie was the right match for Dean. Maybe she called off the wedding because he couldn't love her."

"Or maybe he talked about his ex…you…a little too much."

"What guy talks about his ex to his current?"

Monica shook her head. "OK…well he had to say something. Or maybe she overheard him talking to someone else?"

"I don't think anyone knew about us. I know Jack was clueless. Besides, there aren't many men out there, Dean included, who have soulful talks with their buddies."

"I wouldn't be so sure," Monica said. "Dean could have said something in passing…while having a little too much to drink. You never know."

Maybe.

"Either way, if the mother is Maggie and if Dean is Savannah's real father…then Maggie didn't believe Dean loved her."

"All easy conclusions from what you know about their relationship and this letter." Monica sipped her water and looked around them.

The closest occupied table was three away so Katie continued.

"*I know things about you that I probably shouldn't. I know how much you want a child of your own, how impossible it is for you to do so,*" Katie read aloud. "Dean must have told her about me. How else would she have known I can't have kids of my own?"

"Seems like a personal thing to share."

"Very. I can't think about him telling her this right now or why he did…I just need to work out these facts and deal with the *why* of it all later."

"When two people get married, they talk about all kinds of things. According to Jessie anyway. She and Jack talked about their past sex lives. She even asked your brother if there was any possibility of a kid out there being his."

"Do you think Maggie asked Dean if he could get her pregnant? God, what if she planned this?" She hadn't thought of that.

"Women trap men with pregnancy all the time, but she called off the wedding. I don't think Savannah was a trap. Who knows, I could be wrong, but I don't think that tree is worth barking up, Katie."

Katie looked back down at the letter. "*Her father isn't ready for her, but if my instincts are right, he will be one day. And when he is, the two of you will give Savannah the loving home she needs.*" Katie paused after reading the passage.

"Sounds like Maggie knew the two of you would reunite if she wasn't in the picture."

"Dean has always wanted to be a father. He talked about having a houseful of kids one day, just like the one where he grew up. He had to have talked about these things with her. They were getting married for Christ's sake. She had to know he wanted kids." Anger rose inside her. *How could Maggie be so ignorant?*

"If he didn't love her, she would either have to live a lie with him or raise this child in a broken home. Neither choice is easy."

Monica was right.

"Two parents loving a child will always be better than one."

"Oh, that's crap." The hair on Katie's neck stood on end. Her father had done just fine!

"Really? Most of your life you haven't had a mom. How's that working for you?"

"I'm fine," she bit out between her stiff lips.

"Bullshit. No more than I am about my dad abandoning us. Yeah, we get along…get over it. But that shit still hurts and you know it. Even Jessie with all her brave face about raising Danny alone couldn't love him like a father can. Jack has made it better for both of them."

Katie wanted to deny Monica's wisdom.

She couldn't.

Monica picked at her food. "So Maggie is the mother."

"Looks that way."

"And Dean is the father."

"Looks that way."

"Now what? You obviously haven't told him."

"How can I? What if I'm wrong about him…what if he does love Maggie and wants to try and work it out with her? I could lose them both." Her stomach twisted with the thought.

"I don't think Dean would do that to you."

"One of the things I love about him is his loyalty. He adores Savannah. It's like he feels a connection. Is that possible? That on some level he knows she's his?"

Monica rolled her eyes. "Now you're talking nonsense. If Dean loves kids the way you say he does, then he's enamored with Savannah…nothing more than that."

"This insecure feeling under my skin is itchy, Monica. I don't like it." She hated it.

"Is that insecurity or the guilt you feel from keeping the truth from Dean?"

"I don't know. God, I hate this!"

Monica reached across the table and covered her hand. "I know you do. Just remember who this is really about. Savannah is the innocent one in all of this. You'd never be able to keep this from Dean forever."

"I wouldn't want to."

"I know you wouldn't. And no matter how much you might *think* he'll react, you'll never know until he does. The longer you keep this from him, the harder it's going to be for the both of you. Trust is important in any relationship."

Katie looked beyond the patio to cars passing along the street. Everyone going about their day without stress, without worry. "I love him, Monica. I don't want to lose him again."

Not again.

"Where's Katie?" Jack's voice screamed into Dean's cell phone and made it over the noise of the cement truck that was pouring concrete into the foundation molds of the parking structure.

"What?" Dean plugged his other ear and ducked away from the noise to try and understand what Jack was yelling about.

"I…and…can't find…" The reception kept cutting out.

"Hold up, Jack. I can't hear you over the noise." Dean hustled away from the heavy equipment and tried again. "OK, what's this about Katelyn?"

"Where is she? I can't find her anywhere. She's not at the hotel. Not at Monica's. I called the office and she's not there. Damn it, Dean, I asked you to keep an eye on her."

Oh, boy. He knew this was coming. "She's fine."

"I can't find her. Our dad's frantic. It's never good when Gaylord gets his cowboy boots on too tight."

"She's fine, Jack. You'll have to trust me on this. Did you try her cell phone?"

"She's not answering. I need to talk to her. Do you know where she is?" Jack's voice had lost some of his edge, but he still sounded off to Dean.

Dean felt the web of lies starting all over again. He did this before and he damn well wasn't doing it again. "She's probably at home." *Katie's gonna kill me.*

"Are you not listening to me? She's not at the hotel. I called and they said she's only been there once this week."

Dean started to pace. "I didn't say she was at the hotel. I said she's at home. My home."

"W-what? Your house?"

"Yeah, Jack. She moved in with me last week. We wanted to see how things worked out before we announced the move to anyone." OK, that was a lie. They hadn't told anyone to avoid any unexpected visitors. His bachelor pad had been converted into a romper room with all the baby stuff an infant needs.

"She's living with you? Seriously?"

"Yeah."

"Well, holy shit. I didn't see that coming."

"Not sure why not. I told you I was serious about her."

"I'll kick your ass if you eloped. Don't tell me you—"

"We're not married." Dean laughed.

"Well, hell. I'm not sure if that's better or worse. My dad's not going to like it."

"We weren't asking his permission."

"Which will piss him off."

"Good thing he's in Texas." Dean laughed.

"Yeah, well, he's gonna be there later tonight to pick her up. Fair warning."

Dean stopped pacing. "What? Pick her up?" *No, no, no, no…* Gaylord sticking his nose in was a very bad idea.

"That's why I'm looking for her, Dean. There's been an accident."

The worry about Gaylord finding out about Savannah quickly vanished with Jack's words. "An accident, who? Is Jessie OK? Danny?"

"We're all fine. It's our mom. It doesn't look good, Dean."

Katie's relationship with her mother was almost nil, but he knew she still cared about the woman. "Is your mom gonna make it? What happened?"

"Long story. And we don't know. My dad and I are flying in at six tonight to pick Katie up and then we're headed to South Florida."

"Florida? I thought your mom was in Italy."

"We all thought that. Listen, I've got to go. Tell Katie we'll pick her up—"

"I'll have her at the airport, Jack. Keep the jet on the runway." The last thing Katie needed was more drama. Gaylord and Jack discovering Savannah was a pile of drama just waiting to happen.

Chapter Twenty-Four

Just when Katie thought her day couldn't get more emotional, she walked through the front door of Dean's home…no their home, and life took her for another ride.

"What kind of accident?" she asked when Dean greeted her at the door with the news.

"Jack didn't say. He tried calling you."

She'd noticed several missed calls from her brother but didn't think a lot about it since he hadn't left a message. Her mind was on how she was going to tell Dean about Savannah. Talking to her brother wasn't high on her priority list.

"It sounded serious, Katie. I asked Mrs. Hoyt to stay with Savannah so I can take you to the airport."

"Airport? Why?"

"Jack and your dad are coming to pick you up."

"Is she dying?" Panic spread through her veins. She didn't care for her mother, but she didn't want her dead.

Dean led her to the couch and sat her down. "Do you think they'd insist you go with them if she wasn't?"

"Oh, God." *Not now.* "She's too young to die."

"Do you want me to go with you?"

She gripped his hand. "Yes…but I need you here with Savannah. Will you stay here with her?"

"You don't even have to ask. Maybe we should all go."

Katie shook her head. "No. Not yet. This isn't the time to tell my family about her."

"I wish I disagreed, but if it's as bad as Jack let on, having Savannah there will only make things more complicated."

"Oh, Dean, why is all this happening now?"

He held her in his arms. "I don't know, darlin'. We're going to be OK."

She tried to pull up another emotion about her mother, other than frustration, but she couldn't. "She didn't even go to Jack's wedding."

"I know," Dean said.

"Why should we care if she's hurt?"

"It's what makes you a better person."

"What if I don't want to be the better person?" She knew she sounded like a child but her mother didn't deserve her sympathy.

"I'll support you if you don't want to go. You'll have to live with that decision forever if she dies, Katie."

She wanted to scream. "Mrs. Rock, meet Mr. Hard Place."

"C'mon. I'll help you pack." Dean helped her to her feet.

"I didn't think I'd be flying to Italy today."

Dean rested his arm on her shoulder. "You're not. She's in Florida."

"What?"

"That's what Jack said."

"What happened to Italy?"

"No idea."

The annual Christmas card was always postmarked from Italy. Maybe she was visiting someone.

In their bedroom, Katie removed several slacks and a few blouses. She had no idea how long she'd be. The thought of leaving Savannah for more than a few hours felt awful, but she couldn't avoid it. *At least it's not Italy.* Damn…Katie was leaving her child to be there for her mother. A mother who couldn't be bothered to be there for her.

She was never there.

Katie wanted to feel pain, but anger ruled instead.

Dean placed a suitcase on the bed and helped her shuffle clothes. "There's one more thing you might want to know before your family gets here," he said as he tucked her shoes into the bag.

Should I pack a black dress? Just in case? She grabbed one from a hanger really hoping it wasn't needed.

"What's that?"

"I told Jack you're living here."

She snapped her gaze to his.

"It couldn't be avoided, Katie. He called the hotel, Monica's…"

Dean's look of distress kept her from getting too upset. "I'm a grown woman. I don't need my brother's permission to move in with a man."

Dean walked around the bed and kissed her. "That's what I thought. Besides, it's one less secret to keep."

"Right."

They sat in silence as the plane taxied on the runway before takeoff.

She supposed they were all in a little shock. Dean had shaken hands with both her father and her brother before taking her in his arms and kissing her good-bye. Her family stood by in stunned fascination.

"Call me and I'll come…we'll come," he whispered in her ear.

Katie understood his meaning, kissed him again, and walked toward the plane.

"I guess we'll have to talk about all this when we get back," Jack said to Dean behind her.

"I guess you might need to know when something isn't your business and butt out," she called over her shoulder.

When they reached cruising altitude, Gaylord undid his seat belt and poured himself two fingers of whiskey, neat.

Her dad was a big man who had something to say about everything. His silence had always frightened her. So far he'd only greeted her and walked onto the plane.

"I'll take one of those," Jack said.

"Please tell me we have wine," Katie chimed in. Apparently, none of them wanted to do this without a little liquid courage.

Her father tilted back his glass, finished the drink in one swallow, and poured another one. He fixed one for Jack and opened a bottle of wine from the fully stocked wet bar for Katie.

"Thanks, Daddy."

He offered a forced smile and sat beside her on the leather sofa. "Does he make you happy?" he asked from nowhere.

It took her a minute to realize he was asking about Dean. "He does." *Keep it simple. Don't offer too much information.*

Gaylord sipped his second drink. "Good."

Jack wasn't so quick to applaud. "Really, Dad? That's it? You grilled me for an hour about Jessie before you met her."

"I didn't know Jessie. I know Dean. He's a good man. Hardworking. Hell of a lot better than some of the men your sister's dated."

"I think I should be offended," she teased.

"You should," Gaylord said.

She laughed. Despite the somber reason for the three of them to be on the plane together, she found herself smiling. "Oh, Daddy, I wasn't that bad."

"Yes, you were!" both her father and Jack said at the same time.

Now all three of them were chuckling.

"Dean even has you wearing proper clothes. I hope he burned those skintight jeans and barely there skirts."

She'd left those in the closet at the hotel. But she still loved her high heels.

"Is he gonna make an honest woman of you?" her father asked.

"No one says that anymore, Daddy."

"I do."

She smiled…not sure where she and Dean were going. "You'll be on the list of the first people who will know if that's what we decide."

"I guess that's all I can ask for then."

Katie leaned over and kissed his cheek. "Thanks for trusting me."

"Oh, honey, I've always trusted you. It's the guys I didn't trust."

She sipped her wine and thought of some of the untrustworthy men she'd brought into her life. "I was really bad, wasn't I?"

"Yes!"

"Yes."

Again, they sat there laughing. She couldn't imagine sitting back and letting Savannah make the mistakes she'd made. How had her father done that? With all his money, his power…how did he stand it? Perhaps in the near future she could ask him those very questions.

"So…Annette's in Florida," she finally said, broaching the subject they were all avoiding.

"Show some respect, baby girl. She's still your mother."

"She stopped being a mother too many years ago to count."

Gaylord scolded her with a look.

"OK, fine. So…*Mom's* in Florida."

His face softened and he shrugged. "So I'm told."

"What happened?"

"Car accident. She was driving…it was late. I didn't ask those details." Gaylord spoke in short sentences and stared into his glass.

"Who did you ask? Is she still with that Pierre guy?"

Her dad and Jack exchanged a look.

"What?"

"No. Pierre is long gone apparently," Jack said.

"She was living with him…in Italy, right?"

"Not for a while."

OK, now she was completely confused. "We get Christmas cards from Italy. I think there were a couple years there they came from France. She always talked about Pierre."

Jack shrugged.

Her dad sat unusually quiet.

"You guys know something I don't."

Jack stared at their father.

"What?"

Gaylord turned to her and released a sigh. "Pierre was her cat."

Her father could be speaking a different language and she'd understand him better. "Her what?"

"Her cat," Jack said again. "Mom's been living in Florida for years. There never was a man named Pierre. Or if there was, she ditched him and kept the cat."

"But the cards…"

"Came from overseas, I know. I got them, too, Katie. It was a lie. All of it. Annette's been in Florida most of the time she wasn't in our life."

"Doing what?" Outrage fueled her veins.

Jack hunched his shoulders. "Living, basking in the sun…cruising the Caribbean? How the hell can I know?"

Katie noticed her father studying the ice inside his glass. "Daddy?"

Gaylord stood and filled his glass a third time. "She," he cleared his throat. "She did live in Italy. Visited France. I sent the checks to Milan for a while."

"Sent checks?"

"She never remarried, Katie. I didn't fight alimony."

"She's been living off you all this time?"

Gaylord tilted his glass, spoke through the thick flavor of his drink. "It's only money."

"Money she didn't deserve." *How dare she!*

"She moved back to the States several years ago. Her cards to you children were nothing more than fabricated lies."

"Why? Why would we care if she lived here or across the sea? She couldn't be bothered with us either way."

Her dad moved about the cabin of the plane.

"Stop protecting her, Dad." Jack's voice rose, something he seldom did with their father. "You told me you'd talk to both of us together. Well, Katie and I are both here, so spill."

"She lived in Milan…right after. When the divorce was final, she spent a year in France. She was a dancer."

"A what?" Was her father smoking something? "Dancer?"

Gaylord watched the ice dancing in his glass. "She loved to dance. Hated it when she was pregnant because she couldn't move like she wanted to."

"What kind of mother thinks like that?"

"Ours did, apparently," Jack said. "OK, so she had some unrequited passion for dancing. Great. Moved to Italy, France…what happened?"

"Nothing. Exactly nothing. She blew through her divorce settlement, moved back here. It took a few years."

Katie watched a handful of emotions pass over her father's face. None of which she wanted to experience herself. Gaylord never spoke ill of their mother. Even after all the neglectful times he had to make excuses for her.

"So when she kept the letters coming from Italy, you didn't tell us…why?"

He shook his head. "Wasn't my place. I sent my checks and washed my hands of her. If either of you wanted to know more, you'd have gone and visited her. Neither of you asked to. I figured if you'd looked as adults, I'd have heard about it eventually…from you or one of the pilots."

Katie could only speak for herself when she said she'd lost any desire to know her mother years ago.

"So she's in Florida," Jack said.

"She's dying in Florida," Katie corrected.

"Maybe." Gaylord left his empty glass on a counter and walked to the window. They were moving away from the setting sun, which appeared to be hitting the horizon at warp speed.

"And we're going why?" Because Katie was starting to think this whole trip was a bad idea.

Katie heard Dean's words coming from her father. "Because if Annette is dying, you should see her one last time. Make peace with her."

"She doesn't deserve our forgiveness."

"Katie!"

"No, Daddy. Being a parent is more than having a kid. It's the day to day stuff...the crying, the cleaning, the laughing... it's everything and she was never there. She chose a different life. Somewhere, somehow, she should have been straight with us and cut us free. But no. She was selfish and kept us on a Christmas card leash full of lies."

"Don't you think I know that?" Gaylord yelled. "I'm not asking you to visit her because *she* deserves it." He lowered his voice and Katie saw emotion clog his eyes. "I'm asking you to go so, if and when she dies, you have *no* regrets! None. You have one mother. I never replaced her...God knows I'm sorry for that now, but she's it. If you go, see her, and walk out of the room that's up to you. But damn it, I *will* give you the opportunity to say good-bye."

Underneath all her father's anger was a layer of pain Katie hadn't noticed in years.

Katie glanced at Jack and saw her own anguish staring back at her.

She sucked in her lower lip and realized how hard her father had worked to keep her and Jack from any pain her mother caused.

She unfolded slowly from the couch, placed her wine on a table, and embraced her father.

His large capable hands circled her and held her close. "I love you, Daddy."

"I love you, too, baby girl."

Dean received a text when Katie landed in Florida.

Made it. The nurses in ICU said we could come anytime.

Dean texted back: *Are you going to the hotel first?*

Probably. Dad's on the phone with hospital now.

Good. Better to see her with a clear head. How R U holding up?

Dean waited for her reply while propping a bottle to Savannah's lips.

I'm OK. Lots to tell you.

Call anytime, he told her. And because he knew she could use a smile, he took a quick picture of Savannah drinking her bottle and sent it to her. *Savannah says hi.*

Give her a big kiss for me. I miss you both.

Dean smiled, leaned over, and kissed Savannah as instructed. "That's from your mommy."

Kiss delivered.

I have so much to tell you. I can't do it over the phone.

Dean punched in his reply with one finger. *I'm not going anywhere. Take care of you!*

Talk in the morning.

He stared at the phone for a while, wishing he could offer more support. He tried to remember that Katie had Jack and her father at her side. Dean liked to think he knew Katie better than her family… the adult Katie anyway. She'd be facing a mother who had ignored her most of her life and that wasn't going to be easy.

Dean removed the empty bottle from Savannah's mouth, was rewarded with a nice wet mess when he set her on his shoulder for a burp. He laughed at himself for forgetting the burp cloth and settled Savannah back in his arms while she fell asleep.

"Your other mommy might have given you up," he whispered, "but your real mommy will always be there."

Katie's entire life was filled with motherly drama. Her own mother might be dying, a new infant to adjust to…wondering who Savannah's biological mom was. The worry about all of it.

His phone buzzed on the table alerting him to a text.

It was his brother-in-law with a group message that looked to have gone out to all the Prescotts.

It's a girl.

Syrie and baby Lilly are doing fine.

As the squished-up face of his new niece surfaced on the phone, Dean's smile spread.

Lilly was beautiful. Just like her mother.

Dean glanced at the sleeping bundle in his arms and back at the screen.

Both girls had the same nose.

Chapter Twenty-Five

Dean's head was swimming with too many concerns to go to work.

Katie had called and woken him just after five in the morning. They were all on their way to the hospital. She promised to call when she could.

Their conversation was kept short. Dean offered a play-by-play of his time with Savannah since Katie left. He could tell she was already missing her.

Dean spent the morning playing dad and called his mother to see how his sister was doing. They all still lived in Texas. At times like this, he would have liked to be closer. Visiting his brand-new niece would have to wait. At least for a little while.

The image of his niece and Savannah were stacked back-to-back on his cell phone. He flipped between the pictures so many times since the night before he should have worn out the function on his phone.

But no…the pictures kept coming up.

And the questions he'd started asking himself weeks ago doubled.

He was probably stabbing in the dark, but he had to know.

Dean wasn't much for doctors, but he called his and asked to come in. A few clicks on the Internet provided him with enough information to know that finding out if he was Savannah's father could be confirmed within a day.

Dean sat in the reception area of the doctor's office with Savannah kicking away in the car seat. There was plenty of admiration from those around him.

"Oh, isn't she precious."

"Your daughter is beautiful. I'll bet her mommy is, too."

Dean accepted their compliments and kept his distance from those with obvious colds.

A nurse called him back and placed him in a room. With his chart in her hand, the nurse asked why he was in today.

"It's kind of private. I'd like to keep it between the doctor and me."

"Everything you do here is confidential, Mr. Prescott. But I'll send in Dr. Ellis and await his instructions."

"Thank you."

Dean avoided sitting on the exam table and took the chair.

Savannah started to protest after being in the car seat for a half an hour. She wasn't due to eat, but being cooped up probably wasn't pleasant either.

The handle to the door twisted and Dr. Ellis slipped into the room.

"Hello, Dean."

"Doctor."

Dr. Ellis closed the door behind him and peeked into the car carrier. "And who is this?"

"Savannah."

"She's adorable."

"Ah, thank you." Dean squirmed in his seat, feeling all kinds of awful for doing this without Katie knowing. He told himself she couldn't handle the additional stress. And if he could take one more question about Savannah off her plate, he'd do it.

"My nurse tells me you're here for a private reason. I take it you don't need another tetanus shot."

Dean gave a grunt of a laugh. "No, I'm good there for another five years I think."

"OK. Then what can I do for you?"

Savannah let out a cry that threatened to escalate. Dean found the clasp holding the pacifier and popped it into her mouth.

"It's about Savannah. I need to know if she's mine."

Dr. Ellis's gaze moved to the baby and back to Dean. "The mother says she is?"

"It's complicated."

The doctor leaned over Savannah and made a cooing sound before tapping on her nose. "She has your nose."

Dean stiffened. "Yeah…I noticed that. But I need to be sure. And I'd like a rush on the lab work…if that's possible."

"Not a problem, Dean."

Dr. Ellis removed two sterile swabs and proceeded to take a saliva sample off the inside of Dean's cheek before doing the same on Savannah. Savannah sucked on the swab, squished her nose, then tried to spit it out.

"Not what you're used to, is it?" Dr. Ellis teased.

After placing the swabs in vials and marking on the labels, he turned to Dean again. "I should have the results tomorrow afternoon, the next morning at the latest."

Dean handed him his business card and circled his cell phone number. "Call me on this number."

"I won't leave a message," he said. "I'll wait until you pick up. If it's easier, you can call here. I have a busy afternoon tomorrow."

Dean stood and shook the doctor's hand.

"Paternity tests can be emotional things, Dean. Are you prepared for whatever answers we're going to find?"

Dean lifted the car seat and smiled at Savannah. "I'm taking care of this little girl regardless of what the tests say." That he knew without a doubt.

"And the mother?"

The images of Katie and Maggie popped in his mind. "My feelings for Savannah's mother aren't going to change. I'm in this for the long haul, Doctor. For my own peace of mind, I need to know all the facts."

Dr. Ellis patted him on his back. "I'll talk to you tomorrow. I hope it all works out the way you want it," he said.

A lack of sleep and the stress of seeing her mother for the first time in nearly a decade were thicker than the wet heat of a Florida summer.

The mechanical doors of the hospital opened automatically letting the three of them in. Katie kept her dark sunglasses on when they walked through the lobby. Both her father and her brother removed their cowboy hats in a sign of respect.

The volunteer at the visitor desk directed them to the ICU after taking down all three of their names. As it often was when the three of them were together, they walked through the hospital and people parted from their path as if they were water and the other people were grains of sand. It wasn't that they were pushy, it was more like an energy other people could feel but couldn't see. Katie had noticed the phenomenon by the time she was nine. Her friends would tell her it was because her daddy was rich. She disagreed. There was something much more primal influencing the wide berth people made around them. Something organic that wolves in a pack understood and people didn't.

Instead of concentrating on the coming task, Katie noticed the people parting to let them through and drew in the scents surrounding her. The sterile smell of the hospital walls, part antiseptic, part floor cleaner, met with the unique scent of despair.

"Hospitals always smell so…"

"Awful," her brother finished her sentence.

"Yeah."

He offered a grin, grasped her arm, and linked it through his.

This is just as hard on him as it is me. She was more thankful for her brother in that moment than she'd been in a while.

One day I'm going to have to adopt a brother or sister for Savannah. Just thinking about her daughter helped dispel the sour mood she'd woken up with.

They rode the elevator to the fifth floor in silence.

A large waiting room sat outside a set of locked doors leading into the ICU. Several families gathered in the space, some with pillows cradling their heads. A television added background to the noise of the room.

"Mr. Morrison?" The man who approached them wore a suit and tie and stood a good two inches shorter than Katie. The man was dwarfed by her father yet he lifted his head and offered his hand in greeting. "I'm Dennis Nemo, the nursing director you spoke with last night."

"Yes, thank you for meeting us."

"Not a problem."

Gaylord turned toward them, offering an introduction. "These are Annette's children, Jack and Katelyn."

Dennis nodded to both of them before returning his attention to her father. "There's been a few changes since we talked last night." Dennis opened the doors with a swipe of his ID badge.

He led them not into her mother's room, but to a smaller waiting room where he asked them to wait. Dennis left the room and said he'd be right back.

"What's going on?" Jack asked.

Gaylord shook his head. "I don't know."

Katie managed to sit, but she perched on the edge of her chair and jumped when a young woman in scrubs walked into the room beside Dennis.

"This is Valerie. She's the nurse taking care of your wife."

Katie's gaze snapped to her father.

"We're divorced," he corrected Dennis's mistake.

"Right, you told me that. Sorry. In any case, Valerie was here yesterday when Annette came in and has been here for a couple hours this morning."

Valerie smiled at all of them and encouraged them to sit.

Dennis sat beside her and let her talk. The minute she opened her mouth Katie was reminded of Monica.

Valerie was warm, caring, and had a spark behind her eye that told Katie that she loved her job.

"It would help if I knew what you've been told," Valerie started.

Gaylord repeated what he'd told them the night before. "There was a car accident. I was told she didn't have a seat belt on and she ended up on the street."

Valerie nodded. "Right."

Katie placed a hand on her father's arm as he continued. "The doctor said she had to have surgery right away to stop internal bleeding. Something about a collapsed lung. She was conscious last night...asking to see the kids."

Hearing her father say that a second time set Katie back.

I don't care.

Yet even as Katie heard her own words mumbled inside her head, she knew they were full of shit.

"When I left last night, she was groggy from surgery and heavily medicated for pain. She asked for you...all of you. I told her you were coming and she seemed to calm down. Well, later last night she had a setback. The night nurse report said that at three o'clock she started to drop her oxygen saturation. The X-rays indicated a fluid buildup in her good lung. We had no choice but to intubate her."

"What does all that mean?" Jack asked.

"We placed a tube into her lungs to help her breathe." Valerie paused and looked at each of them. "She's on a ventilator."

"A breathing machine?"

"Yes. But since we put her on it, her vital signs have been stable. I know it sounds bad, and I'm not suggesting her condition isn't critical, but right now she's as stable as she can be in the ICU."

Having spent nearly two months living with a critical care trauma nurse, Katie asked what Monica told her to. "Valerie. How long have you been a nurse?"

"Ten years."

"How is she?"

Valerie looked at Dennis then back at her. "Like I said, she is as stable as—"

"No." Katie took off her glasses and met Valerie's eyes. "One of my best friends works the ER. She told me to ask you what *your* gut says."

Valerie rubbed her hands on her pants and sat forward. "Your mom's fighting right now. I'm hopeful."

Katie drew in a deep breath and looked at her dad and her brother. "Can we see her?"

"Of course."

Valerie stood and the rest of them followed.

The short walk through the department felt like a mile. Every doorway they passed held another patient. All of them were lying in hospital beds surrounded by machines. A series of *beeps* and *dings* was a constant reminder that lives hung in the balance. Nurses and doctors walked around them, nearly ignoring them. The professionals in this department couldn't be influenced by their position, their wealth, the Morrison name. They didn't part the way like those outside the ICU doors. This was a place where any and all of them could end up and it seemed everyone here knew that.

Valerie paused outside a door and turned to the three of them. "There is a machine helping her breathe, lots of tubes going into her, coming out of her. She's pretty bruised up with a cut on her forehead."

Why was it the closer she came to seeing her mother the worse she felt? On the plane on the way to Florida, Katie couldn't have cared less, or so she kept telling herself. Now, standing outside a room that only emitted the sound of equipment, Katie felt her throat clog and her eyes start to fill. She reached for the emotionless state she'd managed for years when she thought of her mother and couldn't find it.

Valerie walked into the room and opened the curtain.

Annette lay still on the bed. The ventilator made a hissing noise with each breath she made. A tube protruded from her throat at an awkward angle.

"Damn," her father muttered under his breath.

"Oh, shit," Jack whispered.

"Hey, Annette. Your family is here." Valerie walked into the room as if Annette were awake.

Annette didn't twitch, didn't blink. The only indication that she was alive was the consistent beep of the machine monitoring her heart rate and the hum of another that worked for her damaged lungs.

Katie's eyes swelled and tears started silently falling.

The three of them sat around the room and watched the slow rise and fall of Annette's chest.

Hours later, Katie stood outside the hospital with her cell phone cradled to her ear.

"I hate feeling like this, Monica."

"Yeah…I know. It's hard. My mom makes me crazy as hell but I wouldn't handle her being jacked up and in the ICU either."

It felt good talking to Monica. She answered questions that only she could.

Her mother was critically stable…whatever the hell that was supposed to mean. According to Monica, it meant she had a snowball's chance but every hour and day made the snowball bigger and the temperature in hell drop. She had a chance.

"She's so small. I remember her being so much larger."

"She's older," Monica reminded her. "And you were a kid the last time you saw her."

"She's so helpless."

"What did the doctor say?"

"Broken ribs…messed up lungs, spleen ruptured. I don't know… bunch of crap I didn't understand." Katie waved her hand in front of her face to find some relief from the heat.

"What about the nurse, what did she say?"

"She's hopeful."

Monica paused. "Good. Your mom has a chance, then."

"Really? I mean…that's good. God, I shouldn't care." Katie hated that she did.

"Yeah…but you do. It's OK. I'd probably feel exactly like you if something happened to my dad and I knew about it. Hell, I don't even know if he's alive or dead."

"That might be better."

"I don't know, Katie. Listen, I'd be happy to talk to the nurse, get a grip on what's going on, if you want."

"Would you?" Not that Katie thought Valerie was keeping anything from her, but it would be nice hearing something from someone who knew more than she did.

"You'll have to tell the nurse she can talk to me. All those HIPAA laws keep lips sealed in hospitals."

"OK. I'll let her know you'll call."

Katie gave Monica the number to the ICU and hung up.

She placed a call to Dean but it ended up on voice mail. She lied and told him she was fine and that she'd call him later.

Later didn't come for several hours.

Chapter Twenty-Six

Considering the fact that Katie had no desire to see her mother a week ago, she was disturbed by her desire to stay close to the hospital now. Her internal debate as to why fought inside her mind when she walked down the now familiar path to the ICU from the hospital cafeteria.

The nurses weren't strict with the visiting hour rules. Some families were forced to stay out of a patient's room so the nurses could work. Since Annette was in a medically induced coma, there was no need to make any of the Morrisons stay away.

Jack and Gaylord had left the hospital about an hour before to grab a bite to eat.

Valerie walked into the room with an IV bag in her hand. "How are you holding up?" she asked.

Katie glanced at her mother from across the room and shrugged. "We weren't close."

Valerie went about her task. "Your friend Monica told me that."

Monica had been great. She explained things in a way that made sense. She kept her explanations free of a bunch of medical terms that no one but those who worked in a hospital understood, and got down to the facts.

"I'm sure it's still hard seeing your mother like this."

Katie sipped her cooling coffee. "I haven't seen her like anything in a very long time."

"Hey, Valerie?" one of the other nurses called from the desk adjacent from the room.

"Yeah?"

"Mrs. Morrison has another visitor."

"No problem." Valerie stepped out of the room and Katie waited for her brother and father's return.

A petite woman walked to the door of the room and gasped when she looked at the bed. "Oh, Annie."

Katie waited for the woman to realize she was there before she said anything. The visitor's tearful gaze found hers and she gasped a second time.

"Oh, my, you must be Katelyn."

"You have me at a disadvantage," Katie said.

"I'm Tina, a friend of your…of Annie's." The woman's hesitation in calling Annie her mother didn't go unnoticed.

"I didn't know she went by Annie," Katie said, making conversation with the stranger.

The woman moved farther into the room and placed a hand on the side of the bed. "She hates Annette. Says it makes her feel old."

Tina pulled a chair closer to the bed and stroked her mother's hand. "You're not looking too young right now, are you, Annie?" she whispered, obviously upset.

Seeing someone holding her mother's hand and talking softly reminded Katie of just how removed she was from her mother. "You've known her for a while?" Katie asked, hoping the woman would paint some kind of picture of the person her mother was.

"At least five years now. We met at the club."

"The club?"

"A health club. Well, you know, a place for a little exercise and plenty of play."

OK, so her mother wasn't completely without funds.

"I'm sorry to say this, but I'm surprised to see you here."

"Annette still has my father on an emergency contact list."

Tina opened her mouth, closed it. "Oh."

If Tina was shocked to see her, perhaps she shouldn't be here.

"Maybe I should go," Katie said suddenly feeling out of place.

"No. Please, I'm sorry I said that. I'm sure Annie would want to see you when she wakes up."

"Really? I'm not so sure. She's not tried to see me in years."

Tina shook her head. "She saw you every time your picture ended up in a paper."

Great, so her mother followed the tabloid crap. "Not the same."

"No. I'm sure it's not."

Katie's gaze skirted to her mother and then out the window. "She told my brother and me that she was living in Europe. Sent Christmas cards from there. Do you have any idea why she did that?"

"No. I thought perhaps all of you had a falling out. I knew about you and Jack…it is Jack, right?"

"Yes."

"But she didn't elaborate as to why she had little to do with you."

"Nothing! She's had *nothing* to do with us. My brother was married two months ago. She sent a gift and a card." Reminding herself of her mother's behavior brought back the anger she'd felt on the plane. The room started feeling a little smaller and the desire for fresh air became a need.

"She's not a bad person, Katelyn. She might have been a terrible mother, but not everyone is built to nurture others."

"Then why have us in the first place?"

Tina offered a sympathetic smile. "You'll have to ask her that."

Katie stood and grasped the handle of her purse. "Not an option right now, is it?" She knew her anger was misguided toward the woman in the room, but it didn't stop her from snapping. Katie hated that this stranger, this woman who had a good ten years on her mother, knew more about Annette than she did.

It pissed her off that her mother waited until something awful happened to remember she had children.

"I should go," Tina said.

"No. I'm going. Please ask the nurse to call me if anything changes."

Katie left the room and the unit in a rush.

Built to nurture others!

Could it be that simple? Could it be that Annette, no Annie, just didn't want to be a mom?

The suffocating heat hit her as she exited the hospital and started walking.

She found a coffeehouse, ordered an iced tea, and dialed Dean. She was never so thankful to have him pick up.

"Hey, darlin'," his voice was low, concern for her poured through the phone.

"I need you to talk me down," she told him.

"Oh, no…what happened?"

She relayed the short conversation with Tina and did her best to explain how torn she was about the entire ordeal. "If it wasn't for Jack and my dad, I'd get the hell out of here right now. *Built to nurture others!* Can you believe she said that? Thinks that?"

"What bothers you more, Katie, the fact she said it or that you already knew it to be true?"

"Both! It's just so infuriating, Dean."

"I know, darlin'. Do you want me to fly out?"

"No. I'm all right. The nurse said they were going to take her off the ventilator and wake her up slowly tomorrow morning. Then maybe she can tell me herself that she could give a shit about us and I can leave."

Dean cleared his throat. "Do me a favor, Katie. Don't let her have the power to make you this upset."

Katie watched a woman walk by pushing a stroller and drew in a deep breath. "I'm trying. I was doing great until Tina showed up. Let's talk about something else. How's Savannah?"

"She's a pooping machine, this little girl."

Katie smiled, finding her happy place. "Keeping you busy with diapers I take it?"

"Oh, yeah. She loves being naked."

She laughed. "We're going to have to work that out of her."

"We'll have a few years to worry about that."

We? She liked the sound of that. With all the high drama she'd nearly forgotten about her recent conversation with Patrick. Maybe Maggie wasn't a nurturing mother either?

Maybe Maggie would have ended up abandoning Savannah later in life and screwing her up in the process.

Then Dean would have been a single father…like hers.

"She's easy to love, isn't she?"

"You can say that again."

Her phone beeped in her ear. She pulled it away and noticed her brother's number. "Looks like Jack is looking for me. I didn't tell anyone I was leaving the hospital."

"All right, darlin'. Everything's good here. Call when you get a minute."

"Thanks again, Dean."

The doctor didn't call with the test results until the morning after Dean thought he'd have his answers.

When he answered the call, his hand actually shook.

"Mr. Prescott?" The voice on the line was a woman.

"That's me," he said.

"Dr. Ellis would like to speak with you. Can you hold for him?"

"Sure." Dean was in his office, hoping that when he got this call he'd be able to continue with his day regardless of the answer. If he wasn't a father, then he would act as if nothing had changed. When in fact, nothing had…but if the answer was yes…well, he'd work through the shock instead of staring at Savannah all day.

"Dean?"

"Dr. Ellis."

"I have your test results. Is this a good time?"

Dean huffed. "As good as any."

"Congratulations, Daddy. Your DNA was a perfect match to Savannah's." Dr. Ellis went on to say something about the accuracy of the tests used today and how Dean had nothing to worry about.

"Are you there, Dean?"

His skin tingled and he felt surprisingly light-headed. "I'm here. I'm sorry. Thank you."

"Best of luck, Dean. Let me know if there's anything else I can do for you."

"You've done plenty, Doctor. Thank you."

He stared at an invoice on his desk for twenty minutes.

I'm a dad.

He thought of Katie, of her holding Savannah and smiling at him.

I'm a dad.

He opened the picture function on his phone and brought up Savannah's picture. So beautiful.

I'm a dad.

Being Savannah's father answered one very important question he and Katie had been asking for weeks.

Maggie's her mother.

Dean turned off his computer and left his office. "I've got to go," he told Jo.

"Is Katelyn OK?" she asked, concerned.

Hesitating, he tried to smile. "She's doing OK. But, uh, I have something I need to do. I'll be out of reach—fire, flood—"

"Or surprise inspection," she finished his sentence for him. When he couldn't be disturbed he'd always said that only a fire, flood, or surprise inspection should interrupt him. "I know the drill, Dean. You all right?"

The shock must have shown on his face. "Yeah. Hold it all down, Jo."

"I do that every day, boss."

Yeah…and today he was damn thankful for her skills.

He drove around the block where Maggie had lived when they were engaged. The condominium complex wasn't secured so he drove into the parking lot and found a visitor spot.

He sat in the car with the engine running, trying to figure out what he was going to say.

He'd driven over without thinking. Why hadn't she told him she was pregnant? Why did she give Savannah up? What the hell was she up to? Was she coming back to get Savannah one day, to hurt him for not fighting to keep Maggie in his life?

Memories of their breakup surfaced. He hadn't thought much about her in a long time. The fact that he'd pushed her out of his mind so quickly, so completely, proved to him they weren't right for each other.

"I can't do it," she'd said less than a week before their wedding.

"Can't do what?"

She'd asked for them to have a quiet lunch at one of "their" restaurants. She would meet him there.

He knew afterward why she didn't want them in the same car.

She removed the ring he'd placed on her finger six months before.

He'd asked her to marry him after only a few months of dating. They had been in a club with some friends, they'd both been drinking. "I'm tired of the dating scene," he'd told her. "Let's get married."

In hindsight, he hardly knew her. She quickly accepted and they both fell into the thought of being married. The closer to the wedding, the more he told everyone how perfect she was.

Then little things started to bug her. *Motorcycles are dangerous.* He hardly drove the one he owned as it was. She wanted it gone.

Are you going camping with your friends again? He and Mikey managed two trips…maybe three a year tops.

The blow to his ego kept him quiet while she told him they weren't right for each other. "You're not ready to get married," she had said. "Not to me anyway. You're not in love with me."

He wanted to counter her…but he couldn't.

He didn't.

He left the café with his ring and drove to a resort town in the San Bernardino Mountains. He parked his motorcycle and found the nearest bar. Jack and Mike found him and helped him drink to forget. Then they helped him sober up and kicked his ass back to work.

In the days and weeks that followed, he was thankful Maggie had called it all off.

She was right. He wasn't ready to marry her…he didn't love her.

But God damn it, he didn't know she was pregnant with his child. He would never have let her walk away had he known. He took care of his responsibilities and Savannah now topped the list.

Anger started to build in his blood. If he confronted Maggie now, who knows what he'd do.

With his truck still running, he pulled out of the parking space and decided to go home first. He needed a level head before this conversation.

Chapter Twenty-Seven

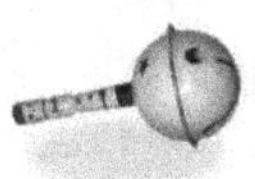

The doctors extubated her mother before the three of them arrived at the hospital the next day. A new nurse walked them into her room and explained that she was groggy but coherent.

"Has she asked about us?" Jack asked.

"She asked about what happened. She doesn't remember the accident. Which is probably a blessing."

"Which means she hasn't asked about us." Katie paused outside of the nurse's station. Jack and her father stopped along with her.

"You don't have to go in there," her father said.

"No. I'm not a child."

Less medical equipment filled the room and instead of looking half-dead, Annette looked like she was sleeping.

"Annie?" the nurse called as they all breached the doorway.

Her mother responded by slowly opening her eyes. It took a few blinks before she focused on the three of them.

"Your family is here."

"Hello, Annette," Gaylord said.

The monitor above the bed beeped a little faster. Katie had watched the monitor for hours the day before and knew her mother's heart rate was speeding up with their presence.

The nurse pressed a button and glanced at them. "This will have to be a short visit. Annie needs to rest."

"We won't be long," Jack told her.

"Th-they told me you were here," Annette's scratchy voice stuttered her words.

"The hospital called the night of the accident. They said you were asking for the kids."

Katie and Jack stood back and let their father do the talking. It seemed the two of them were paralyzed.

"I thought I was dying, Gaylord." Even with her hoarse words, Katie could tell her mother had little to say to her father.

"The doctors say you're doing better," Katie found her voice.

Annette moved her gaze to Katie. "I heard. Guess this life isn't done with me."

No, Katie wouldn't need that black dress quite yet.

"Why did you call for us, Mom?" Jack asked with thinly veiled anger in his voice. Now that they all knew she wasn't dying, it was easier to return to the emotion they'd all identified with the woman in the bed.

Annette turned her head away from them, stared out the window. "If I had died, I didn't want you to think I've never thought of you." Her delivery of why she called was as cold as the woman on the bed.

"Do you think of us?" Jack asked, his jaw tight.

"I do."

"You waited until now to tell us?"

Katie placed a hand on her brother's arm, hoping to calm him.

"When your life flashes in front of you, like clips from a movie, you pick out things. I'm a terrible mother. I was an even worse wife." Annette lifted her eyes to their father.

None of them corrected her.

"That's not an excuse," Jack said.

"I'm not making excuses, Jack. I know you think I walked away and never looked back, but that isn't completely true. I knew your father was the better parent. That I was a failure. You both were better off with him than me. We both knew that."

"So you gave us up," Katie mumbled. She thought of Savannah. A poor innocent child who may have a biological mother just like Annette.

"I thought about coming back. To get to know you both. I figured that time had passed. I didn't deserve a second chance."

Annette blinked a few times; the medication she was on could be seen in her face. She looked worn out and used. Katie couldn't tell if her cool demeanor was a defense or the real her.

Some of the anger burned off. Her dad's words from their trip sounded in her head. Her being here…all of them being here was so that they didn't have regrets. So she could say good-bye.

"Tina stopped by yesterday."

Annette glanced up. "That's nice."

Katie took a deep breath. "She told me you weren't an awful person. And I know Daddy isn't a bad judge of character so there has to be someone in there that I might want to know someday."

Her mother blinked several times as if deciphering Katie's words.

She stepped closer to the bed and tilted her head. "You closed the door on being our mother a long time ago. I don't know if that door will ever be opened again. But for some reason you thought of us, you called for us. When you're better, if you want to pick up that phone, I'll answer it. I'm sure we'll fight. I'm positive I'll call you all kinds of names for leaving me." Tears collected behind her eyes as she ripped her heart out of her chest. "Maybe on the other side of all that, we can be friends. Or maybe we can't. The only way you're going to know is if you try. If you don't want to, that's fine with me. But, Annie…if the very next time you call me is to say you're on your deathbed, I won't come. I'm too old for mind games and I won't be used."

Her mother nodded slowly.

Katie felt her brother's arm move around her shoulders as he led her out of the room.

Their father stayed behind a minute longer.

"Damn, sis, remind me never to get on your bad side," Jack teased.

"Was I awful?" *Did I go too far?*

"You were perfect. She knows where you stand, and you're giving her a chance. At the same time, you're not going to let her lie or use you. Wish I thought to say all that."

Katie leaned her head against her brother's shoulder and sighed. She was done with hiding parents, lies, and secrets.

Their dad met them in the lobby. He walked a little taller when he approached. Katie hugged her dad, thankful again she had him.

"I'll never make you come again," he told her.

"Do you think she'll call?" Jack asked their dad.

"I don't think she knows what she'll do. Are you going to be OK if she doesn't?"

Katie dug deep inside to find his answers. "I'm going to be fine."

Her dad winked at her.

They climbed into the back of the limousine they'd traveled in from the hotel to the hospital.

Her phone buzzed in her pocket and she noticed a text from Dean. A new picture of Savannah greeted her and the cold brought on by her mother melted into a puddle of warm love.

"Must be good," her brother commented.

"The best," she said.

I'm done with the lies.

She handed the phone to her brother and confusion marred his brow. "Hi, Mommy?" he read the text aloud.

Jack handed the phone to her dad.

"Who's *Mommy*?"

"I am. That's my daughter."

Jack's and Gaylord's mouths dropped.

Dean swallowed his guilt as he pressed Send on the picture of Savannah.

He intended to confront Maggie today, now that his thoughts were in some semblance of order. Seeing Maggie without Katie knowing about it felt wrong. Yet he couldn't exactly tell Katie what he'd learned…not over the phone. Besides, she had a full day of drama ahead and didn't needed more piled on.

After retracing his steps to Maggie's condo, Dean knocked on the door and waited.

A woman in her sixties answered the door. "I'm looking for Maggie Reynolds," he told her.

The woman offered a kind smile. "There's no Maggie here. I moved in six months ago."

"Oh, sorry to bother you." Dean left the complex and switched on his phone. He'd deleted her number from his phone and sadly couldn't bring it up in his memory.

He sat in his car for a while flipping around the Internet with his smartphone. He came across an old e-mail out of a sent file and found her cell number.

He dialed it and was met with a *No longer in service* message.

"Well, damn." *Guess she didn't want to be found.*

Dean called up the investigator he'd hired to find Savannah's mother and brought him up to date on the facts.

"I need to know where she is and I need to know yesterday. Katelyn should be back tomorrow and I want to have this conversation with Maggie finished."

"I'm on it, Mr. Prescott."

Unable to go home to wait, Dean drove around town to see if any of Maggie's friends knew where she'd gone.

It was midweek and early in the day so the nightclubs they'd gone to a couple of times either weren't open or didn't have a familiar face in the room.

Maggie's parents had both passed away when she was very young. He remembered her aunt lived north of LA, but he didn't know the exact address. A phone number was out of the question. Hopefully Nathan, his PI, would find the information. And find it soon.

The day ran on with a silent phone. When it did ring, Katie was on the other end, her voice tight with emotion.

"It was awful, but I'm done. It's up to her now," Katie told him after she relayed everything about her conversation with her mom.

"I'm proud of you, darlin'. That couldn't have been easy."

"It wasn't. But you know something? This whole ordeal reminded me how lucky I am to have my brother and my dad on my side. They've been great."

"I've always thought of your dad as a linebacker that would tackle anyone who even tried to hurt you."

Katie giggled. "Yeah...he would. Listen, I—I, ah, told them... about Savannah."

"You what?" His grip tightened on the phone.

"I couldn't keep lying to them. All this drama with my own mother made me realize that there are women out there that can't be a mom. Emotionally. Maybe Savannah's mom couldn't handle it."

Dean thought of Maggie and couldn't rule that reason out. They'd talked about kids, having them someday, but nothing stood out as a sign that Maggie wasn't mother material. Come to think of it, she always brushed off the *kid* conversation. He'd told her about Katie. About their child. Those conversations were short, however. Dean thought their limited conversations on the subject were because they included Katie. Talking with his fiancée about his ex had been met with hostility. He didn't blame Maggie for that.

Now that Maggie was part of his past, Dean could see that he'd always loved Katie. Maggie must have sensed that.

"Dean? You there?"

"Yeah, I'm here. How did they take the news?" The last thing Dean needed was the Morrison men digging too deep in Savannah's parentage…not yet. Not yet.

"They were shocked. My dad thinks someone is gunning for money."

Dean hadn't ruled that out either. If Maggie wanted money, why hadn't she gone to him? Sure, his pockets didn't run as deep as Gaylord's but he wasn't without means. Millions of them.

"What about Jack?"

"Jack got stuck on the fact that I can't have kids. I didn't know my brother was such a softy. He was excited about Savannah though, and can't wait to tell Jessie."

"Do you think your dad will launch his own investigation?"

"I—I told him to wait. I…I…" Her voice trailed off. "I can't wait to get home."

"Me, too." He glanced at his watch.

"We were going to leave tonight, but there's a tropical storm cutting down air traffic. The pilot said we could leave in the morning so long as the bulk of the storm passes overnight without a ton of damage."

"That's probably better anyway…in case something changes with your mom."

"They moved her out of the ICU shortly after we left. I think she'll physically be fine. I insisted that we stop in Texas tomorrow and drop off my brother and dad. They both wanted to come and see Savannah, talk to you."

Dean laughed despite the nerves fraying the edge of his psyche. "I didn't think your family would let me off with a *We'll talk about this later* warning."

"Just leave them to me. After I told my mom off, the two of them aren't so quick to jump on me."

"It's not you they'll be jumping on." Not that he was worried. His intentions when it came to Katie had always been honorable.

Only now he had a new dilemma…he had the mother of his child to deal with.

He gave up on his search for Maggie and drove home. After relieving Mrs. Hoyt and making sure she could return the next day, Dean spent a little time in his office before Savannah woke from her late nap.

A message greeted him from Nathan. "I found Maggie's aunt living in the Valley. Like you said. Looks like Maggie was living with her before she had the baby. I have a new address. Call me."

Chapter Twenty-Eight

Dean approached the door to the bungalow style home and hesitated before he knocked.

He rapped three times and stood back. Maggie's car was in the drive but the house was quiet. He hoped she was home. He didn't want to have to come back later.

He knocked again and heard footsteps.

Maggie opened the door with a rush, the smile on her face quickly faded when she recognized him. Her hair was swept up into a ponytail, her face free of any makeup. She looked younger than he remembered. He'd forgotten that she was six years younger than him. Just out of college when they'd met.

"Hi, Maggie," he said. Trying his level best to keep his voice even.

"Dean."

She looked beyond him, searching for Savannah maybe…or Katie?

"I'm here alone," he told her. "Savannah's with a sitter."

Her attention shot to his and her shoulders sagged. Without words, she opened the door farther, walked into the house, away from him.

He followed her inside and closed the door behind him. His heart beat so rapidly he found himself breathing hard.

She stood with her back to him, her hands poised on the edge of the kitchen sink while she looked out a window.

Dean waited for her to say something. He didn't trust himself and had learned long ago that silence often worked better than words when trying to get someone to open up.

"So…you and Katelyn are back together." *Was that hurt in her voice?*

Instead of answering her question, he asked his own. "Why, Maggie?"

She took a deep breath and still had yet to turn around. "Do you know how much you talked about her when you were with me?" she asked.

Dean flinched.

"You tried to hide your feelings for her. I convinced myself that it was natural for you to slip once in a while and call me her name."

"Twice. That happened twice." And they'd only been dating a few weeks when he slipped. Maggie had laughed it off and told him it wasn't a big deal.

She twisted around, met his eyes. "You talk in your sleep, Dean. I told myself that you weren't responsible for your dreams. Reminded myself that it was me wearing your ring. But it wasn't me you loved. It was her."

Dean's teeth clenched together. He couldn't deny his feelings and didn't see a need to shelter Maggie from the truth now.

"I cared about you."

"But you loved her."

"You had my baby."

She blinked a few times.

"I would have stuck by you," he said softly. He wasn't raised to walk away from his responsibilities.

"And I would have hated you for it. Having a child isn't a reason to get married."

"I'd already asked you to marry me." He ran a frustrated hand through his hair.

"To what end, Dean? You may have been ready to get married, but you weren't ready to be a father."

"The hell I wasn't!" he yelled.

"Not a single father. Do you remember the night you told me about Katie's miscarriage?"

He'd been drinking. Trying to move on with his life. He thought if he'd told someone about Katie he could do that. Since he was engaged to Maggie, he felt it was right to let her know about his past.

"You were heartbroken. I told myself it was because of the baby, but it wasn't. It was because Katie walked out of your life. You told me then that a child isn't as important as being with the right woman." Maggie crossed her arms over her chest. "I lied to myself for months about us. The wedding was coming up fast. I couldn't do it."

He remembered the empty feeling when she'd returned his ring. His ego was so friggin' bruised he couldn't see straight. A bigger part of him was relieved.

"When did you find out about the pregnancy?" he asked.

"A few weeks before we broke up."

"Why didn't you tell me?"

"I didn't want your pity. I wanted your love but you couldn't give that to me."

"So you dumped our daughter."

"I did *not* dump Savannah. I placed her in the care of someone who wanted her more than I did. This may come as a shock to you, Dean, but I didn't want kids. Not yet anyway."

Dean thought of Katie, of the ongoing drama with her mother. Not everyone was cut out to be a mother. How fair was it that Katie wanted kids and couldn't have them and Maggie didn't want them and could.

"You never told me that."

"It wasn't until I was pregnant that I realized I wasn't ready. You never attempted to contact me after we broke off the engagement…didn't try and get me back. I knew why. I wanted to hate you. I couldn't." There were tears in Maggie's eyes. "So instead of terminating my pregnancy I decided to have Savannah and give her to the one person that would love her unconditionally and without regret."

"You didn't even know Katie."

Maggie smirked. "She's rich, beautiful, stubborn, and in love with you. I watched hours of that stupid reality show she was on when she was a teenager. Do you know how often she talked about you on that show?"

He shook his head. He hadn't thought of that show in years.

"Even then she adored you. I kept up with her brother Jack's story, knew he was getting married in Texas and that you'd both be there. I had my doctor induce my labor so I could get Savannah to Texas before you both left.

"Leaving Savannah was one of the hardest things I've done in my life. I thought it would be easy."

Dean's heart squeezed in his chest. This was where Maggie was going to ask for her back. He thought of Katie, her angelic smile when she watched Savannah laugh.

"Katie's a perfect mother," he told her.

"I'm not going to ask for her back. Leaving her was hard, but I know I did the right thing. She'll be raised in a loving home with two parents. If I'd kept her I would have hated sharing her. I didn't want to share her daddy either." Maggie's sadness was palpable. Dean cursed himself for her grief.

"So that's it? You walk away and never look back?"

"Now that I know the two of you are together I can go on with my life."

His brow pitched together. "You went through a lot of trouble keeping your identity hidden. Are you saying you would have told me eventually? That you did all of this so Katie and I would get back together?"

"I loved you, Dean. Once I realized it wasn't your fault that you didn't love me I knew I could at least give Savannah a chance at a good life. Savannah can only be icing on the happiness cake, not the glue that holds it together. You and I weren't that cake."

Here he thought Maggie was the most selfish woman in the world for leaving their daughter. "I wanted to love you," he whispered.

She brushed away her tears and forced a smile to her lips. Maggie pushed away from the counter and walked over to him. She lifted up on her tiptoes and placed a soft kiss to his cheek. "Good-bye, Dean. Take care of your girls."

Katie dropped her bags in the doorway and rushed into the living room where she heard Mrs. Hoyt and Savannah.

"Oh, look, Mommy's home," Mrs. Hoyt said when Katie hurried in the room.

"Where's my little girl?"

Savannah smiled and Katie pushed away all the crazy emotions she had harbored over the past several days. "Did you miss me?" Katie kissed her tiny nose and held her tight.

"She's such a good baby. There was a little extra fussing. I think she missed you."

"Lord knows I missed her. Is Dean home?"

"He left early. Said he'd be back this afternoon."

Katie caught up on Savannah's day. She put aside her own unpacking until nap time. No reason to spend those precious moments doing chores. She loved her baby girl. She loved her baby girl's daddy.

By three in the afternoon Savannah couldn't hold her eyes open any longer.

Katie had called and left a message on Dean's cell phone letting him know she was home. When he didn't call her back, she decided to see if maybe he'd left his phone on his charger in his office. Something she'd brought with her to work a couple of times since they had moved in together per Dean's request.

There wasn't a phone at the end of the charger that sat on his desk. She sat in his chair and picked up his landline to call the office.

Jo reported that she hadn't seen him in the office for a couple of days.

Katie's skin prickled when Jo told her that he informed her that he didn't want to be notified unless there was an emergency.

"I thought maybe it had something to do with you," Jo told her.

"Um, well, I guess maybe...he didn't come with me to Florida."

"Well, he's not here. If you see him, let him know that I'm holding off the hounds, but he might want to make an appearance tomorrow or Friday at the latest."

"I'll do that."

What the hell is going on? Everything sounded normal on the phone.

Right now she had wine chilling in the refrigerator so that at dinner tonight she could tell him about his daddy status.

Katie turned to leave the office and noticed the blinking light on the message player. She hit it twice accidentally and the player started to play old messages before finding the new one.

There was a message from her early in her trip. One from Jo at the office. *Must have come through before he asked for phone silence.*

A voice she didn't recognized made her drop back into the chair. *I found Maggie's aunt living in the Valley. Like you said. Looks like Maggie was living with her before she had the baby. I have a new address. Call me.*

"He knows." Katie looked around the room. "He knows."

The next message that played was a hang up. Then the in-box was empty.

As empty as everything inside of her felt in that moment.

There was no doubt in her mind that Dean was with Maggie right then. Talking to her, confiding in her...the mother of *his* child.

"Oh, God."

Katie left the office and walked into the living room. She paced, thinking. Worrying.

They'd been engaged. What if he wanted to make that work now that he knew the truth? Did he know that Katie had kept the information from him...was he upset with her for not telling him?

Minutes ticked slowly past and turned into an hour. She tried his cell phone again but didn't leave a message.

Savannah woke early from her nap and fussed more than normal. Or maybe Katie's stress didn't tolerate it. What could she do if Dean wanted Savannah? That one part of the entire equation that neither of them had considered was: *What if a daddy showed up?*. There was no showing up necessary. Savannah already lived with her father.

Katie was the expendable link.

Several hours ticked by, each one more painful than the last. Could she force herself to walk away if Dean asked her to? Everything had been going well...moving in the right direction.

Why this? Why now?

The sound of the garage door reached her and her palms started to itch.

Dean walked through the garage door, dropped his keys on the counter, and entered his house in a daze.

He wanted a quiet moment. One without his mind running, reaching for impossible solutions. As soon as he revealed to Katelyn who Savannah's mother was…or more importantly, who the daddy was, things could change.

Dean moved into the den, poured that stiff drink, and collected his thoughts. Today should have been a homecoming. He hadn't seen Katie in three days…three nights. He missed her.

"I tried calling you." Katie's wavering voice brought his thoughts into focus.

He swiveled and saw her standing in the doorway, holding Savannah.

"I'm sorry. I've been—" He lowered his gaze, sipped his drink.

"With Maggie," Katie uttered.

His gaze collided with hers. "How did you know?"

"There was a message on your machine."

He'd forgotten about Nathan's phone call. Dean poured more whiskey down his throat and tried to burn the image of Maggie from his mind. "Maggie is…Savannah's mother."

Katie winced, as if the words hurt. "I know," she whispered.

"What?"

"And you're her father." It was Katie looking away now.

Dean gripped his glass. "You knew? How long did you know?"

She moved into the room, placed Savannah in her swing, and buckled her in. "I spoke to Patrick right before I left for Florida… wait, that's not entirely true. A couple days before."

Guilt started a quick fuse to anger. "You knew?"

Katie turned on the swing and gave it a gentle push. "He found video images of Maggie in the hotel…that night. I guessed about who the daddy was."

"Why didn't you tell me?"

"I would have."

"When?" he raised his voice, darted a look at Savannah, and lowered it again. "How long would you have kept this from me, Katelyn?"

"I thought about it when I was in Florida. Wanted to say something to you then…but I couldn't do it on the phone. I couldn't stand the thought of you going to her when I wasn't here. But you did anyway. I've been here all day thinking you're with her. The mother of your child." She ran a hand through her hair. "Where do I fit into that?"

"Dammit, Katie."

"Dammit, what? Savannah is *your* daughter. I'm a substitute for the real mother."

"You're not a substitute."

"I am. Now that you know Savannah belongs to you more than she can ever belong to me, what do I have? You've been with Maggie, were ready to marry her. You have a child with her. I can't compete with that."

He'd never seen Katie so vulnerable and scared. As torn as he was about Maggie's decision to keep Savannah from him…for leaving his child on Katie's doorstep, he wasn't at all torn with who he wanted to live his life with. Dean set his glass down, crossed the room, and tried to put his arms around her.

She shrugged away with tears in her eyes.

He cringed with her rejection.

Katie wrapped her arms around her own waist. "I won't stand in the way. I love you both too much to break up your family."

All he could think of when driving home was how he and Katie could work this out together. They would decide together if Savannah would ever know who her real mother was.

"Look at me, Katie. You're my family," he said. Dean moved in front of her a second time, didn't let her shrug away again as he pulled her into his arms. "You're Savannah's mother."

"You spent all day with Savannah's mother. You didn't take your calls from me." Katie tugged back.

Dean kept her close and stared into her eyes. "I spent the day getting answers. Maggie had my child and didn't tell me. I had to find out what she was thinking. After I left, I drove around trying to figure out how to tell you about this whole mess. I don't have any romantic attachment to Maggie. Something she knew long before she had Savannah."

Katie's struggles to get out of his embrace froze. "You didn't love her?"

"No, Katie. It's impossible for me to love two women at the same time. Maggie knew I was in love with someone else."

Katie blinked through her tears. "Me?"

"Of course you," he said with a half smile. "She saw through me. When she found out she was pregnant she decided to give you Savannah because she didn't think I was ready to be a dad…and she knew you wanted to be a mom."

"How could she know that, Dean?" Katie trembled but he refused to let her go.

"Somewhere in the rulebook of guy I forgot the rule on talking about my ex. I talked a lot about you…a lot. Something in those conversations…or what I said in passing, made her realize how much I still loved you. Maggie believed that we'd find each other eventually, make amends."

"What if we'd never figured it out? What if I'd taken Savannah and left the country?"

Dean ran his hands up and down Katie's arms. "Maggie would have told me…eventually."

She'd stopped shaking and the tears were fading. Dean followed Katie down to the couch.

"Does…does she want Savannah back?" Pain laced Katie's question.

Dean kissed her forehead. "No. She's not ready to be a mom. I'm not sure I like her explanation for leaving Savannah, but it is what it is."

Katie stared at Savannah. "There are plenty of people who can have kids and not be a parent."

Both of them watched Savannah in her swing, lost in their thoughts.

Katie squeezed his arm. "I'm sorry, Dean. I should have told you about Savannah the minute I found out. My own selfish insecurities stopped me."

He hushed her. Katie didn't own the title of insecure. "You're not the only one feeling guilty. I took Savannah to my doctor and had a paternity test."

"You did? When?"

"The day after you left. I kept thinking about the letter left with Savannah and the conversations I'd had with Maggie. I couldn't believe she'd have my child and not tell me. But then there's that little bundle." He nodded to his little girl, smiled. "She has the Prescott nose." He saw it now as sure as the one on his face. "I knew it was possible Savannah was mine."

"She does have your nose. Your appetite, too."

"I didn't want to tell you over the phone either," he said.

Katie offered a coy smile.

Dean placed his palm on the side of her cheek. "I wouldn't have gone back to Maggie. Yeah, I was raised to take responsibility for what's mine, for what I created. But I wouldn't leave you for her. It's you I love, Katie. Not her. It's you I want to be the mother of my children…Savannah and any others we may choose to have. You are my family and I'm not giving you up ever again. Either of you."

He kissed her then, sealing his words, and doing everything he could to burn his conviction into her brain.

From the baby swing, a clapping sound shortened their kiss. Savannah sat with a smile on her face as she clapped her hands together.

Katie's laugh warmed the part of him that had been chilled all day. "Looks like Savannah approves."

He kissed her forehead and hugged her close. "I love you."

"I love you, too, Dean." They settled into the couch and watched Savannah watching them. "This means we're getting married... right?"

Dean found her question funny and started to snicker.

She pushed away and offered a playful frown.

His laughter reduced to giggles. "I wanted to have a ring before I dropped to my knee."

"A ring?"

"Yeah, shiny thing I put on your finger before I ask. A ring."

She frowned and leaned back into his arms.

"You know," she said a moment later, "you don't have to have a ring to ask."

"We already have a child before the wedding. I don't want to mess up all those traditions." He'd search out the perfect ring first thing in the morning. He'd already had one in mind before she left for Florida.

She huffed out a breath. "But you are going to ask..."

Oh, boy, he could see they weren't going to get far. "The question isn't *if* I'll ask, it's if I can get to it faster than your father and my best friend show up at the door with a shotgun. That's the question."

Now it was her turn to giggle. She kicked her legs under her bum and wrapped her arms around his waist.

"What...that's it? No more drilling?"

"Nope."

"Why not?" It wasn't like her to give up so easily.

"I told my dad and brother they had to wait two days before they came to meet Savannah."

Dean tipped his head back and laughed. When Katie joined him, the weight of the days and weeks faded.

Epilogue

Katie had Savannah playing in a playpen while she burned yet another meal on the stove. "Remind me to hire a cook," she said to Savannah.

Savannah babbled to herself and jumped at the side of the playpen. She was ten months old and close to taking her first step.

"Cooking shouldn't be this hard."

Savannah muttered, "Da Da."

"Yeah, he's a better cook. Don't remind me."

"Da Da."

Katie lifted the sticking pasta from the pot with a frown before taking it to the sink and letting the garbage disposal eat it.

"Da Da."

She tucked her hair behind her ear and flattened her hands on the sink. The three-carat square-cut diamond set in white gold with a matching diamond band twinkled on her hand. So she was a lousy cook. She had the wife thing down and loved everything about being a mother.

Life could be worse.

Maggie had moved out of state without a good-bye. Katie thought about her from time to time but no longer worried that she'd return and demand custody.

With some legal help, Dean's name was added to Savannah's birth certificate. The three of them were a real family now…in every way.

The floor squeaked behind her before a bouquet of flowers was thrust in her face.

"For my beautiful wife," Dean whispered behind her. His lips found the nape of her neck and she leaned into him.

"What are these for?"

"Do I have to have a reason?"

She twisted in his arms and cocked her head to the side. "A husband brings a wife flowers on Valentine's Day, birthdays, and anniversaries…or if he's feeling guilty for something." She sniffed the flowers and smiled. "So what has you feeling guilty?"

Dean's strong jaw dropped in mock offense. "I'm offended."

"Ha! Takes more than that to offend you. I know. You eat my cooking and you're not offended."

He looked past her and into the sink. "Looks like I'm off the hook tonight."

She poked him with the stem of the flowers "Hey!"

"It's OK. I'm taking my Prescott girls out tonight."

"You are?"

"Yep, and pack a bag, cuz we're staying overnight."

"We are?"

"Yep." Dean leaned over and turned off the water, which was still running.

"Wow," she said. "You must have done something awful for this kind of guilt. Flowers, dinner…overnight stay."

Dean took the flowers from her hands and placed them on the counter. He leaned his body into hers, pinning her to the sink. "You're forgetting one holiday on which a husband buys his wife flowers."

She pinched her lips together and tried like hell to take him seriously with him pressed so close. "Can't think of one."

"What's tomorrow?"

"Not my birthday."

He kissed her nose. "Happy Mother's Day, Katie."

Her mouth opened, closed, then opened again. "I forgot." She'd spent years ignoring the holiday because she had no one to celebrate it for. She'd seen some of the commercials on the TV and they'd both joked about this being her first Mother's Day as a mom…but she'd forgotten. "It is Mother's Day."

"It is. And I'm taking you and our daughter to the happiest place on earth."

Katie's eyes flew wide open. "Really? I haven't been there in years."

"I couldn't think of a better place to celebrate."

She tilted her lips to his, thanked him with a kiss. "I love you."

"I love you, too."

He kissed her again and then retrieved Savannah from her playpen. "Did you say Happy Mother's Day?" he asked.

"Da Da."

"She has that down. One of these days I'm going to hear Ma Ma." Katie sponged out the pot and set it on a towel to dry. *Yep, it's time to hire a cook.*

"There's mail on the counter," Dean told her.

She picked it up and thumbed through the junk.

In the stack was a card-shaped envelope addressed to Katelyn Prescott. It was postmarked from Florida. She opened the envelope and found a floral card with *Happy Mother's Day* written on the front.

Dear Katelyn,

I hope this card finds you well, and that you're happy in your new life. May this and every Mother's Day bring you the happiness you so richly deserve. You've grown into a strong and beautiful woman, one I would be honored to have as a friend.

I've been a lousy mother, but I would like a chance of being a halfway decent grandmother. If an invitation arrives, I'd love to visit you and meet your family.

All my best,

Annie

"Katie?"

She waved the card in the air. "It's from my mom."

Dean stopped bouncing Savannah. "You're kidding."

"She wants to visit." The note was clearly an olive branch. Katie smiled. The ice in her heart in regard to her mother began to thaw.

He moved beside her, glanced down at the card. "What do *you* want?"

Katie looked into the eyes of the man she loved. "I think it's time. Put the past behind us and move forward."

"It won't be easy," he reminded her.

"The good things in life never are."

Dean pulled her into his arms, squeezing Savannah in between.

"Da Da."

Katie groaned. "Mama. C'mon. Can I have a little *mama*?"

Savannah giggled. "Ma."

Katie squealed. "Did you hear that? She said *ma*."

Delighted with the praise, Savannah said it again. "Ma."

"Ah," Katie screamed, kissing Savannah over and over. She grabbed Dean's arm. "C'mon, guys. Let's pack. We're going to Disneyland."

"Ma Ma."

A big thank-you to my fans who have embraced this new series with open arms.

As always, thanks to my agent, Jane, and her team, for making this book possible.

For Montlake, and my editor Kelli, who wanted a story where I tied in Mother's Day to the theme. Everyone has read the secret baby story. I thought it was about time for a baby to be left on a woman's doorstep.

This book was as much about motherhood as it was about family.

I will end my acknowledgments with the person I dedicated this book to, Kayce. You're more than a cousin, more than a friend. I can count on you anytime, day or night...and know you'll always be there. I hope your daughters know how lucky they are to have you as their mother.

I love you!

Catherine

About the Author

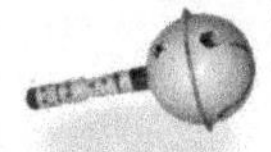

Photograph by Lindsey Meyer, 2012

New York Times bestselling author Catherine Bybee was raised in Washington State, but after graduating high school, she moved to Southern California in hopes of becoming a movie star. After growing bored with waiting tables, she returned to school and became a registered nurse, spending most of her career in urban emergency rooms. She now writes full-time and has penned the novels *Not Quite Dating*, *Wife by Wednesday*, and *Married by Monday*. Bybee lives with her husband and two teenage sons in Southern California.